THE ORANGE ENVELOPE

The Orange Envelope

Mario Soldati

TRANSLATED BY *Bernard Wall*

A Helen and Kurt Wolff Book

Harcourt, Brace & World, Inc.

New York

THE ORANGE ENVELOPE

PERHAPS nothing would have happened if I hadn't run into my old school friend, Alessandro Rorà, at Brignole Station.

Now he's dead too. And I've changed his name as I've changed the name of nearly every character in this story: because time rushes on so fast as to wipe from the memory of the living the genuine and affectionate loyalty they feel for dead relatives or friends, yet not fast enough to overcome vanity about names and the fear of offending that vanity.

Alessandro was very rich and aristocratic and he inherited a great family name. He was good-looking, intelligent, cultivated, and sociable; and then, toward the age of forty, he mortified his true nature in an unexpected and violent way, renounced the only happiness open to him, surrounded himself with a false peace and the protection of an artificial family, wrapped himself up in silence and respectability, and lived out to the end as a lonely and desperate man, with hell in his heart. And all this because at a given moment, through fear of scandal and under the influence of a French missionary priest, he became convinced that his particular abnormality—though anything but rare—indicated that he was the object of the malevolent attention of Our Father in Heaven, a particular case of the tragic outcome of Adam and Eve's sin.

In our days at Moncalieri, now so long past, Alessandro had developed a habit of confiding in me rather than concealing his tastes from me, and not just because we were classmates or had adjoining rooms in our last two years at school. The truth is that we both suffered from the same illness. We went on suffering from it even later, during our university days and in the years after that. In those days it was the sickness of all upper-class adolescents in Turin and Milan, and our "fevers," though of opposite kinds, were particularly acute. Once Alessandro had overcome the difficulty and shame of his early confidences, there was nothing particularly strange about our finding an outlet and a comfort in confessing our pains of lost love to one another.

In the beginning Alessandro had made up his mind to talk to me because he thought that I, as he did, liked men: and I, in slight bad faith, had let him believe it. My bad faith could be explained, if not excused, by snobbery. Alessandro's family belonged to the high aristocracy. And snobbery was the lesser of the two poisons that my mother, the good Jesuits, and the good Barnabites had instilled drop by drop into my blood; the other poison, much more disastrous, was fear of women.

I couldn't resist the temptation of making capital of the occasion and winning his friendship—the friendship of the Marchese di Rorà's only son. Immediately afterward, less perhaps out of loyalty than out of stupid vanity (when will we free ourselves of the wretched prejudice of thinking manliness in itself superior to womanliness?), I explained to him that there had been a misunderstanding, that of course I felt as terrified of the sexual act as he did, but my feelings were for women. As luck would have it, Alessandro didn't believe my retraction either then or later; he never showed complete conviction about my normality. I have said "as luck would have it" because in this way my vanity ended up by seeming less guilty.

According to Alessandro I was afraid of women because I believed I liked them, but my fear was a false fear—it concealed indifference or downright disgust and was the sign of another really deep and unconscious fear: fear of what I really did like.

Just imagine! After all that has happened to me, I can only say: Just imagine! God may have wanted Alessandro to see right into me, but that didn't happen, alas. At the stage I've now reached there's no doubt about it. Women have been the sole source of my pleasure; and two women the sole source of my pain.

But when I got out of the train at Brignole Station and recognized Alessandro's wide shoulders and disproportionately thin, almost concave, neck, as he paused in front of a newspaper kiosk, thirty long years had slipped by since that painful and absurd time of frenzy and anguish which was our adolescence. Thirty years. Long enough for a number of changes to have been wrought within us; long enough for our friendship to have altered and come to an end some years previously.

We were together at school and together at the university during the four subsequent years, he studying law, I philosophy. Owing to our custom of almost communal life, our friendship was continuous, and so were our sexual ambitions—only my ambition was more absurd than his for I was merely grasping after the normal. On his father's death the following year, Alessandro came into an enormous fortune and began traveling in comfort. He had a special taste for North Africa, Greece, Asia Minor, and the East. From the first he made up for time lost at the university, learning—when far from home—how to transgress without remorse all moral commitment to himself, and how to overcome without hesitation all that restraint by which society would have bound him owing to his name.

In those days stories about his extraordinary insatiability used to be passed around in "upper-class" circles in Turin, Milan, and Rome, but the location of these stories was Bangkok, Kyoto, or Marrakesh, and their origin lay in the confidences he himself made to his friends, all of whom, with one exception, shared his tastes.

I was the exception. Alessandro emerged from his prolonged adolescence on the death of his father, and I emerged from mine at roughly the same time. The nature of my tastes had become clear to me and was obvious to everyone who knew me, so there was no longer any excuse or motive for even the most malicious people to suspect me. On the contrary, everyone knew perfectly well that though I was over twenty-five and had already taken my degree, my mother still maintained a ruthless domination over my private life or, rather, attempted to dominate it and believed she was successful. Though really my private life wasn't at all what she thought it was.

When Alessandro's father died and left him rich he had unwittingly provided him with the best possible medicine for dealing with his unhappiness and finding a quick cure for it. Unfortunately, things worked out quite otherwise for me. When my father died my mother was the heir, and she knew full well that if she was generous with me the money would be used for my amusement and would help me to become adult—as, in a different way, it helped Alessandro. For the same motive my mother never encouraged me to look for a permanent paid job, for she knew that if I began to make money I would soon become independent of her. No, my passion for music suited her down to the ground. Admittedly, there was one disadvantage: the Scala. My constant trips to Milan, sometimes lasting several weeks, hardly appealed to her. But she realized that she had to give way to me about something!

After getting my degree I'd expressed a wish to go and settle in Milan—alone, of course. This she opposed with all her strength, saying, among other things, that we couldn't afford a second home. Finally she decided to leave Turin, sublet our apartment on the first floor of our house on Piazza Bodoni, and retire to Levo with Costantino and myself: it was understood that I'd have "leave" to get away to Milan every time I wanted to go to the Scala. In those days there was very little traffic and the trip by car took hardly more than an hour, and it was understood that I would always stay with Alessandro. And indeed he put a bedroom and bathroom at my disposal. My mother suffered horribly every time I left Levo, but she found balm for her snobbery in the knowledge that I was a guest in the Marchese di Rorà's mansion. To be sure, I could have taken action in law against my mother and obtained what is called my "legal share." Especially in the early years when she counted out a few ten-lire notes into my hand every time I set out and wanted to know every detail about what I intended to do with them. Then I really did feel tempted to bring about a final break, with the legal consequences I have mentioned. But in the end a friend in Milan began lending me money, and later, with my agreement, he opened a credit account in a bank, both he and the bank having ascertained that someday I would have a substantial margin merely from selling the Turin house. So without my mother's knowledge and without the knowledge of the upper classes—whom, incidentally, I had almost completely ceased to frequent—I rented a *garçonnière* in Via Pasquirolo, and there I put up my successive girl friends, one after another. They were whims, adventures that lasted at most a couple of weeks and usually only a night or two. But they involved me in assiduously returning to the same "motifs," indeed in an almost regular alternation of the same "motifs" during a whole season or during a given period of time.

I was also influenced by the necessity to put in an appearance at Levo as often as possible, if only to maintain my mother's illusion as to my way of life and prevent her from thinking up some plan for having me followed. Of course alternatively my mother could telephone Alessandro. Or come to Milan and catch me unawares. She was a woman quite capable of that, and she did so a couple of times; but I had warned Alessandro's servant, Paolo, and Paolo showed ability in rising to the situation.

My girl friends were usually minor actresses or show girls; more often than not they worked in brothels, or "houses," and they spent several hours with me during their afternoons off or during their ten days' holiday.

After our useless and ridiculous attempts in our university years, and while Alessandro was discovering his vein of eroticism in Algiers (almost as in a famous chapter of a famous book by André Gide), I discovered my own more modest path in a brothel at Novara. I don't know about Alessandro; but as for myself, perhaps I should make clear that already even in those days, my times of bliss, though genuine and authentic, were of very short duration.

Until I had money in the bank and could rent the *garçonnière* in Via Pasquirolo, I seem to remember making love only in brothels or small provincial hotels with the chambermaid or the barmaid. This habitual way of seeking satisfaction, this tendency of mine, may help to explain why I went on visiting brothels later on—for I always did so, as long as they remained open; and why with the girls I found in the corridors of the Lirico or the Odeon I insisted on picking out the oldest and most *routinières*. If I am to descend to detail I should add that I liked those who were tall, handsome, dark, and strong-willed by temperament. Then, if I am to attempt to interpret my preference, I should add that my mother was tall, handsome, dark and strong-willed by temperament, and that I think I loved her up to the age of twelve or thirteen with all the passion with which I hated and feared her from that age onward and ever increasingly until her death, and even after.

Some modern experts who depend in part on Freud's theories consider that a person's character is completely formed at the age of two—all his essential physiological and psychological choices have already been made. In other words, we have no exact memory of what most determines or at least influences our decisions, and it is our fate to remain in ignorance of the very thing that it would be most useful to know so as to correct our defects and cure ourselves of our follies. . . .

It was only after the death of my father that my mother began to pour out her morbid love on me. Earlier, above all in the first years of her marriage—when I was very small, that is—my mother was very happy and therefore took very little notice of me. It was at that time, when I felt neglected, that I began adoring her. What I am going to say may seem almost absurd, and my recollection of that time is so vague as to border on hypothesis, but the first of the two of us (my mother and myself) who began to love the other was myself.

On gloomy winter afternoons in Turin, with the weak light filtering in through the thick olive-green curtains of the boudoir, she used to sit at her writing desk, hurrying through her correspondence, while I sat "well-behaved" in a corner where she'd left me, playing with a teddy bear or a toy train, which I found much less interesting than her back.

I pretended to play—especially on the rare occasions when my mother turned around, her suspicions perhaps aroused by my silence—but really I was gazing at her powerful back, her strong neck, and the mass of her black, carefully done hair. I was studying the well-rounded shape of her arm and elbow. I was following the exact nervous movements of her white plump hand as it traced mysterious signs and pushed the pen along. Even the grating of the nib in the plush silence of the boudoir, even the almost silvery vibration of the paper when my mother tore the leaf from the pad, filled me with enchantment; and so did the green cloth of the writing desk, the sheets of blotting paper, the well-ordered writing materials in their various pigeonholes which rose one above the other and crowned that shrine like a portico: the visiting cards, the invitation cards, the writing paper, the orange envelopes for official and important correspondence, the little boxes of stamps, the sticks of sealing wax, the seals, the tiny bottles of ink, the pencils.

Sometimes, in the evenings, my mother used to dress herself up to go to the theater with Papa.

On those evenings my parents dined out after the show.

At that time they were still fond of one another and often went out together. I ate alone, a little earlier than usual, perhaps imprisoned in my high chair or perhaps in the servants' quarters, instead of being allowed into the dining room, where it was thought pointless to set the table for me alone. The minute I had finished eating I ran into my parents' bedroom.

In the glitter of the lights around the three looking glasses of the dressing table and the big mirror of the *armoire-à-glace,* my mother used to dress with leisurely, detailed, and elaborate care. She certainly took strict precautions not to be seen even half naked by me; but occasionally I caught her by surprise. Then she scolded the nurse roundly for not being quicker running after me and stopping me from making an unexpected entry. She didn't realize that it was she herself who was being imprudent by scolding the nurse and so conferring an extraordinary value and a marvelous mystery on what I absolutely oughtn't even to have glimpsed. But in any case that glimpse was more than enough to fascinate me. My mother never appeared as lovely as she did then. Her full naked shoulders, the bracelets and the bejeweled rings, the sapphire cross that hung from her neck emphasizing the insinuating shadow between the double exuberance of her breasts, the raven-black hair, the brilliant chestnut eyes . . .

She was doing the "final touches"—penciling her eyebrows and the corners of her eyes, applying cream, powder, lipstick, scent, long operations that took up a whole extra half-hour. And I was always in a corner, or even between the bed and the wall, or on the carpet or goatskin where I was supposed to tumble around with my teddy bear or toy train or some other ridiculous thing. I played little or not at all; I was content to stare open-mouthed at my mother.

My father dressed in the bathroom, as quick as lightning. He hurled himself back into the bedroom to put on his tails, and she tied his white bow tie.

For what mysterious reason are grownups so absurdly ready to think that a child doesn't listen to their conversations, whereas he is all ears? Worse still, why do they think he doesn't understand them, whereas their meaning is only too clear?

"Where's Carlo?" murmured my father. "Surely he ought to be in bed."

"Don't worry; he's here; he's being good," murmured my mother in reply. They both murmured, as though that were enough, as though I were deaf.

"Where?"

"I can see him in the mirror; he's being so good it's as though he doesn't exist . . . as though he doesn't exist."

But I existed all right. I was happy to hear that it was as though I didn't exist—was forgotten, that is—whereas I was really there, present, very present indeed, there, intoxicated by the French scent that exhaled from my mother's body, and that even from a distance seemed to enfold me like some immaterial and voluptuous substance.

The same substance almost drowned me every night when my mother came to give me the ritual kiss and bent over my cot in the darkness. "I can't sleep if you don't come and kiss me," I had said. And as soon as she had kissed me and gone away with a light rustle, I moistened my thumbs with saliva and put them on the exact place on my cheek where my mother had kissed, then transported her kiss, so to say, over my whole body beneath my pajamas: I rubbed her kiss directly and accurately onto all my skin, onto the rest of my face, onto my chest and stomach. When this operation was over, and only then, did I fall into blessed sleep.

And what about the afternoons when she went out shopping and I was still too small to go with her? I stayed at home with the nurse and the maids. I can truthfully say that in the first two years of my life I spent by far the greatest part of my time in the company of servants. Naturally, the maids and the nurse called my mother "the mistress." Sometimes I myself called her that; and when I turned to her and said "Mistress" she burst into a mad fit of laughing. And when I saw her going out with her hat, her veil, her umbrella, her beaver fur or her miniver, the fact that I wasn't able to go after her in the rain, through the city that I found so huge and wonderful, but had instead to stay with the servants, was a laceration, an extreme humiliation, and my love was all the more inflamed.

But the reason for my hatred, which continues to this day, alas, I would be unable to explain. By instinct I blame my mother for all the misfortunes from which I have suffered, and for the calamity that overtook me and even dragged my brother in all his sweetness and innocence in its wake. This is instinctive and perhaps unjust; yet I can't rid myself of it.

True, my mother must have suffered deeply from my father's death. It was terrible for a woman like her to be a widow at such a young age, she, the daughter of a high civil servant, who'd grown up in a family entirely composed of high officials and stiff bureaucrats, very religious in her feelings and at the same time extremely sensual and impulsive. One always finds the same story, one way or another. Perhaps all the cruelties to which a human being gives way are only forms of revenge; the consequence, that is, of the cruelties which that being underwent in his turn at the hands of destiny or of other people who in their turn were made cruel by other destinies or other people . . . and so on. But where does this lead us?

To go back from one evil to the next may serve as an explanation, but it isn't an excuse; not for anybody, not even for my mother. We show virtue by the gentleness with which we accept a destiny, by the goodness with which we respond to the wickedness of others. My mother was hurt by the destiny that took away her husband, and was driven to despair by her solitude, but she was never able to resolve the problem, never able to free herself from this curse. Sometimes I thought she even took pleasure in it. With almost diabolical pride she refused either to marry again or to take a lover. And she concentrated all her passion on me: she wreaked on me all she had suffered or was suffering. Her vengeance was all the more cruel and efficient the less it was conscious. My father, who died in a railway accident when I was little more than a child, had been what is called a great womanizer. What I most remember about him were his sighs, his silences, his desperate glances toward the ceiling when my mother reproached him in front of me at mealtimes. For him, family life was a continual and exasperating series of jealous scenes inflicted on him by my mother. I was hardly surprised that he went off traveling so often. He was representative in Northern Italy, Switzerland, and Bavaria for one of the best brands of champagne and one of the best cognacs. And I have now become convinced that this occupation, which brought in very little money, constituting at best a modest supplement to the income left him by my grandfather, was really only a pretext to travel and thus loosen as much as possible the stifling embrace of my mother's jealousy.

Even his death, for my mother, was a final proof of his infidelity, for then the wound of jealousy, which tormented her so much, became gangrenous and there was no possible cure.

The railway accident occurred on the line between

Modane and Paris: my father was found in a sleeping car with a girl. . . .

My mother always kept the memory of my father's death alive, but she transformed it into a terrifying ground for revenge. The revenge was this: that at all costs I should never resemble my father. As soon as she judged that I was of an age to hear the truth, she didn't hesitate; she determined to tell me every detail: her arrival on a winter's night at Ambérieu Station, between Chambéry and Dijon, not far from the scene of the accident, her identification of my father's body, and the presence of the body of the woman. "Your father, unless he repented at the very last moment, and I don't know if Our Lord was so merciful as to grant him this, your father died in mortal sin." She recollected herself; lowered her eyelids; then reopened them and amazed me with her fine chestnut eyes, fixed strangely on me, and, beyond me, on a vision of horror. "Your father may be in hell. Do you understand what that means? Answer me, do you understand?"

Thus, with the violence natural to her, my mother began to terrorize me and impregnate me with the fear of mortal sin. Naturally, mortal sin, for me, could only lie in having erotic relations with a woman before marriage. Whatever woman I might run into, there was the danger of my being led into temptation. And then there was also the mortal sin of desire. But there is no real way of conveying my mother's folly, except by pointing out that she was addressing a boy of thirteen or fourteen. Imagine whether, in the innocence of that age, I could conceive of a mortal sin; that is to say, the will to offend God with the full knowledge and full consent of all my faculties. To tell the truth, I don't think any human being is really capable of mortal sin. Even in the frenzy of the most horrible vengeance, the motive force driving an unfortunate man to action is not so much hatred of the good as its very opposite, an illusion of justice; as a result of suffering and humiliation, he has ended up by turning reality inside out and looks for peace in crime. But it was not this evil that my mother feared in my case. If sin became for me something more than a verbal expression, if the evil against which my mother warned me touched me, then it was my mother herself who charged that word with meaning and planted within me the seed of that corruption. When I was a boy it was my mother. And a year and a half ago, at Brignole Station, it was my friend Alessandro.

My mother began terrifying me with the idea of mortal sin and hell, all the while putting me on my guard against women. According to her, the only dangerous ones were those I liked. And they were dangerous precisely because I liked them. The desire I had to see them, approach them, talk to them, and the tenderness I experienced if, in the end, I yielded to that desire, were nothing but unhealthy symptoms and signs of temptation. . . .

EVEN before my father's death my mother and I were inseparable friends—Costantino was too small to accompany us and was almost always entrusted to a nurse. Every day, as soon as I'd finished my homework, I went out with my mother to "do the shopping." The custom—normal with all children when they go for a walk with grownups—of "holding your darling hand" was complicated with my mother and me by a secret and exquisite little game, probably invented by my childish instinct, but which my mother never even dreamed of discouraging. She even showed signs of clinging to it in excess. And when I delayed she would be the first to say, "Luccio, when are you going to put your finger in the little hole?" For the invention, the complication, the little game, lay in this: while I clasped my mother's gloved hand with my own small one, I stuck my forefinger in the little oval hole in the glove; I stuck it in until I had immersed it completely in that warm smooth crevice between the two plump little cushions formed by my mother's hand within the glove. Oh, the warmth and supreme sweetness of that contact! The texture of the glove varied, sometimes chamois and sometimes kid—two very different sensations but both equally intoxicating. If the glove was chamois, when I put my finger into the little hole the change-over to contact with the living warm skin of my mother's hand was almost imperceptible. If the glove was kid, there was a little hem around the hole, but even that hem, when I caressed it with my thumb, gave me intense pleasure, as did the small, sharp, mother-of-pearl buttons which closed the cleft between the wrist and the little hole. But the most real pleasure of all was to feel my finger stretched, almost immersed, almost lost in my mother's soft warm tapering hand, and at the same time to be able to wiggle it about within that scented and enfolding mass.

In the early stages, it was fairly natural that my father's death should serve to cement that passionate bond between me and my mother. But even later and for several years the bond, instead of loosening—which would have been natural—tended to grow stronger. I was slow at growing up. I was slow at finding a friend among my companions at school. For none of my schoolmates seemed to offer me that tenderness and sweetness given me by my mother; none seemed to promise me that trust and extraordinary union.

So certainly my mother and I prolonged beyond the proper time, and perhaps until after I was twelve, habits like that of "shopping" in town and "the finger in the little hole." I can't remember exactly when or how I began to draw away. Perhaps it was during the *terzo ginnasio*, when I saw that none of my schoolmates went out walking with their mothers regularly, as I did, but only on special occasions. Possibly I had met one of them when I was with my mother, and he had looked at me, or I had thought that he had looked at me, with a smile of pity, and so for the first time I had felt a certain uneasiness, a certain shame. Finally a phrase, some ironical comment, would have been thrown out, words I can't remember now but which would have been decisive: my eyes were opened, I was suddenly aware of my incipient male dignity. I can imagine a conversation like this:

"Carlo, who was that woman with you yesterday under the arcades of Piazza Castello?"

"It was my mother. Who did you think it was?"

"Ah, your mummy . . ."

There you have it. That would have been enough—the babyish caricature with which my companion emphasized the word "mummy."

When my mother realized that I was beginning to draw away from her, she began by making one or two brief and uncertain attempts to hold me back. But she wasn't so stupid as not to understand that if she persisted in that sort of attitude she would soon become hateful to me. Besides showing increasingly marked signs of his incurable apathy, my brother Costantino had in recent months gone from one fever to the next and had become so weak that the doctors feared for his life and advised that he should live in the open air as much as possible; and there was the villa at Levo which seemed very suitable for this purpose. My mother had central heating installed and left Turin, provisionally shutting down our Piazza Bodoni home, and finding a courage she would never have found had circumstances not forced it on her: courage to separate herself from me and send me to a boarding school. I was thirteen, and was to go into the fourth *ginnasio*.

Never shall I forget the last day I spent with my mother before leaving for Moncalieri. It was, I think, the last day of our old love—I can't think of any other word for it. In the evening, she wanted us to go out together, and she wanted us to go to confession in the same church, together, even if to different confessors. It was the church of the Santi-Martiri in Via Garibaldi, served by the Jesuits. It was early evening, shortly before half past seven, the hour when they closed the church. From inside the house a distant bell was ringing, summoning the Fathers to the refectory. We finished our two confessions almost at the same time, and knelt down some distance away from one another to recite our penances: my mother in one of the first benches near the altar, as was her habit; myself, perhaps recalling the "pharisee" and the "publican," and so as to differentiate myself from her, or even to oppose her, in a bench nearer the back and rather to the side. From this place I could make out in the darkness of the church, faintly enlivened here and there by the fluttering of a candle flame, not only the well-known outlines, strong and ample, with full shoulders, waist well modeled by the stylish coat and skirt, and the marked roundness of the behind, but also the fleshy and overbearing profile, only just softened by the network and beauty-spots of the veil, and the smooth band of black hair surmounted by a wing of the three-cornered hat (also fashionable) which endowed her with a bizarre and stern authority.

Now my mother with a quick, decisive gesture of her two hands—emerging naked and bejeweled from the fissures of her gloves, which curled up her forearms and hung from her wrists like huge beige-colored flowers—

rolled up her veil, arranged it on her forehead, and, pressing her face against the palms of her hands, threw herself violently forward on the elbow-rest as though hurled by the very fervor of her prayer.

She was praying for me, I knew it and could feel it. But my period of freedom and self-rule had already begun. And my mother's figure thrown hurtling toward the altar, as if to use violence with God too, was no longer admired and loved by me as it had been during all those long years of childhood and early adolescence. In those days, more or less consciously, I saw in my mother, when she was praying, only the impetus of her immense affection for me, and rather than respecting I venerated and adored even the outward manifestations of her who was venerating and adoring God for my good. But now her prayer irritated me. Secretly, I criticized my mother's attitude, I judged it to be exaggerated and ridiculous; and the beauty and ornamentation of her face and hands and body, and the elegance of her coat and skirt, deeply disturbed me; they seemed to contain something false, ambiguous, almost fraudulent. Now, when my mother prayed, I no longer saw her love; I saw the overbearing and bullying violence with which she tried to impose on me—at all costs, with all means, and for the whole of my life—a very precise choice of ideas and emotions; her choice, not mine. All this for my good, always. My mother was in good faith, of course. But the worst crimes are those committed in good faith.

My mother was praying. And I, from my bench, once I had mumbled my penance, watched her without feeling. The streetcar passed in Via Garibaldi: I heard it gradually approaching, then just outside with its thunderlike climax of noise but muffled by the church's double doors and thick curtain, then I heard it going away. In the evening silence of the dark, deserted church it seemed to me that a deep sigh arose now and again from my mother's direction. She was sighing as if to collect her strength and pray with greater violence. It wasn't possible, my mother must have been saying, it wasn't possible that God shouldn't hear someone who prayed to him like that. "Lord, you know it," she must have gone on, reasoning in her secret dialogue, "my life has been so different, oh, how different, from my dreams as a girl. And you know that I have nothing to blame myself for. If my husband committed the atrocious sin of betraying me from the very first year of marriage, you know, Lord Jesus, that I never justified his behavior, not even with the slightest misdeed of any kind. You know that with your blessed help I have always resisted every temptation, and you know that there has been no lack of temptation, quite the contrary. If I have sinned in anything, it was perhaps precisely through pride, which is blameworthy, of course, but not gravely so, through my awareness of my just and virtuous behavior, and once again I humbly ask your pardon, as I have asked it so often before. But it seems to me that I have already paid the reckoning. You have already punished me enough by making my son Costantino a backward creature and mentally handicapped. You cannot go on punishing me. I do not deserve it, Jesus. Now you must, you must help my elder son, in whom I have reposed all that remains of my earthly affection, and all the remaining hopes that my life will not be a complete failure. Carlo Felice must not be like his father. You cannot allow it, Lord Jesus. I know, I feel in this instant that you in your infinite goodness will protect him from the evil of all these women and will save him in this life and for ever and ever. Amen."

Just as sometimes, at night, a wave breaks stronger and higher on the shore than all the others, so, now and again, I heard a great, deep, isolated, sorrowful sigh coming from my mother. It was accompanied and prolonged by the low silky rustle of the lining of her coat, moved by the heaving of the breast. I imagined that powerful and generous breast which in the past I had been unable not to adore, and I felt myself beginning to detest it.

My mother extracted a small handkerchief from her sleeve, dried her tears delicately and at length, softly blew her nose, lowered her veil again over her face, and finally got up from the bench. With her somewhat heavy but so sure step, she came down the nave toward me. I got up, preparing to go out. My mother took my arm, squeezing it tightly above the elbow, and leaning against me: I could feel the warmth and mass of her breast and the delicate French perfume that escaped from it.

"My Carluccio," she said, letting go of my arm and feeling for my hand, pressing it convulsively, "my Carluccio, give thanks to Jesus. Isn't this the greatest moment in our life? Think: we're both pure, both near to his heart. If we died at this moment, we'd go straight to heaven. Tell me, isn't it wonderful, isn't it beautiful? Don't you feel this joy, too, this immense peace inside you?"

"Yes, Mamma," I said in a low voice, calculating that in her mystical intoxication my mother would interpret as reserve accompanying strong feeling what was really my impatience and disgust.

As soon as I could I freed myself from that embrace which, though it had taken over only my hand, made me feel it was stifling the whole of me. I profited by the nearby holy-water stoup. I leaped toward it, reached it. I moistened the fingers of my right hand and presented them to my mother, just brushing her fingers with a brief light touch which was the extent of my desire. I am not going to say that that was the last time I touched my mother. Alas, no. But certainly from that time I began avoiding all occasions of physical contact between her and me, and always controlling, watching, and counting them.

The following morning I was to go to my boarding school. My mother woke me up early. I realized at once that she intended to resuscitate a custom that we had abolished by common consent some time before: that of her being present while I had my bath, and helping me to dress. I protested and tried to rebel; she felt offended; and I saw that, what with humiliation and rage, she was on the point of tears. I remembered my father; so as to avoid scenes he used to fall in with my mother's desires as far as he could. I behaved like him.

So once again there were my mother's hands drying me after my bath, pulling on my shirt and my socks, touching me gently, almost caressing me.

At the main doorway a black, plushy, funereal limousine (a 510) was waiting, the one my mother always hired for solemn occasions, and above all for visits to the cemetery. It took me to the heart of old Turin, the Sanctuary of the Consolata where, as prearranged, we heard Mass kneeling side by side, and received Holy Communion elbow by elbow at the altar rail.

After which, in accord with an almost sacred custom of Turin families when they "went to Holy Communion at the Consolata," we entered a little chocolate shop that stood on the other side of the square, opposite the Sanctuary. We sat side by side in old leather chairs at a round marble-topped table. Oh, the fragrance of that hot steaming chocolate, as thick as cream! Oh, the crunch of the wafers and their slow dissolving when dipped in the chocolate! They were sensations I had experienced, in that same place, every time I'd "gone to Communion at the Consolata" with my mother; sensations repeated identically, infallibly, throughout the long sad years of my childhood, solitary except for my mother's company; sensations, alas, no less vivid in my memory—after such a lapse of time— than the mystical ecstasy that regularly preceded them by ten minutes. I think this must have been rather the same for many Turinese of my generation, of generations close to mine: the religious impulse must have preserved for them, through their whole lives, the delicious flavor of creamy hot chocolate and wafers, and the radiant recollection of childish appetite satisfied.

My mother had now reached the age of thirty-six, but she was as greedy as a little girl, and the "chocolate at the Consolata" was unquestionably, among all the pleasures of the palate, the one to which she gave herself with the fullest enthusiasm and the lightest conscience.

And even on that morning it was the same. As she dipped the wafer into the thick cream, she forgot everything for a while. But once the first cup was finished, she raised her eyes to mine and memory came flooding back: within an hour, even less, she would have left me at Moncalieri; within an hour we two would be separated for the first time.

Her eyes filled with heavy tears, while a drop of chocolate and a pale crumb of wafer decorated absurdly, though not unpleasantly, her firm round chin. Yes, I must confess it. Though I had begun to hate my mother, at that moment her tears, or possibly not her tears but the drop of chocolate and the crumb of wafer, this lapse, this transitory disorder in her always immaculate make-up, had the power to arouse my emotion. And to arouse my emotion with thoughts of my mother, not of myself. For I was not at all dissatisfied at going to boarding school. I was attracted by the elegant military uniform with the yellow bands, the wide belt, the kepi. Life at home, in view of Costantino's illness, was one long sadness. I loved my brother; but I was still too young; for the time being I was almost exclusively an egoist. I couldn't imagine forming a close friendship with a boy of my age, as would certainly happen at boarding school. Above all, I could hardly wait for something to change in one way or another, even though I realized that change might be for the worse.

We went back home to get my two suitcases. I went upstairs to brush my teeth and to kiss Costantino and the nurse. Then, once again in the 510 limousine, we went to Moncalieri.

During the journey she wept the whole time, without being able to stop and without saying anything. The veil was up. She was continually drying her tears with the lace-edged handkerchief, now a little ball in her hand. With her free hand she clasped my right one, clasped it and tortured it as though wanting to break it.

"Mamma, you're hurting me."

"You're hurting me, too. I see that you just don't care about leaving me alone."

"That's not true," I said, but my calm proved my lie: at that moment, at least, I was thinking solely of the great novelty of boarding school. I tried to give another meaning to my negative attitude: "It's not true that I'm leaving you alone. There's Costantino."

"Oh, Costantino . . ." She smiled through her tears, a bitter, almost mocking, smile. I saw that she was on the point of saying something more, of saying that poor Costantino didn't count; but she restrained herself, sure that I would have understood that, and not wanting to mock my brother still further, and needlessly.

I can still picture the great hall, light and many-windowed, the moment before we separated. I remember my mother saying to the Rector:

"I entrust him to you, Father. God has given him to me

25

and I give him to you. I know; I'm giving you a terrible responsibility. But God will surely help you. I will pray; I'll pray every morning. From tomorrow I'll go to Communion every day and hear Holy Mass for Carlo Felice, and I'll pray for him every hour, an ejaculatory prayer every hour, I assure you. . . ."

She was unable to go on or she would have burst into tears. The Rector smiled gently:

"Don't worry, Signora. Everything will be all right. All the boy needs is the will to study."

"Oh, if that's all . . . I think I can guarantee that," and my mother looked at me with pride.

With two fingers, the Rector delicately loosened a watch-chain that passed between one button of his habit and the next, and looked at his watch.

"You still have a few minutes, Signora. If you'd like to go with Carlo Felice to the parlor . . . there's no one there now."

My mother turned her eyes on me, tearful, suppliant, anxious. I understood the meaning of that look. "Yes, my Carluccio, let's go into the parlor and be by ourselves. But I'd like you to agree, and come of your own free will. . . ."

My mother's tears exasperated me, but I was also afraid that at any moment they might become nervously catching and overwhelm me too. I said no, but just with a look and a slight negative gesture which was imperceptible except to her. Once again, as on the previous evening, I counted on an equivocation and profited by my state of mind to deceive her and free myself from her tedious affection. I told myself that in all probability I was already showing my nervous emotion, so my mother would believe in the sincerity of my feeling and in the will with which I was trying to overcome its outward expression, and would think that was why I didn't want to be alone with her in the parlor. Whereas I only felt uneasiness, embarrassment, and impatience to be left in peace.

The Father Rector went away toward the glass enclosure. My mother threw herself on me and hugged and kissed me at length, sobbing. I could feel her heaving breast against me, that breast, that skin, that perfume I knew so well. She bent over my ear and began whispering strange words, words that she hadn't said for years but which neither she nor I could have forgotten, a whole private language invented by her and me during my childhood, and known to nobody else in the whole world. There were even the joking, sweet, and tender names that we gave to our kisses, to differentiate between the various kinds:

"Luccio, darling," she whispered, "don't forget, don't ever forget the Long Kiss, the Little Bird Kiss, the Snake Kiss, the Biting Kiss, the Wind and Rain Kiss, the Good Night Kiss, the Hidden Kiss," and each time she kissed me with the kiss whose name she had just whispered in my ear.

"And the Holy Love Kiss . . ." which was the slightest and most delicate of them all, on the tip of outstretched lips, like the infinitesimal explosion of cyclamen petals at the moment of opening. But as I remember, I wasn't able to give it; I, too, was sobbing at last and clung to her for the last time.

SCHOOL life began. From then on I rarely went out walking with my mother through the streets of Turin; yet I went on seeing her regularly—on visiting days at school, during the Christmas holiday, on Shrove Tuesday, at Easter, and then at Levo during the summer vacation from June to November.

The women in whose presence my mother had the opportunity of observing my behavior were of two categories only: one, the maids in our house; two, my young cousins, and the daughters of friends or more distant relatives whom I met at receptions, teas, and dances during carnival time. On those occasions my mother kept me under constant vigilance, though she tried to hide her maneuvers and expedients so as to convince herself, and then maintain shamelessly to me, that she had been very discreet and that I couldn't reasonably be annoyed. If any of those girls happened to show some sign of interest on their part, then, according to my mother, they were girls who were only apparently normal.

"Yes, yes," she said, "of course they lead ordinary lives, ordinary daily lives. I'm not saying that they're not nice girls. No one can be certain, and I don't want to make rash statements. But among those nice girls, those very nice girls, it's the easiest thing in the world for there to be one who isn't like the others. And she'd be enough. One is enough. There could be one who is apparently a girl but who really is sin, that is, the devil disguised as a girl; the devil for herself and for others, and hence also for you. Especially—now listen carefully to what I'm saying— especially if you have some special feeling for her, such as, for instance . . ."

In my first year at boarding school I was still entirely under my mother's influence, even though I was no longer in love with her and was positively rebellious where her caresses and tender advances were concerned. I hadn't yet become friends with Alessandro. My mother was still my main confidant. So I hastened to complete her sentence:

"Such as shyness, darling Mamma? Such as a kind of fear?—as though I weren't able to look that girl in the eyes?"

"That's it, my good boy, that's how it is. And do you know why you're afraid? It's because that girl is in a state of sin and would mean sin for you. Oh, a mother's heart is never mistaken. I didn't say anything to you, but I saw everything. And even if I hadn't seen, even if I hadn't been there, I would have known all the same."

"But how, darling Mamma?"

"When I look you in the eyes, after you come home, I immediately observe everything. And I know that up to now you're pure. And something here inside me tells me that, with Our Lord's help, you'll always be pure."

In July of the following year I passed the exam for the *licenza ginnasiale* with very high marks. Soon after my arrival at Levo my mother noticed that she no longer occupied the position of my main confidant. That place had been taken by Alessandro, and I have already said how. A fortnight passed and my mother noticed something else: for some reason unknown to her my religious faith had become slightly weakened, slightly tarnished: since my arrival at Levo I hadn't yet been to Communion.

In the village there was a girl of about twenty called Pierina, a dark beauty, florid, with very bright eyes. Her family was poor, and her father always ill. They lived in the first house in the village, just in front of the gate of our villa. We only saw Pierina late in the afternoon if my mother and I went out for a short stroll as far as the presbytery, or else on Sundays, for she was a working girl and went to Baveno every day by bicycle, and then on by bus as far as the cotton factory at Fondo Toce. But this year Pierina always stayed at home. Everyone knew that she had become the mistress of Aglietta, the firm's boss. Two or three evenings a week the boss would come by car to pick her up, and he brought her back late at night when everyone was asleep. It was also known that he was jealous and insisted on Pierina's going out as little as possible. So Pierina spent the whole day on a little balcony at the corner of the first floor of the cottage, half hidden by wisteria leaves and stretched out on a chaise longue, reading or sewing. And she peeped out through the leaves and greeted my mother and me with a big smile when we passed. My mother hardly answered; but I, I must confess, failed to hide my perturbation, I was fascinated by the beauty of the girl and "tempted" because of the very thing said about her.

My mother had certainly observed the effect Pierina had on me, but she was too astute to broach the subject head on. Merely to utter Pierina's name in connection with me would be to admit the possibility that there could exist between Pierina and me even the most shadowy vestige of a relationship, whereas such a possibility ought to be, and hence, according to my mother, was, totally excluded.

So my mother judged it opportune to set about frightening me not with the idea of mortal sin and hell, but with the specter—much more immediately agonizing—of venereal disease.

"You must be careful, Luccio! If you knew what that doctor told me . . . ," and she lowered her voice to give me the name of a famous specialist in Milan who had examined my brother some time earlier. "He told me that it isn't at all unlikely that Costantino's illness is a result of your father's crimes. Of course I have had myself checked. And you too, all those visits last year before you went to Moncalieri. In a word, we can be at peace, we have nothing. If you knew what an appalling thing those illnesses are! Take care, for the love of God! Evil women, women who misbehave, those who give themselves for money . . . Take care. You have a terrible danger before you!"

And naturally, by the very fact of admitting that this danger from women who misbehaved existed for me, she removed into the distance the danger of other women, of well-brought-up girls, of those who were not usually ill, but with whom, from the religious point of view, sin was no less grave or mortal: quite the reverse!

By shifting emphasis to the danger of disease, my mother —though without intending it or realizing it—relegated religion to a secondary plane and directed my tastes, my senses, perhaps for my whole life, precisely and exclusively to "evil women, women who misbehave." For I remember that up till that time, that is, up till the summer holidays between the *quinta ginnasio* and the *primo liceo,* the women I had thought about most had been four: Contessa Dessalles, a friend who was only a little younger than my mother; Delia, the pretty niece of our cook who had recently come to work for us; my cousin Poupette; and Gabriella, a friend of my cousin's. But as soon as my mother began frightening me with the specter of syphilis, which was strictly bound up with the specter of "evil women," I immediately began to be attracted as if by enchantment to evil women, or women who had the air of being evil.

Except for the permanent wave, always in place, a little lipstick, and one or two silk shirts, Pierina was exactly the same as the year before; but for me, now, she was like a divinity to be secretly adored. I never passed the little balcony without my heart's pounding. I found excuses and went out several times a day so as to be able to see her, so as to be able to greet her, so that she might answer my greeting: but I didn't dare to greet her always, that is to say at too short an interval beween one time and the next; and so I sometimes contented myself with walking under the balcony and raising my eyes to see her legs, which were large but excellently shaped, with sturdy calves and delicate ankles. Those legs, glimpsed between the wisteria leaves, and always, despite the summer heat, well sheathed and modeled by the silk of her stockings, with her small black shiny shoes with high heels, still remain among the dearest and most hopeless memories of my life.

Why have I written "hopeless"? God knows that later, and especially after my mother's death, I made up for it. But no, I don't know . . . I vaguely feel that that vision was the culmination of a supreme and mysterious voluptuousness, full of a desire which, in the years that followed, I perhaps never recaptured with the same force. And the reason could be this: that since that time I have perhaps never felt so far removed from the possibility of satisfaction!

To desire and to know for certain that the desire will never be fulfilled: it was the very cruelty of this contradiction that transformed Pierina's legs into something sublime: into an image which, for me, was at the same time totally natural and supernatural.

Not so very different was the religious impulse with which, until a few months earlier, I had adored the Host and the chalice raised up by the celebrant at the moment of consecration, or the monstrance during benediction, or the particle held suspended over the pyx between the thumb and the forefinger before the distribution of the Eucharist. That was what my mother had taught me every time I went to church with her. I was kneeling down beside her and only needed to imitate her. Every time the sacred species were shown to the faithful, you must gaze at them. You mustn't lower your eyes or pray with your head between your hands. And the Jesuit Fathers had taught me the same thing—it was with them that I had attended primary school and lower *ginnasio* "as a day boy." Many years later, when it seemed to me that I could make the comparison in my thoughts without trembling at the profanation, I admired the cleverness or, if we prefer, the wisdom of Catholicism in nourishing Faith by means of Communion; that is, by means of an act both physical and metaphysical, which confers on mystery a breath that is palpable, a taste not only symbolic . . . Rather as if I had been allowed to take away with the tip of my tongue the dust which sometimes veiled the shiny surface of Pierina's small shoes.

When I had finished school, I signed on at the university. My mother had never given up our quarters in Turin, and during the winter holidays it was there that she awaited me and welcomed me. She reverted to living there regularly, on purpose to be near me during my university years. My brother was a bit better and, more important, we had found a trusty woman who was at once nurse, maid, and cook and had become devoted to us, and especially to Costantino.

Angela wanted nothing better than to look after Costantino and live in our villa at Levo. She came from near Lake Orta; she was thirty-five, good-looking, not needy, but unmarried and unhappy. For ten years she'd been engaged to a young man of the region who, like so many others from those parts, worked as a waiter in a London restaurant and had made a solemn promise to marry her as soon as he'd become a *"maître."* But when that day arrived, the new *maître* preferred an English girl who was prettier, younger, and richer. Angela had suffered much; less from the disappointment than because, the first year after his marriage, her ex-fiancé had come back to the lake with his English wife and a baby and opened a hotel-restaurant; it was a continual pretext, even among the least malicious people in the village, for teasing poor Angela. So she had wanted to get away, but not too far: her parents were old and alone. Levo, which was less than an hour by bus, was a gift from Providence. Years later, toward the outbreak of the war, Angela fell ill. When she began to suspect the nature of her illness, and to realize that she could no longer take care of Costantino as in the past, she summoned a nephew of hers who in his turn had good reasons for leaving the region. This nephew was Giopa, an abbreviation of Giovanni Battista. Giopa was an only son, and his mother, having been left a widow since his babyhood, had gone to live with a man who couldn't marry her because he was married already. He was contractor for the jerry-built houses at Bolzano Novarese. He was rich, he made plenty of money, and he was separated from his lawful wife. He couldn't abide Giopa. Giopa returned his hatred wholeheartedly and so was only too ready for an opportunity to leave home. He grew as fond of Costantino as his aunt had been before him. And when she died, he took her place in our house.

SO MY mother's baneful influence on my childhood and adolescence went on, and even now hasn't left me. My other great confidant, Alessandro, who at first almost neutralized my mother's influence, was fatal for me too, in the end. It is strange. But not all that strange, if I reflect that after his conversion Alessandro became, in some way, like my mother after the death of my father.

The secret of the most concealed homosexual always leaks out in the end, even in his family circle, among relatives and old family acquaintances. But sometimes, when the adventures that are talked and laughed about have happened not locally but under distant skies, then the outbreak of scandal is delayed. And this was how it was. But before the scandal broke, and because he could see it coming and did not think himself strong enough to face it, Alessandro had suddenly decided to change everything, to give up travel, amusements, the gay, spendthrift, and abandoned life—always lived on the dangerous tightrope of blackmail—and had married a woman rich and aristocratic like himself, but ugly, boring, and stupidly austere. I must make this clear: his conversion was religious, even mystical; but a component part was the fear of scandal and a concern for social decorum.

Throughout his most dissipated period, which was all the years that elapsed between his father's death and his conversion, our friendship had remained unchanged: solid, lively, affectionate, unbounded. Though I always talked about women, and he always talked about boys, each of us had gone on genuinely upholding the role of confessor and consoler as regards the other. I always listened to him with a touch of bad faith, as if I shared his particular anxieties and joys, at least in part; that is to say, I displayed a degree of interest and emotion that was greater than I really felt. For his part, he always listened to me with a trace of skepticism, with an uncertain smile or, at most, one that oscillated between commiseration and disbelief: commiseration until I seemed sufficiently seriously in love, yes, and with a woman; disbelief when his prevailing opinion was that I was deluding myself or pretending.

My troubles with my women were unquestionably more expensive but infinitely less risky than his with rough young men, workers, sailors, airmen, policemen: above all, unlike his, they were not complicated by sentiment or sentimentalism. The situation about which I complained in all my so-called love affairs was invariably and uniquely the same: that—on my side of course—they did not last longer. There was no woman capable of making me happy for more than one or two nights. And two nights was a record that I reached with great difficulty and never went beyond. It sometimes even seemed to me that the feelings of disillusion, coldness, and disgust that followed making love were worse in proportion as the act of love had been intense and total, and forgetfulness had been bliss. A woman who "before" had been for me a queen and more than a queen, a goddess to whom I would have sacrificed all my possessions and life itself, became in the space of a few hours, and despite all my efforts in the opposite direction, an abject, ignoble, and extremely boring creature whose mere company I could no longer endure and from whose presence I madly tried to free myself. But I had another and deeper problem: I attained the complete and intimate pleasure I've just mentioned only if, at the time of expectation and preparation, I was utterly and sincerely convinced that this time would be miraculously different from all the times that had gone before: and I had that conviction even when it was supremely irrational to have it—that is to say, regarding a woman with whom I had previously been, and with whom I had already experienced the usual fatal and final disillusion. Hence on every occasion I promised the woman that I would devote much more time to her, and give her much more money, than the time or money I was afterward inclined to accord her. I made up detailed programs of communal life for a fortnight or a month. I would study a journey in detail and would reserve railway tickets and hotel bedrooms in Monte Carlo, Nice, or Venice. On the second or third day, on any kind of pretext, I would break off everything and go back home. Usually I didn't go back to Milan but straight to Levo, to my brother, who, regularly after each adventure, I was tenderly anxious to hold in my arms. But if each time it was easy enough to get out of the time commitment, the promise of money had to be kept, down to the last lira. And in order to win forgiveness for the humiliation I was inflicting on the queen, whom I had so brutally dethroned, I often gave even more than I had promised.

I have already said that it was anything but rare for me to return and lose my head over a woman whom I had already, and more than once, despised after adoring. There was even a time when the bed in Via Pasquirolo became a sort of altar on which three or four specific goddesses regularly took turns. And then the extraordinary thing was this: while every time, with obstinate good faith, I reverted to the belief that this was the real time, and made the usual promises and the usual commitments, scrupulously fulfilling the usual rites of preparation and propitiation, as if I was about to form a relationship lasting at least a short month, my partner, having already passed through the curious experience, knew perfectly well how it would end up, and hence nearly all of them rebelled against playing the game. "Why did you make me bring the big suitcase? Why did you make me bring the trunk from the bathroom? I'm sorry, but this is ridiculous; you know perfectly well that you'll be sending me away tomorrow." "I swear I won't, not this time. I love you and adore you for ever. I can feel it." And almost all of them, convinced that I was pretending, answered with a burst of laughter or shrugged their shoulders. But some of them didn't. The most intelligent and nicest of them understood that I was being sincere, and extended their own professional seriousness to the backing-up of my caprice: they arrived at Via Pasquirolo or at the rendezvous at the Central Station with an avalanche of suitcases and trunks, though knowing perfectly well that they would never open them. They knew

37

that, before a night of love, nothing depressed me more than to see that their luggage consisted of a single grip or a single beauty case—a sad and incontrovertible sign of the separation destined for the following day. Of course such intelligence or professional skill always ended up by being translated into economics: they knew that they belonged to a superior class and insisted on being paid accordingly.

Just once, one of them tried to be clever: she arrived with two brand-new traveling trunks from Franzi's. She said she had bought them specially for the occasion, and, when she saw my enthusiasm, asked me to give them to her as a present: that is to say, refund her the money she had spent on them. I agreed, though the sum was far from small. I gave her the money at once, then asked her to open the trunks. She searched for the key in her bag but couldn't find it. Suspicious and angry, I prized the lock open with a knife and discovered, as I feared, that the trunks were empty. In a rage I called for a taxi and sent her away on the spot. I paid her the agreed-on sum without making love and without letting myself be moved by her tears.

When I told Alessandro these stories, he smiled and sighed as if they didn't completely correspond with the truth.

"What do you want me to say, my dear Carlo? After all, a madman knows more about his own house than a sage about someone else's. But have you ever asked yourself why you're dissatisfied with women?"

"But I'm so content. They give me so much joy."

"Before, yes; but what about afterward? It isn't normal, my dear Carlo; you mark my words, it isn't normal."

"And what's your idea of normal?"

"Oh, Carlo, Carlo . . . If only you weren't such a

hypocrite with yourself! If only you didn't try to be different from what you really are!"

"Why? What ought I to do, in your opinion, if I were sincere?"

"My dear boy, go to a psychiatrist. Go to someone who can help you see yourself clearly."

Out of a malice common enough to those who like men, Alessandro envied men who like women, and thus affected to despise women. It was rather the fable of the fox and the grapes, but naturally in a subtle version, where the object of desire was replaced by the capacity to desire.

Alessandro was still convinced that the reason I didn't practice homosexuality was that I lacked the courage, not the vocation. And as I was unable to provide a proof of the mistake to which he so obstinately clung, I ended up by almost agreeing, and by seeming to admit that he was right. Our friendship was genuine and had now lasted for twenty years: but at its base there was always the old equivocation—on my side a touch of snobbery, on his a touch of malice.

Alessandro's conversion took place in Algeria, in the Ahaggar region of the Sahara. He had gone there in pursuit of quite another aim and inflamed by quite another passion. He happened to fall seriously ill. In 1937 the comforts of transport and air services did not exist as they do today. Alessandro was taken in, nursed, and brought back to life by a missionary, a young French friar, a follower of the famous Père de Foucauld. He stayed there for a whole year, perhaps because of his illness, perhaps even after he was cured: his letters, in this regard, had been very vague and contained no allusion whatsoever to the possibility of a moral or religious crisis. But when he got back to Italy he was a different man. I was aware of it at once, a few moments after having embraced him, and in any case before he started telling me about himself.

He had let me know, in a telegram from Marseilles, of the date of his arrival in Milan. I had already been a couple of days in Milan, at Via Pasquirolo—my mother thinking, as always, that I was living "in my room in Alessandro's house." Alessandro arrived later in the evening. We talked on the telephone and I went to see him next morning.

We were in his study and it was getting on toward noon. The large solemn *fin-de-siècle* windows, framed by a valance and ocher damask curtains, were open onto the park, onto the green of the tapering poplars, onto the red of the Castello, under the May sun. We had just embraced. He had come down to open the door himself, perhaps he had looked for me from the window, and now we had just entered the study; we were there, face to face. A whole year! We had never been so long without seeing each other since we had first known each other. We looked at each other and laughed. Now we tried to observe, in the clear light of spring, what in the shadow of the ground-floor entrance we had not been able to see: whether, and in what way, we had changed.

Alessandro was thirty-five, two years older than me. The Sahara and his illness seemed to have aged him: he was very sunburned and much thinner, but his thinness was nervous, uneasy.

There was a knock at the door. It was Paolo, asking if I was staying to lunch.

Yes, of course, Alessandro said. And seeing Paolo, I asked him the usual question: Had my mother by any chance telephoned from Levo asking for news of me?

Then suddenly I saw Alessandro's face become sad: his eyelids lowered over his fine blue eyes, his sensual upper lip sagged inertly. Anyone who didn't know Alessandro well, and wasn't used to him as I was, might have guessed at a shadow, or a wave, of secret melancholy. All I saw was a worldly grimace of boredom. Unbelievable! So was Alessandro "fed up" with my mother telephoning his house for news of me, as she had always done? Once the servant had gone I lost no time in removing my doubt: "What is it, Sandro? Is there some reason that I don't know, and that you don't want to tell me, why you prefer that my mother shouldn't call me up here . . . or perhaps that I shouldn't have my room here any more?"

"If you had one, I should feel the very opposite. . . ."

"What do you mean, the very opposite?"

He gave a deep sigh, lowered his eyes again, and went on without looking at me:

"My dear Carlo, I'm fully aware that I have no right to preach you a sermon; I, alas, have been . . . I've made more mistakes than you, very many more . . . and I'm only just beginning to see the extent of the abyss in which I used to live so horribly peacefully. I'll tell you, I'll tell you everything. It's been the most wonderful thing that could ever happen to a man, I think. And I only wish that you, too, could now share my new sense of security, and share the joys that I didn't know existed before; if someone had mentioned them to me I might even have made fun of him, without understanding."

"Joy? You seem to me to have become sad."

"I'm sad for you. I'm not ashamed to tell you that at Tin-Tuatin and El Golea, on Père de Foucauld's tomb, I, we, prayed for you. I said that I would feel *the very opposite* because I'd like you really to live in your room here, I'd like you to become a serious person. . . ."

"A serious person?" I think I had to make an effort not to laugh, not to show that I was becoming genuinely amused. Alessandro, who knew me as well as I knew him, caught this rakish gleam in my eye.

"No, I'm not joking. I'd like you to come to feel the bitterness of living as you live, and as, alas, I lived up till last year. I understand"—and he glanced at the door where the servant had departed—"that you still have Via Pasquirolo, or something of the kind?"

"Yes."

"And everything is going on as before?"

"Yes."

"And are you content? Content with yourself?"

"Very much so."

"Poor Carlo. How long do you think you'll be able to go on like that? Life has meaning only if you accept renunciation and pain, in sacrifice, whereas you think that a human being's life can be the same as that of a spider, don't you? Perhaps, yes; perhaps there are wretched and ignoble individuals who are content to be like that; waiting in their lair, or in their web, for their daily fly . . . as you have done till now."

"I swear that at least as far as the victims are concerned no comparison could be more mistaken. But perhaps it wouldn't have occurred to your mind if . . ." It was a malicious thing to say, so I hesitated for a moment before saying it; then I made up my mind. At first his absurd preaching tone had surprised me, then amused me; now I'd had enough; I was annoyed: ". . . yes, perhaps the comparison wouldn't have occurred to your mind if the victims had belonged to the other sex."

He tightened his lips and said nothing, as if he were savoring the intimate bitterness that my phrase had caused him. We looked one another in the eye: perhaps in the half-hour since we had met again and embraced, this was the first moment of absolute truth. It was also the last, and for ever. As soon as he managed to speak, he immediately began to veil that cruel light both from me and from himself, to filter it through error and make-believe. With a bland smile he said:

"Just the opposite of what you think, this time too. I've decided to get married."

It was so gross that at the moment I didn't believe it. But I was wrong. He kept his promise within the year.

There was no real break between us: it was just that a coolness developed. That day I stayed to lunch. He told me everything in detail: his illness, and how he had caught it in a remote fort in the Ahaggar desert; the vision of Our Lady of Lourdes that he saw like an apparition in his delirium, though it was really a little clay statue standing by chance in a niche at the foot of the bed; and another apparition, this one accompanied by cures; Père Jaboulet was a member of Père de Foucauld's order, but he also had a degree in medicine and had specialized in tropical diseases, and was fairly young, as I could see from the inscribed photograph already squatting in its frame on Alessandro's writing desk. Alessandro added that Père Jaboulet was a fascinating person: his beard was like gold, his eyes were green with flecks of gold, and quite magnetic. . . .

Of course I was not impressed, and made no effort to appear so. Gone for ever were the days when I tried to win Alessandro's confidence by letting him think that I shared his tastes, at least partially. And now Alessandro could hardly expect me to follow him in his conversion, along the road of sacrifice and mysticism; but he expected that his story would move me a little, perhaps disturb me, or at least awaken my respect and leave me thoughtful and perplexed as to my own affairs. Whereas he saw on my face an expression of repressed irony, not to say mockery, and he was deeply disappointed, even offended.

Our relationship quickly changed. When I left Levo to go to Milan, I no longer told my mother that I was going to stay with Alessandro. I said I was going to a hotel because Alessandro could no longer put me up; he had the builders in and was altering his apartment.

From the day of his return from Africa, we began seeing each other much less often. Above all, we gave up confiding in each other and listening—sometimes with real interest, sometimes with disguised boredom—to each other's detailed account of his adventures. And whereas, before, he had never hidden from me any escapade of whatever intensity or conclusiveness or length—so that, I fully believe, no fleeting glance from sailor or airman caught during an evening stroll by the sea or in town, no faint current from a policeman's hand just brushed in a crowded streetcar, occurred without Alessandro telling me at the first possible moment, trying, by dwelling on it and telling it, to compensate in some way for the obligatory renunciation of action—now he didn't even feel the need to tell me about the "nice young lady" who first became his fiancée and then, a few months later, his wife. He never spoke of her to me. I only heard of his marriage when it had already taken place.

True, as I have often told myself, his silence could be interpreted as a proof of friendship, the last he gave me. He felt the falsehood of his own conversion, knew the skepticism with which I viewed it, feared the frankness of some intervention on my part, preferred to confront me with the accomplished fact, and, still more, perhaps he was ashamed of his wife and didn't want me to see her. As it was, I only got to know her after the wedding, and by a sequence of events that was both unforeseen and inevitable. She was worse than ugly; she looked almost repulsive. I was unable to suppress the malicious suspicion that Alessandro, in his unconscious, had chosen someone as awful as this owing to his old hatred of the feminine sex. Formally, I was only obliged to suppose that he had applied the Christian theory of renunciation and sacrifice, and to pass over the detail that he hadn't thought it necessary to apply it globally. But there you have it; although Alessandro's fortune needed no props, his wife was immensely rich in her own right, the heiress of an ancient and noble Genoese family that had married, two generations before, into a family of shipowners.

Alessandro had seven children in a little over ten years. He didn't live in Genoa, but in a castle on the sea, at Bergeggi. He spent his time educating his offspring in historical and religious studies. In 1946, on the thirtieth anniversary of Père de Foucauld's death, he published a life in novel form entitled *A Saint and Hero*. He sent me a copy at once. The dedication was: "To my old Companion Carlo Felice, so that he will understand for what new Companion I abandoned him." The book was among the very few that I salvaged from the sale of my library. I can see it as I write; it's here on a shelf in my study in Auckland; the only one, in my very small collection, that has no literary value. Or perhaps I am mistaken, because it is also the only one with uncut pages.

. . . I WAS coming from Florence, from the capital's May festival, and was on my way to Genoa for a concert conducted by Celibidache: they were to play for the first time one of Zafred's compositions, which I found very interesting and had to review.

I had just got out of the train at Brignole. Preceded by my porter, I was making for the exit. Then I recognized the broad shoulders of Alessandro as he stood by a newspaper kiosk; and, beneath the Mossant brown felt hat, the disproportionately slender, almost concave, neck, scattered with thin silky curls, gray, almost white.

I swear that my first instinct was to hurry past. If I had followed it, perhaps I might have saved myself. But at the sight of his neck, and those thin little curls, now almost white, a feeling of tenderness swept over me. I stopped a step or two away from his back; for a moment I was undecided as to whether to speak to him or not, and then I suddenly resolved to give destiny one more chance: if he turned around, well and good. If he didn't, then I would continue on my way after a moment or two.

The sides of his spectacles were sticking out behind his ears: perhaps he wore them all the time now? I rapidly calculated how long it was since we had seen each other. Two years. He had come to Milan to hear Callas, or rather to see her the first time she was directed by Visconti.

He was rather bent, and seemed to be scrutinizing the newspapers' front pages with close attention: then, with the tips of the fingers of his gloved right hand, he lifted up the corner of the papers one after another and cautiously turned them over, with the obvious aim of reading the headlines. It occurred to me that he was one of the last people in the world to wear gloves at the end of May. And I thought that the cautious and furtive maneuver with which he was reading the headlines came from his increased avarice: rather than buy an extra paper or two . . . This was another defect that had come to him only with his conversion. As a boy he had never been mean; just the opposite.

All these thoughts seemed as one, and took only a few

seconds. How many more seconds would I have stayed there, waiting for him to turn around?

I have never had any doubts as to the importance of chance. Even on much more futile occasions than this one, I have always had the habit of playing a little game with myself. For instance. A leaf carried by the wind lands on the window sill: if it comes into the room, it's a good sign; if it doesn't, it's a bad sign. Whether, when I'm in my car, I do or don't succeed in getting past the lights before they turn red. Whether a woman dressed in white, standing in front of a shopwindow, will have moved, or not, before I, continuing at the same pace and along the same sidewalk, arrive at the same window. Whether one match will be enough, or not, to light my cigarette in the open air on the Laveno-Intra crossing.

Sometimes the game is faintly disturbing, because I find myself uncertain as to the positive or negative significance to be attributed to each of the two opposing eventualities.

And so it was now. The porter went on slowly toward the exit in the midst of the crowd. I wanted to call to him to wait. But that would have been against the rules of the game; in all likelihood my voice would have made Alessandro turn around. I therefore decided to remain there for the few moments needed for the porter to disappear from sight. The moment after that, if Alessandro hadn't turned around, then good-by to all that, I would have gone off.

I swung my head from left to right, like someone watching a tennis match, looking first at Alessandro as he went on examining the papers, then at the porter as he moved away. It was one of those cases I've mentioned, in which I wouldn't have been able to decide which of the two signs brought good luck, which bad. But I remember perfectly that I was only thinking of "a sign," and it never even crossed my mind that if Alessandro turned around before the porter disappeared this would cause a whole series of woes: woes which his not turning would have avoided.

Of course he turned around. He felt he was being watched. When he saw me, he blushed, as though caught red-handed.

"Look who's here!" he exclaimed: and I immediately recognized, in the unnaturalness of the phrase and the Tuscan, an initial aggressive irony with which he perhaps wanted quickly to correct his involuntary and, for me, mysterious blush. Meanwhile I went toward him. He came toward me in his turn, carefully pulling off his right glove. But instead of shaking hands we embraced, by a common and simultaneous initiative. This had ceased to happen at our meetings, rare and well spaced out though they were.

He immediately took my arm, leaning on me rather too heavily, as he used to do, and pushing me in the opposite direction from the one in which I was going. I stopped.

"No, I'm sorry, I must go that way. I have a porter with my bags at the exit. I've just arrived."

"And I'm just leaving," he said.

"Have you time?" And I began to make for the exit.

He didn't move. He delicately raised the edge of his glove and glanced at his watch on his left wrist—still the same tiny almost feminine watch.

"Not much, I'd say. I must catch the first train going to Principe. At eleven there's the fast train from Principe to Savona. I'm going home."

I noticed that he had picked up a slight Genoese intonation. I again made toward the exit.

"Come with me, I must find my porter. Then I'll stay with you until you leave."

He came with me, but seemingly unwillingly. As we passed in front of the kiosk I said:

"You know, I'd been watching you for some time, standing in front of those papers."

He bent toward my ear, sighed, murmured:

"It seems it really was he who shot and killed the cinema proprietor."

"He? Who?" I asked, not understanding at all.

"Mumi," he breathed in answer.

Mumi was the unforgettable nickname of a boy of unforgettable beauty who had been his lover, and whom I had known very well though I never knew his real Christian name and surname and so couldn't have thought of Mumi when I read the papers that morning. The robbers who'd been arrested in Alessandria the other night had burgled the cashbox of a cinema, killing the proprietor. They had confessed. On the first pages there were photographs of them all. But how could I remember Mumi's face when I hadn't seen him for twenty-four or twenty-five years?

It was clear that Alessandro was upset, and it hadn't yet dawned on him that I mightn't be aware that Mumi was among them: a second too late, perhaps he regretted having spoken.

I still had *La Stampa* in my hand, with a sheaf of magazines I'd been glancing at on the journey. I slowed my pace, wanting to have a look at the photographs.

"Don't do that; forget about it for the moment," he whispered almost in supplication. "It's he, there's no doubt about it."

"Why?" I too lowered my voice, instinctively adopting my former tone of complicity. "Have you seen him again?"

There was nothing malicious about my question: I was only thinking of the photograph in the paper that I hadn't been able to recognize. But to my great surprise, Alessandro looked around him and answered:

"Yes, on Sunday. Twenty-four hours before the . . . the event. Here in Genoa. By chance."

We had gone out onto the piazza in front of the station. The porter was already loading my bags. I told him to unload them and wait for me at the buffet. Meanwhile, I paid the taxi.

"I'm sorry about that," said Alessandro, somewhat dismayed that I hadn't hesitated about that little unforeseen expense. And I realized that his avarice had grown more than I thought.

"Still, it's better to talk here, outside," he added as soon as the porter had gone off. He was obviously afraid that someone might overhear us. And it seemed to me that at the same time he was relieved not to have to pay for a drink in the buffet, an expense that would naturally have fallen to him. For the same reason, as I later discovered, he chose to wait for a train to take him from one Genoa station to the other rather than avail himself of a taxi, which would have been the natural thing. He must have calculated that if he included the trip across the city in his ticket to Savona, doing it by train cost a little less.

He had again taken my arm, leaning on me heavily, and was making for the steps in Via De Amicis, on the wide pavement flanking the station. I wanted to look at Mumi's photograph, but he again implored me not to.

"Later, you can see it later. The whole thing is too painful to me."

He told me the whole story. Mumi had stopped him under the arcades of Via XX Settembre. He was in need of a shave and was very badly dressed. Like me, Alessandro had not seen him for many years and did not at once recognize him. Mumi said that he had a family, a wife and small children, and that he was in trouble. He wanted to give the details, but Alessandro refused to listen. Whereupon Mumi asked for a large loan.

"So as to get rid of him I didn't argue the point but handed over everything in my pocket; about fifty thousand lire. I didn't argue; for, as you'll understand, I didn't much want to be seen under the arcades with a fellow like that. All my wife's relatives live in Genoa, and I myself am very well known now."

"You could have suggested meeting him somewhere else."

"What an idea!"

"But how much did he ask you for?"

"Twenty times as much as I gave him. Quite absurd. Fifty thousand lire was a huge sum, as it was. But what could I do? He was threatening."

"He was threatening you?"

"No: if I didn't give him a million, he threatened that he'd be obliged to do something silly. I thought he was referring to suicide. The papers say that he's been in jail several times already, but only for minor theft, or swindles. Whereas this time it's a very different matter. I'm feeling very low, as you can imagine."

We continued to walk up and down, slowly, in silence. I could feel a bitter taste of some kind rising within me, but wasn't yet sure what it was. I asked Alessandro:

"What are you planning to do?"

"Nothing. What could I do, at the moment? Pay a lawyer? I've got a family too."

I immediately countered:

"You could pay a lawyer without anyone knowing, if that's what's worrying you."

"There's that. And something else."

"You could help his wife and children."

"That too, without anyone knowing where the money's coming from? Please be sensible!"

"I can't see what's so very strange about it," I said bitterly, with that curious anger I could feel growing inside me, though at the same time I was aware that I was only suggesting good and just actions.

His conversion, his marriage, his return to order and conformity, his consuming avarice, the speed with which, the very day after his return from Africa, he had put an end to our affectionate and long-standing friendship—these things had offended me, and every time I thought about them they continued to irritate and disturb me. Now, suddenly, an opportunity for revenge had presented itself. Revenge, I repeat, with justice. Alessandro had not only hurt me as a friend; worse still, he had betrayed himself, his love of truth, his trust in life, all that was best in him. As nasty as only a man can be who knows he's right, I said: "Don't think I'm preaching at you. You, on the rare occasions when we've met in recent years, have always tried to preach to me, of course. But I've never done so to you. But if Mumi has arrived at the point he has arrived at, you share a part of the responsibility. . . ."

"Why?" For a moment, in his agitation, he raised his voice, again adopting the Genoese intonation. "Why? Should I perhaps have given him all the money?"

"No, I'm not talking about the here and now; I'm talking about your responsibility then, when he was no more than a boy, when he was still a sailor, and immediately afterward, when he traveled with you, when he lived with you."

"Oh, don't worry about that, I've already done penance for it and for all the rest, and I do so every night and every day, and have done for years and years, my dear fellow. Ever since I got married. You mustn't think I have a happy life. Of course my children give me joy, but—how shall I say it?—it's a gray joy. As for my wife, we now live in silence; total silence. The few words we exchange are violent ones. Ah, if I didn't know that everything comes to an end someday! But I accept the pain, I accept the daily torture, slow as it is, because I've understood what you haven't yet understood, my dear Carlo: that is, that the basis of life is nothing else but this, for everyone. Evil is within us, and sooner or later it emerges. If we've lived for a time as I once did, and as you still do now, ignoring or rather believing we ignore this evil, this hell, then the day always comes when we realize everything, when we see what the end will be, indeed when we feel that the end, in us, has already begun; then we understand that there's only one thing left: to live the years that remain with our eyes wide open and our feet firmly planted on the ground."

Once in my life, I, too had come near to marriage. It was by pure chance that I didn't marry. Destiny separated us: the death of my mother, and the Allied landing at Salerno. I lost Meris and never found her again, though I looked for her for a long time and using every means. Perhaps I didn't love Meris—who can tell? Certainly I had liked her better than any other woman, certainly I had desired her, and deep down I still desired her: I thought of her constantly.

Whereas, plainly, Alessandro should never have got married, given his liking for men; besides, of all women, he had chosen one with whom he knew he would find it very difficult to get on. He had chosen her for reasons of social and financial convenience.

And now his bitter words were producing in me a strange, unforeseeable, adverse effect. I thought that if destiny had allowed me to find Meris again, and to marry her, I would not have come to Alessandro's end. Pleasure, if not love, would anyway have given an element of warmth and humanity to our union. I thought once again of the tenderness of nights no longer solitary; of the sweetness of dedicating one's life to a single creature, even if not loved, even if only desired . . . Meris! Where was Meris? Was she still alive? Could I really have lost her for ever? I discovered that I was still not resigned, even after so many years of fruitless search. And meanwhile, death was approaching. Youth was far in the past, even for me. Alessandro was right: death had already begun inside me, I felt a sudden need to avoid thinking of what lay ahead, to affirm, to seize the reality of joy again, and at once. As soon as Alessandro was on his train, I would deposit my bags in the hotel, but I wouldn't even go up to my room: the Suprema is only a few steps from the Bristol . . . And then I remembered, with sorrow, that this simple and potent consolation was no longer allowed me: some months ago the "houses" had ceased to exist. So, I asked myself, was my life a failure like Alessandro's? Probably so. But the failure was less gloomy: it lacked hate, that was it.

Though there's no marriage between men, there are nevertheless examples of men who live together harmoniously for years, perhaps even for life. In the early stages it is only passion, and only on the part of one of the two; then they become friends and love one another like husband and wife. Perhaps Alessandro's great mistake was to have lacked the courage for this: precisely with Mumi, perhaps.

So many confused and heaped-up thoughts had passed through my mind during the few more moments of silence while we still paced up and down along the pavement outside the station. Beside us the huge piazza spread out as far as the sea, noisy and teeming with traffic on that morning in May. Once again, I was the first to speak:

"I had my suspicions that you didn't love your wife, but not that it was as bad as that."

"Love her? What an absurd idea! How does love enter into it? The truth is that there's only one true love. But unfortunately there are very few who achieve it."

"Do you mean the love of God?" I hazarded, but not without, I fear, a slightly ironical overtone.

"Leave it alone. All of us, at least you and I, we're all damned souls, wretched damned souls; that's the truth."

There was something exaggerated, something false, in this tragic negation. Did total pessimism allow him to pretend to feel rather less guilty about Mumi?

If all life is an ineluctable evil, if hell is already with us, what does one crime more or less matter, or one man more or less condemned to forced labor, even if he's the father of a family and even if he's an old boy friend? That's what he seemed to be thinking.

But I hoped for his sake that he wasn't really convinced: that he would be the first to note the hypocrisy and cowardice of beginning to reason and philosophize that very morning, immediately after getting the news about Mumi from the papers, in however pessimistic or Manichaean a fashion.

I looked at him. We had been together for twenty minutes now, and up till then I hadn't dared take a really good look at him. He was an old man. Not only his temples, but his whole face was gray. Was he suffering? Was he suffering enough? That is, as much as he ought to be suffering? To what extent was he a hypocrite? How far did he believe, as he said he believed, in everyone's guilt, and in the general and inevitable guilt of the human race? And how much did he feel the weight of the precise, particular, and anything-but-inevitable guilt of failing to help Mumi? A guilt not so much of not giving him unconditionally the money he'd asked for, but of being ashamed and afraid of him, of not conceding him a little trust, of not stopping to talk to him a little longer, of not having gone to a café with him to talk in a human way, of not having been willing to listen to the story that Mumi wanted to relate of his miseries and misfortunes. I remembered Mumi as a loose-living boy: lazy, dissolute, and as corrupt as you like; but he was also good-natured, incapable of malice.

Alessandro looked at the time.

"I'd better be off. My train goes in five minutes."

Perhaps it was the repetition of the delicate movement with which he'd lifted the edge of his glove; perhaps it was seeing that feminine little watch again; or perhaps it was my own urgent yet vain thought of going to the Suprema, and the equally vain memory of, and desire for, Meris: "Be sincere, Sandro," I would have liked to say. "When you saw Mumi again, did he merely cause you fright and horror, or did the possibility cross your mind, if only for a moment, of making love with him?"

Of course I in fact said nothing. I looked him in the eyes once more, but only fleetingly. And he seemed to have guessed. He took my arm again, this time holding it tightly as he dragged me toward the station entrance.

"Come to the train with me. I haven't told you the worst. When I saw him under the arcades, almost before I'd recognized him in all his filth and shabbiness, I felt for him something that I hardly ever feel nowadays, and always manage to overcome pretty quickly. It may have been just for this reason that I was so frightened, and that I rid myself of him so quickly, as if he were Satan himself. And that's another reason why I'm sad, so terribly sad about what's happened. . . ."

"I can well believe it," I said in spite of myself.

"Yes, but I don't regret it. One never regrets not having yielded to Satan."

What else could I say? I changed the subject:

"Haven't you got a car? Isn't it more convenient to go from Bergeggi to Genoa by car?"

"I've got a car, the driver is coming to meet me at Savona. There's nothing to be done with this traffic, especially getting across Voltri . . . whereas with the train it's all so simple, especially without luggage. I came to bring one of my sons back to school; the third. He's been convalescing at home for a few weeks. Nothing serious. Now he's got to get ready for the *licenza ginnasiale* exams."

"Is he with the Jesuits?"

"Of course, at the Annunziata, like all his brothers."

THE wisteria on Pierina's house was in full bloom: a thin, delicate lilac which, high on the hills around the lake, indicates the sweetest and briefest moment of spring, and seen from afar it looks white: but I knew at once when I saw that whiteness after the turning near the wash-house that it was the wisteria.

Unlike my usual custom, I had traveled by train because the car was being repaired. This was another of destiny's signs: otherwise I wouldn't have been at Brignole Station the day before, and I wouldn't have seen Alessandro again. As soon as I got to Stresa I fetched the car from Caldi's garage. I traveled by the usual road. On the last stretch, from the Gignese crossroad as far as Levo, the road wasn't paved, as it isn't to this day.

For me, the house with the wisteria was still "Pierina's house." Whenever I returned from some journey to my old village on the lake, memories overcame my resistance at that point: the turning was so narrow and the surface so rough that I always had to shift gear in the end. But many years had passed since Pierina lived there. She had finally made a regular marriage with Aglietta, the cotton factory boss: children, family, comfort, all was fine. I had rejoiced at this, as on every occasion when reality gave the lie to my mother's apocalyptic forecasts, and made nonsense of them. Pierina's parents, pleased at no longer having to feel ashamed in the village, had stayed there till the war, and then gone to Pallanza, to the daughter's villa. And evacuees had come to the house with the wisteria. Now there was a Calabrian family; both father and sons were builders and worked for a firm in Baveno.

When I'd had to take my *licenza liceale,* I'd left school, like many of my school friends, and retired to the country to study in peace. Alessandro was my guest. We did our "reviewing" together. At that time my mother was in England with Costantino, in a special clinic reputed to make use of the very latest methods for curing my brother's kind of mental illness. So for the first time I was free, not only from the supervision of school, but from the much sterner supervision of my mother. And I had profited from the occasion to pluck up the courage which till then had failed me in spite of all my efforts: I'd gone to a rendezvous with a girl.

Pierina again. The girl, that is, with whom—had I been normal—I would have had to say I was in love, whereas I only dared think of her in terms of "adoration." She was an unapproachable divinity! I had made no progress whatsoever since the summer three years before when I'd begun to go back and forth under the balcony so as to admire her legs. I had gone on sadly and obstinately excluding any possibility of one day finding myself alone with her. So when Angela mentioned a rendezvous, I thought I was dreaming: the enterprise was mad, ludicrous, far beyond my powers. Nor would I have listened to Angela if she hadn't assured me that the idea had come from Pierina herself; in fact Pierina had entrusted Angela with a message; Pierina, who had become aware of my long-standing devotion.

It may have seemed strange to me that it was she who took the initiative, but not that she hadn't taken it earlier. Until the year before I had still been a boy; now, at least in appearance, I was a man. She, too, had changed. Perhaps owing to her sedentary and inactive life, a real "kept woman's life," she had grown much fatter, although she was still extremely young—twenty-two or twenty-three. To me she was more pleasing than before, and for this very reason. Fatness seemed to me the supreme sign of her exceptional voluptuous power. With large breasts and large thighs, she was opulent, soft, yet sufficiently tall not to lack grace. Her ankles were still thin, and her feet were tiny and very lovely. Her raven-black hair was cut baby-wise, according to the fashion of the time, and looked like a high compact helmet; and the long, thick commas of the so-called "kiss curls," seductively framing her cheekbones, were in perfect harmony with her full lips painted crimson, with her laugh showing teeth as white as white, and with her big black almond-shaped eyes.

The meeting was to take place at eight in the evening, in the meadow beneath an inn called La Parúsciola, which still exists. After a day spent studying, I had a bath, shaved, put on a complete change of clothes. When Alessandro saw the fervor with which I made these preparations, he shook his head as though he was sorry for me. I asked him to let me have a little of his lavender water. In those days he wasn't at all mean, and immediately complied with my request, only when he held out the little bottle he murmured:

"But what do you think you're up to? It's all illusion. Do you by any chance think that girls like scented men? Have you any idea who do like scented men?—Policemen! Look, I don't envy you." He seemed an expert in his own vice. But I knew perfectly well that it was just the opposite, and that he was talking without reticence precisely because he hadn't yet "done" anything with anyone.

Angela had told me that Pierina wanted me to take her a present of two packs of Giubek cigarettes. I had already bought them. I put them in my pocket and went down in the direction of La Parúsciola with my heart in my mouth. It was not yet night, but the leafy boughs of the never-ending chestnut trees that bordered the road made it almost completely dark. I could only see things in the distance: the lake, the lit-up boats, the Maccagno hills, blue at their base, and blending to violet as they rose, and finally to pink in the last rays of the sinking sun. For some time the triangular rock of Caldè gleamed white in the dusk, like a huge sail standing on the bank of the lake. I walked quickly, unable to put from my mind Alessandro's ironic and by no means propitious words, and I felt my hopes gradually diminishing as I drew nearer to the place of assignation. That I might succeed, on that very evening, in losing my virginity didn't even enter the fringes of my mind. A simple kiss seemed to me the highest goal I might aspire to.

I reached the meadow. I left the road and proceeded swiftly over the newly cut grass. There was still a smell of hay in the air. As I pressed on, I carefully scrutinized the darkness all around me: the place was so open that, if there had been anyone about, even a distant shadow, I would have seen them at once. But all I could see were the fire-flies, wandering here and there, with their uncertain and seemingly pointless flight. I wasn't upset at seeing no one. On the contrary, I felt almost relieved. I gazed at the fire-flies, and the fireflies, I don't know why, seemed to me happiness: it would have been too wonderful if Pierina had really been there. I lit a match to look at the time: there were still five minutes to go before eight. As soon as the match had gone out I heard a whisper, without know-ing where it came from. I stood still, so as not to make a noise with my footsteps, and held my breath. The whisper was repeated, and became clearer:

"Master Carlo . . . Master Carlo, here I am." And a faint shadow detached itself from a stone hut, or rather a barn, that was at the end of the field near the wood going down toward Carpugnino. I remembered the stories about Aglietta's jealousy. It was unthinkable that Pierina would be ready to risk losing him! It was more than natural that she should be prudent like this. I ran across the field toward the barn, where meanwhile the shadow suddenly disappeared. I ran, and even now I could hardly believe in my good luck, in the reality of what was happening. I realized that I'd always thought of the possibility of a trick or, at best, of some setback at the last moment.

But no, it really was Pierina. I stopped in front of her so as to see her in the dark, so close that our bodies almost touched, and I could smell all the scent of her body, a thing I had never imagined, not even in my most detailed and persistent fantasy-weaving. She laughed, and looked straight at me with her great black eyes. I would have liked to say something, but all the words I could think of seemed absurd, stupid, and so I said nothing and pretended to be getting back my breath after running. But she spoke:

"Are you pleased?" she said.

"Yes," I answered. "Here are the cigarettes."

She immediately slid one out. I lit her cigarette with a trembling hand. Like that, in the light of the match, I could see her better. How beautiful she was! If I had followed my instinct, and not been afraid of seeming ridiculous, I would have thrown myself on my knees in front of her, I would have clasped her legs, kissed her feet. She spoke again:

"How about you, do you smoke?"

"Yes, yes." I hurriedly lit a cigarette in my turn, just as if she had issued an order. The first mouthful of smoke gave me some courage. I said:

"Thank you, Pierina."

"What for?"

"For . . . for this."

"I knew you liked me. I always knew it. But you do know, don't you, that it's only for a little petting. That's all right, isn't it?"

I was perfectly aware of the significance of the expression "petting," which means "making love but without ever getting down to brass tacks." Nevertheless, I felt my heart miss a beat as if that word alone suddenly opened the mysterious and celestial door to pleasure or vice, which up till now I had always seen from afar, darkly closed. And it was only many years later that I understood that it meant the opposite: that is, that it implied a genuine invitation to brass tacks, but given in the most delicate way, as if jokingly. Because it had been she who had proposed the meeting, now Pierina, out of pride and reserve, hastened to declare that she intended to limit its consequences to petting, thus attempting to correct the bad impression she feared she might have made on me by taking the initiative and talking to Angela.

It was the first kiss of my life, since the last one I had

given my mother, five years before, in the school entrance hall. In any case, it was the first kiss on the mouth. Perhaps I never again experienced anything so sweet, so tender, so intoxicating. I hugged her around her ample, solid, yet soft waist. I could feel her large breasts pressed against me. Instinctively I began to try to caress her skin by slipping my hand between her blouse and skirt.

"You're tickling me," she said after a moment, laughing and shaking herself free.

"Oh, forgive me," and I took away my hand, terrified that I had offended her.

"Only a bit of petting . . ." she repeated, and started kissing me again; without guessing, alas, that I wouldn't dare caress her again; without guessing that if, now, she left the initiative to me, we would never get beyond kissing.

And that's in fact how it was. Pierina had obviously grasped that I was timid. "A timid young gentleman who goes to church," she must have thought of me. And if she'd spoken in confidence with one of her girl friends, I'm sure that's how she would have described me. But her education and experience, as a country girl, a working girl, and as mistress of the boss, and her previous petting—and more —with the village boys, were not enough to enlighten her: she couldn't possibly imagine that my shyness, my gentlemanliness, and my "churchy air" wouldn't be overcome and overthrown, when the moment came, by my desire to make love, once this desire had come to me.

And so the sad smile which appeared on her face, when our lips drew apart after the umpteenth kiss, seemed to me, then, a first hint of boredom; the sign that she had suddenly decided "not to do any more petting." It was only many years later that I realized that it was a smile of humiliation and delusion. "The young Master Carlo thought he wanted to, but he didn't like me enough. . . ."

And even this equivocation became part of my destiny.

MY MOTHER came back with Costantino at the end of September. She was disappointed and frustrated. The cure had yielded up no practical result. Indeed, my brother's moods seemed to have got worse in England; but after a few days at Levo he returned to normal, to his gentle and melancholy indifference. The atmosphere, the forms of treatment, the apparatus of the clinic, the foreign language, and the uninterrupted presence of my mother had obviously taken their toll. Whereas the old villa, the garden where he had played since childhood, the serene grandeur of the landscape, the shapes and colors of the mountains so familiar to him, the blue depth of the lake lying between the mountains like another sky, my company, and—still more, perhaps—that of his beloved Angela, restored him to peace if not joy. Costantino wasn't, and isn't, what could be called "dangerous": he is humble, very gentle, even intelligent; only in certain things he is like a baby of three: left alone, he would die from boredom, or from one of the countless dangers provided by our daily life which he has never learned to recognize—street traffic, gas, electricity, a bottle of disinfectant, stairs, a window, a balcony. . . .

Costantino desired nothing, and never had desired anything, except to live near Angela and me. With my mother he was in constant altercation about every trifle. Costantino's life consisted of trifles, it was a repetition of tiny problems and futile doubts—which for him, however, were serious and could become a matter of anguish from one moment to the next if someone whom he trusted was not there to dissipate them. Ought he to fold his handkerchief when he put it into his pocket, or ought he to put it in unfolded? And if folded, then folded how? There might perhaps be no lemon: should he drink his tea just with sugar, or with a drop of milk? He was going on a walk on the road to Someraro; it was overcast: should he take an umbrella, or a raincoat, or both? He trusted only two people in the world: Angela and me. He loved his mother really very much; but he systematically opposed her, he went against her in every plan, and scolded her for every timid piece of advice she dared put forward. And our mother, though knowing full well that Costantino was ill, didn't know how to behave with him as though he was. Their conversation, from morning till night, consisted of an endless bickering which was painful, embarrassing, incessant, and exhausting. . . .

My mother had enjoyed England: first, because it stimulated and satisfied her indomitable snobbery; and second, because Costantino was unhappy in England, and although my mother loved him with her whole being and longed for his cure with her whole soul, she had convinced herself—in accordance with her ancestral faith in discipline and authority—that this cure was possible only if one day Costantino achieved "doing precisely what he didn't want to do." The doctors had of course explained on a number of occasions that his apathy, his indifference, and his lack of will power were merely the symptoms of the illness from which he was suffering. But my mother insisted on regarding these symptoms as the illness itself, and with unintentional cruelty reiterated: "Oh, if only you were capable of mastering yourself, of making an effort with yourself, of showing your will power."

Now that Costantino had been entrusted to Angela, and all extraordinary efforts to cure him had been suspended, my mother returned to lavishing her attention on me, on venting her need for love on me, and concentrating on me her tireless activities. I went to the university; I had enrolled in the faculty of philosophy. My mother reopened the apartment in Piazza Bodoni and decided to live in Turin with me. It was all very odd: she hadn't seen me for most of the time during the years I'd been at school at Moncalieri, and just recently she'd been separated from me for some months while she was away in England; and now, as if all this hadn't happened, she started again to direct me, control me, oppress me. Of course while I was at school she had put blind faith in the Barnabite Fathers. And it hadn't occurred to her that great temptations would beset me at Levo, even after I'd taken my *licenza liceale,* when from the end of July till the end of September I had all time and all freedom at my disposal. And unfortunately she'd been right. Pierina remained a botched and isolated episode. But when we were in Turin, and after dinner I went out to join my friends, she thought it her right to know how I had spent the evening, and stayed awake late into the night so as to hear an exact and detailed account. This went on during all the time I was at university; she never loosened her grip, as would have been natural as I grew older, but treated me at the end of the period, when I was twenty-two, exactly as she had treated me at the beginning, when I was eighteen. So military service was necessary for me to contrive to lose my inconvenient and stupid virginity. And in order to begin living with a little freedom at last, I needed the trick about Milan, and the fiction that I was being put up by Alessandro.

I had a friend and fellow student, Ettore, in whom I wanted to confide; but I was ashamed. He was very nice, very "experienced," and well known for all his women and girls: dancers, dressmakers, friends, and even married women. I had sought out his friendship precisely because I'd hoped he would help me achieve the great experience. Alessandro was studying law, and I saw him all the time; but naturally I couldn't count on him.

One night—I can't remember whether it was during my first or second year—after a big drinking bout around the wineshops, Ettore and others went off as usual to a brothel. When that moment arrived, I had a burning desire to go with them, but I lacked the courage, so I left them. As usual, I said good-by with the excuse that I was sleepy and wanted to get back home. But that evening, either because they were drunk, or because I'd said my piece too often, or because Ettore felt inspired to try a decisive test and help me once and for all, my friends made me go with them, by shouts, laughter, threats, and finally force.

On the threshold of the brothel, I jibbed. But they chased me with pushes and punches up the stairs. I seized Ettore by the arm, having managed to get beside him for a moment. I whispered in his ear:

"It's the first time, you see. . . ."

I watched for the expression on his face. He didn't seem surprised; he looked as though he'd guessed as much already. Or else perhaps he disguised his surprise, out of kindness and tact, so as really to help me. He answered evenly:

"There's no necessity for you to go into the room. Come up and sit down, calmly. That way you'll be able to see. Wait for us. By no means all of us go into the room. Then we leave together. Pretend nothing is happening. Cheer up."

I obeyed. I was very drunk and have only the vaguest recollection of what I saw: the pink, exhausted flesh, the filmy veiling, the death masks of women. I stayed sitting in a corner, just as Ettore had told me: and when we all left together, I gave a sigh of relief, almost feeling as though I had escaped a great danger. At the same time I began to regret not having dared. There'd been a tall, dark, plump girl who'd given me a long look without speaking: perhaps I should have gone with her. . . .

We separated from the others. Ettore went home with me. At the main entrance I felt sick and vomited. I was afraid to go upstairs, afraid of my mother. She had made me promise not to get home later than one. It was now three. On previous occasions when I hadn't got home by three, my mother had started telephoning the police and the hospitals. I implored Ettore to come up with me. In telling my mother about my university friends, I'd told her the truth about Ettore; that is, I'd described him as the most broad-minded of the lot. I had perpetrated this thoughtlessness, this idiocy, partly because I always felt weak with my mother and unable to give up entirely my childhood habit of confiding in her, and partly for the opposite reason, so as to wound her, cause her displeasure, give her new worries on my account, and show her the independence I'd almost attained. What did I hope to achieve by asking Ettore to come up with me? I certainly didn't hope that his presence would serve to mitigate my mother's anger; if anything it would do the reverse. What I really intended was that Ettore should come to my home unseen, that my mother should not know that he was there. But I wanted him to come because I wanted him to hear the shouts and reproaches whose violence I had more than once described to him, for I was unconvinced that he entirely believed me; I felt he thought I was exaggerating my mother's violence so as to cut a less weak figure myself. I admired Ettore, and every day was more ashamed of my virginity. I had an absolute need for him to understand me. I needed to give him material proof of the difficulties I had to overcome. He would never believe unless he heard with his own ears. Of course I couldn't admit all this to him. There had to be a pretext. So I told him that my head was swimming, that I would be incapable of putting the key in the lock, that I was feeling sick again, that I was afraid of falling and not having the strength to get up again. I begged him to come up with me to my room and help me get undressed.

We went in very quietly. We moved softly along the hall, on tiptoe. "Let's hope she's asleep . . ." I'd said to Ettore, which involved two lies: I knew it was almost impossible that my mother should be asleep; and on this occasion I didn't even hope that she was.

We had gone only a few steps when a strangled cry could be heard from the other end of the apartment:

"Carlo, is that you?"

"Yes, darling Mamma, it is."

"Thank God," my mother replied still shouting.

Then suddenly nothing more. We pushed on through the dark hall on tiptoe. We stopped. We thought we heard from the silence of my mother's room the sound of a number being dialed on the telephone. And now my mother's voice, extremely calm, saying: "Is that the police? . . . Yes, Inspector, yes, it's I . . . I wanted to inform you . . . yes, thank heaven, yes, just now . . . Just this moment. It's for me to thank you, Inspector. Do please forgive me for bothering you. I'm terribly sorry, but you will understand a mother's feelings . . . Thank you." Then the receiver clicked back, and immediately the furious voice resumed: "And now come here at once and tell me whom you've been with and what you've done. You must tell me everything. It's your solemn duty. What have you been doing? I want to look you in the eyes! Come here at once. I order you. You're killing me. I've taken ten drops of coramina. You promised to be in by one. It's now four."

"Three," I corrected her as I went into my room.

"Ten past three!"

The door communicating with my mother's room was ajar; a bar of light filtered in. In the half-darkness I began getting undressed, with Ettore's help. I really did still feel ill. My mother heard something which she possibly took for a hiccup. She began shouting again:

"Come in here, I said. Don't you know that God has special punishments, terrible punishments, for those who make their parents suffer? Come here."

"You'd better go. Go, go . . ." Ettore whispered to me. I examined his face in the dimness. He seemed to me sufficiently impressed. I said:

"Yes, I'm going. But don't you stay any longer now. And be careful to shut the door quietly."

Ettore nodded, and went toward the hall while I entered my mother's bedroom.

My mother lit the main light so as to see me better. As soon as I went in she shouted:

"Carlo! What have you been doing?"

Even after so many years I still can't explain why, but as soon as I saw my mother I was treacherously assailed by unforeseen emotions. It was as if, before, when I only heard my mother's voice, I'd imagined that I would find her less young and less beautiful; or else perhaps more disagreeable, more similar in appearance to the frenzied and ridiculous voice and the possessive significance of her words: above all, it was as if I'd imagined that I would find her different, that is to say I would find only the hateful and domineering mother who tyrannized over me and not, also, the sweet and affectionate mother, the mother who at times seemed to suffice for my emotional life. But no, the two mothers, the one who seemed to be for my good and the other who worked for my harm, were inextricably tangled up in one single creature. When I saw her, an extraordinary tenderness welled up in me; this was genuine and probably the result of my drunkenness, but I could have dominated it, withheld it, concealed it, if I had wanted to. I waited a moment or two more. I listened. I wanted to hear the muffled click at the end of the hall that Ettore would inevitably make when he closed the front door, despite my warning. To tell the truth, that was what I was waiting for before I could let myself go; Ettore mustn't be there as a witness to my collapse. And by now I wanted to collapse. I needed to. I regretted that I hadn't gone off with the women. I regretted that, having at last entered one of those houses, nothing had happened to me. But, since this was, alas, the truth, I hadn't got the strength to face not being believed by my mother, or to endure the unjust accusation expressed by her piercing look and summarized in her simple and terrifying question: "Carlo, what have you been doing?"

"Darling little Mamma!" I threw myself on my knees by her bed, and now I sobbed, hiding my face in the coverlets.

"What's the matter? What's the matter with you?" Barely recovered from the exultation of waiting, my mother willingly returned to indulging another exultation: this time, of unhealthy curiosity and baleful foreboding. "What's happened? Say something. Talk!"

I was torn by an overriding and absurd uncertainty, though it's only now, thirty years later, that I realize how absurd it was. I continued to be tempted to tell my mother the whole truth, and now, just as I was on the point of doing so, I realized that, on the contrary, I ought to remain silent; I ought to let her think anything whatever, even that the very thing she most feared had happened. I would have deceived her, not myself; for I would have taken a first step, short but decisive, toward concrete independence. So I was sincere, but with a merely formal sincerity, when, between sobs, I began (and even now I'm almost ashamed of setting it down):

"Darling Mamma, you must know that I'm pure, you can kiss me. The others did it, but I didn't. I went in, yes, but I didn't want to. I didn't do anything. I didn't even want to go in, but they forced me. But I'm pure, I'm pure! Tomorrow morning I can go to Communion!"

"Tomorrow morning! You don't know what you're talking about! When you've been drinking. And you've certainly been drinking *since midnight*. I can smell from here that you've been drinking. And why are you talking about Communion? It's weeks and weeks since you've been to Communion."

I had gone on attending the services and receiving the Sacraments for a year or two after "losing the faith." But I had gradually withdrawn from this, little by little slowing down a practice that by now lacked all fervor and lived on only through habit. At that moment what my mother said was true: how many weeks was it since I had gone to Communion? Without her knowing it, naturally, and without her even imagining it, I no longer even went to Mass on Sunday. But for her sake I had to invent, every time, what church I had gone to and at what time. But why did I mention Communion that night? Was it connected, perhaps, with the warmth and comfort of the bed, of those coverlets containing the soft majestic body of my mother, a sensation that I knew so well and hadn't experienced for some time, and which probably linked up, deep down in me, with all the sensations of religious practice?

Meanwhile my mother kept insisting:

72

"What have you been drinking? Wine, spirits?"

"I mean that I could, not materially, but from the point of view of *purity of soul*, go to Communion." These words, uttered with a certain inner shame and a certain conscious falsity, nonetheless moved me, by the mere fact that I heard myself saying them. I burst into tears again. "Darling Mamma, forgive me! Tell me that you forgive me! I'm pure, you know. I'm still pure. Say that you forgive me."

"Yes, dear, yes, I forgive you. . . . But you have nothing to be forgiven. Come, look into my eyes. There, yes, I know it, I see it. My darling Carlo isn't lying to his little mother. My eyes can see everything in your eyes, you know."

"Yes, I know, Mamma."

"I only have to forgive you one thing, for having drunk too much. Health is so precious. If only you knew what a terrible poison alcohol is. Do you know what Perroncito told me? Senator Perroncito, the most famous pathologist of the university?"

I already knew Perroncito's words by heart. Nor could my mother have forgotten that she had quoted them to me more than once. Perhaps she thought that owing to my drunkenness I had forgotten them; or perhaps she thought that they would be particularly effective if I heard them again at this moment, when I was feeling so ill owing to having drunk too much.

"Well then, this is what Perroncito said. He said, 'Be careful, Contessa, that your son doesn't drink. For alcohol destroys the nerve cells, and once the nerve cells are destroyed they can never be recovered.' And the harms of alcoholism are transmitted to the children. Your father always drank too much. That's why Costantino isn't yet well, and perhaps never will be well all his life. . . .'"

My drunkenness didn't prevent me from remembering that, on various other occasions, my mother had solemnly told me that Costantino's infirmity was due to an illness of my father, yes, but one of a venereal nature. She suddenly saw this memory in my eyes and hastened to correct herself, adding with a deep sigh:

". . . For this reason, and for another, as I've already told you."

I would have liked to chime in with something that I already knew: that it was much more likely that the cause of Costantino's illness was the close affinity of blood between my parents, who were first cousins and children of the Tholozan sisters. My father and mother had needed an ecclesiastical dispensation to get married. Costantino and I are the children of first cousins, and it is not out of the question that this is the cause of Costantino's troubles as well as of my own vagaries and manias. I was to reach the age of fifty without excessive difficulties. I was to believe myself "immune," safe. But I was mistaken. A sickness, a weakness, was lying within me, with which I had grown accustomed to living, but which I had always ignored— and which I still ignore now as regards its inner substance.

The two Tholozan sisters, that is to say my mother's mother and my father's mother, were not of a noble family. They were, as the saying goes, Tholozans *tout court*. But in Turin there were also the Tholozan de la Baumes, and the sisters were perhaps distantly related to them. So it came about after my father's death—he himself would never have agreed—that my mother decided not to forgo any longer the delight of being called Contessa, and of repeating remarks addressed to her when they contained this usurped title. Usually I was irritated by this, indeed disgusted; and I showed it, and told my mother so. But that night, oiled by tears, I even let the word "Contessa" slip by.

"Will you promise me you'll never drink again in this way?"

"Yes, darling Mamma . . . I promise. But give me a kiss."

"Yes, dear, yes."

"And let me stay here a bit, like this. . . ."

I buried my head again among the coverlets. My mother's hand caressed my hair. We were silent for a moment. A light, rapid footstep could be heard; a step in the hall. My mother reared up into a sitting position, terrified.

"Who is it?" she cried in a strangled voice.

The steps immediately stopped. I got up. I was sure it was Ettore, and moved toward the hall. When we came in I'd made the mistake of closing not only the wooden door but the glass door as well; and Ettore had feared, not without reason, the noise of this glass door. Therefore he'd come back to close the communicating door between my room and the hall. But he had had to take off his shoes to avoid making even more noise. Unless, when he gave me this explanation the following day, he wasn't being truthful, but was hiding from me that he'd delayed owing to curiosity. I went back to my mother and told her everything: how I wasn't feeling well, how Ettore had helped me upstairs. My mother surprised me by her unexpected and perfect calm.

"Bring him in," she said, "I want to talk to him."

Though convinced that my mother would make a ridiculous scene, I hadn't the strength to disobey her. I asked Ettore to come in: I felt ashamed, but there was, after all, a fairly plausible justification: on hearing the footsteps in the hall my mother had been frightened and thought it was a thief. . . .

When I went back into my mother's room with Ettore, I noticed that the main light had been switched off. In the rosy shaded glow of the bedside lamp at the head of the bed, my mother was waiting, reclining on various pillows, her shoulders draped in a shawl, calm, smiling, and in every way like a convalescent receiving a social visit. I was astounded at the speed with which she had composed herself. It even seemed as though, in those few seconds, she had found time to comb her hair. In those days she hadn't a single gray hair. In the warm half-shadow, her black and lustrous hair was in harmonious contrast with the soft pink mesh of her shawl.

Ettore was tall, athletic, dark, his hair naturally curly, his eyes large and slightly protruding.

"Good evening, Contessa," he said in a loud, firm voice. He must have heard everything while hiding in my room just before. He had met my mother briefly once or twice already, and had never shown that he knew about her weakness for the title.

He bent down and kissed her hand. My mother smiled, looking at him as if weighing him up sensually.

"I'm grateful to you," she said, using his surname, "I'm grateful to you for bringing Carlo Felice back home: but not for . . . for the rest."

That was enough to let Ettore know that she knew where we had been: and not merely on a round of drinks in the wineshops! It even seemed to me that, in the short hesitation or pause before saying "for the rest," her dark brown eyes shone with a suppressed glow, betraying a smile, a kind of mischief.

I believed with absolute certainty—indeed I could say that I knew—that my mother had never had a lover, either before or after my father's death. I was not lacking, however, in another certainty. On various occasions, as for instance this one, there was evidence, visual evidence. I saw that my mother considered the possibility of having lovers, a possibility that she immediately and fiercely drove from her mind: but she thought about it; she would have liked them. Her shameless and unconscious flirtatiousness did not seriously disturb me, but it irritated me, and disgusted me. In her looks and gestures at that moment my mother, though without realizing it, resembled a prostitute: precisely because, in sensuous reality, she never allowed herself and never would allow herself the smallest pleasure.

EQUALLY vain attempts to have a first, full, erotic experience followed one on the other as long as I stayed in Turin. I was incapable, inhibited. The causes that even then seemed the most obvious were my religious education and the violence of my mother's affection: but probably there was an additional one, a secret, sweet, soft, penetrating cause which was almost a daily enchantment.

In Via Carlo Alberto, not far from Piazza Bodoni and on my daily walk between our home and the university, there was a little tobacco shop; and behind the counter of this shop there was a woman whose beauty seemed to me supreme. It goes without saying that she was dark, tall, plump, well-proportioned, not young, and in general bearing and expression outstandingly imperious. Usually severe, but sometimes smiling, her gestures, her glances, and her words—in contrast with the routine banality of her tasks (greeting the customer when he came in, asking him what he wanted, turning around to take the cigarettes from the shelf or extending a ringed hand to push the tray of Tuscan cigars toward him, telling him how much he owed, counting out the change on the counter, then thanking him and saying good-by) —revealed the leisureliness, ease, and calm of a queen.

She had a low voice, not hoarse, but as though refined by a strange vibration that resembled the sound of a precious crystal with a tiny fault in it. Such was the magic of that voice, such was the pleasure I experienced when listening to it, that sometimes I put questions to her so as to hear it a bit longer—questions that I knew were perfectly futile though I'd prepared and studied them in advance.

"Haven't the Black Cat cigarettes come in yet?" I knew that Black Cat had not been in stock for some time.

"No, sir, not yet. I'm sorry. We have Three Castles, if you would like them."

And this was an example of a marvelously long answer which went on vibrating within me for days and nights. She had a Turin accent, but her English pronunciation was almost perfect.

For four years, from November to July, I dropped in at that Tobacconist's at least once a day. For all that, I never discovered anything about her. I heard them calling her "Signora" but I never saw her husband: only the mother, a bent and dried-up little woman, who was usually in the back of the shop and occasionally took her daughter's place at the counter. The truth is that I never made the slightest effort to discover anything. In the first place, whom could I ask? The girls or barman in the nearby cakeshop? I would never have dared. In the second place, I now realized that I preferred things that way, that she should remain surrounded by mystery for me. I never even knew her Christian name.

Independently of my trembling and adoring state of mind, there reigned a genuine air of witchcraft and secrecy in the tobacco shop, especially in the evenings after dinner. Standing in corners, leaning against the shelves or the counter, one or two men were always there, motionless and taciturn, their eyes fixed on the Tobacconist, following every movement she made, and now and again exchanging an odd phrase in dialect, in low voices, and sometimes with a short chuckle. To me it seemed an allusive and conventional jargon of their own; often I couldn't understand a word of it. I can only remember one of these men either because he was the most assiduous or because his face was more striking than the others: he was elderly, pale, bald, extremely thin, with sunken cheeks and blue twinkling eyes.

Sometimes, after I had been at the tobacco shop around nine, I would go back at half past ten, or eleven, or even later, and I would find the same person immobile in his corner: either the pale, thin gentleman, or else someone else, and sometimes even two men, again the same ones, so that spending the evening in this way must have been a regular part of their daily round: standing still, looking at the Tobacconist, and now and again exchanging the odd word with her.

I began envying those men.

Another extraordinary fact was this: the Tobacconist dressed differently every evening. I can't remember ever seeing her dressed the same way. She was always very elegant; and, when the good weather started, she was also provocative, though with ladylike discretion and perhaps a little severity: blouses that were transparent but not excessively so; low-necked styles that gave a reasonable and not exaggerated prominence to her abundant breasts; bare arms—these were plump but very lovely, exquisitely rounded with gentle curves up to the point of the elbow. The colors she preferred for her clothes were first of all light blue, then black, beige, and on rare occasions pink and red. Her skin was dark; but it seemed to be of an extremely delicate quality, of an artificial brown tanned by long sunlight even in winter, and in an even tone, between sepia and chestnut, with no trace of copper or rose. She had thin wrists, especially when compared with the fullness of her arms and all her parts; her hands were small, soft, as though without nerves, and with backs darker than the palms; her fingers were long and tapering; her nails were pointed, shining, not colored, and, in their paleness, they were in precious and hard contrast to the dark skin of the fingers. On her knuckles, between the small bones of her fingers, the corrugation of the skin was such as to give almost an impression of dirt, but I saw that it had nothing to do with dirt, nor with age, and those little dark nests of creases, with their mysterious and microscopic monstrosity, fascinated me and intoxicated me: they were, who knows why, the high-water mark of the effect of her beauty upon me. She always wore jewels, and more in the evening— earrings, bracelets, rings—but only jewels made with brilliants, whether genuine or artificial, and set in platinum or white gold.

If only I could have spent the evening in the tobacco shop, like those men! I was still naïve, to be sure, but not so naïve as to suppose that afterward, at midnight, when the shop was closed, nothing happened over and above that public contemplation and adoration. Toward midnight I took up a position some distance away, at the corner of the Madonna degli Angeli: I saw that it was never she who pulled down the heavy shutters, but always one of her friends, either the thin old gentleman or another. And everything in her expression and behavior combined to exclude from my imagination the suspicion that she was a woman who didn't enjoy life to the full. Her eyes were not brown like my mother's, but darker, black and very bright as though lit by an inner fire, and sometimes they seemed laden with shadows and surrounded by seemingly bruised skin. I never thought for a moment of the concrete possibility of regarding myself as one of those men, even for a single evening. It was a life, it was a world into which, for the moment, I was not allowed to enter. I would have been satisfied with spending the evening in the tobacco shop: leaning up against the farthest and darkest corner, near the entrance, staying quite quiet and almost becoming invisible, whether she looked at where I was and saw me, or behaved as if I didn't so much as exist. But even this was extremely difficult, or so it seemed to me, except for a few minutes at a time. After I had bought a cigar, and after I had withdrawn to light it precisely in that corner near the entrance as if to avoid the wind in the street, and after I had lit it as slowly as possible, I lingered on, like that, silent and motionless, smoking and watching her.

I could see her there, a few steps away, in the serene yellowish light, against the neat multicolored background of the shelves. Customers came in, went up to the counter, bought cigarettes, went out again. And every action made by the Tobacconist seemed to impress itself on my memory for ever: her slow way of turning around, the look of her shoulders and neck, the half-naked arm stretched up for the pack. It was a whole ritual that was taking place before me: that counter was an altar, and she was at once the priest and the divinity.

It sometimes happened that the pack asked for was beyond her reach. Then, but always slowly, she got up and took a step or two behind the counter; but it seemed as if this was only to show off her majesty the better. Of course she saw me: she saw me standing there in my corner, and she looked at me without surprise, almost with indifference. It was certainly not because of this glance of hers that I regularly went off after a minute or two. Her glance would have told me clearly enough that I could stay. But near the counter there was always at least one of her friends: either the old man, or another. It was his stare that drove me away; he rested it on me with growing frequency, and in the end with irritation, as much as to say, "Well, and what are you doing here? Be off with you. It's bad manners."

I mumbled "Good night" and bowed in her direction, and also in the direction of the friend or friends, and went out without turning around, as if I were dragging myself away from what, at that moment, seemed the only reason for living.

I went home, and to bed; and feverishly in the warmth of the bed I reconstructed the scene, I put it together piece by piece, I saw the Tobacconist once more, I achieved a materialization which was more effective, for my senses, than the reality itself: until there appeared, drawing me to the culmination of the orgasm, the small, lined, black, soft intricacy of the skin of her finger knuckles.

The Tobacconist is still alive within me. When I'd finished at the university, and after my military service, I moved to Milan. I rarely went back to Turin, but, every time I did, I never failed to visit Via Carlo Alberto and go into the tobacco shop. Each visit was so removed from the one before that I can say I saw the Tobacconist grow old in pitiless stages. But she was always very beautiful, and I always desired her. And I couldn't believe that, before, I'd had no idea of what to do to get straight to my goal: at least to have a try, and in the politest of fashions, and with the greatest possible likelihood of success. Yet when I was again face to face with her, the old fear took over. Her greeting, as she recognized me, was very different from the enigmatic or indifferent one of those bygone days: she now gave a gentle smile, slightly emotional, very typical of Turin. I realized with this new greeting and smile that I, too, had changed: I had become a man, whereas before I was a boy.

The old fear: and also perhaps the doubt that I might destroy everything, if I really tried to achieve my goal, and succeeded. And I didn't want that. It was earlier, precisely when I was a boy, that I should have approached her: to know the silk of her skin, lose myself in the black diamonds of her eyes, kiss her eyelids and the soft little folds of her knuckles, feed myself on her. Who knows? If I had started off with an experience like that, my whole life might have been different: perhaps I would have been saved. Now, nothing mattered much. I wasn't able to follow the more reasonable inclination of my adolescence. But at least I didn't lose the sweetness of a memory.

And one final time when I returned to Turin, the Tobacconist was no longer there: the shop had passed into other hands. The city had grown. Industries and technology were rapidly increasing. It was a new life. I realized that the enchantment of the Tobacconist had been the result not only of her beauty and my almost childlike inhibitions but also of the emptiness and deep silence of Turin in those days, in the evening after dinner—except on some major festival or at carnival time. The night life of a big city in those days was more provincial than that of any provincial city today: darker, stranger, more closed in, more desperate; and here and there, in all that dark and silence, it covered up and brooded over hidden, fervid hotbeds, like the mysterious little tobacco shop in Via Carlo Alberto.

ONE OF my mother's uncles, now dead for some years, was a General in the army; my mother's paternal grandfather also held a high military rank. All her relatives on her father's side were bureaucrats, civil servants, or army people, and this was perhaps the font and origin of her authoritarian character, and of the discipline she imposed on everyone at home, but it was not enough to broaden her maternal love to the generous scale of love for her country. Hence she had made up her mind that I shouldn't do my military service, and at the first medical examination she managed to have me declared "temporarily unfit." I would have been "invalided out" at the second had I not dared, at last, to play a cunning game against her. When I had been turned down as temporarily unfit, I had hidden my disappointment from her, at least in part; knowing myself to be healthy and strong, I had hoped that her maneuvers would fail. She had recommended me to a General of her acquaintance, who in his turn had recommended me to an army doctor of the district, with the rank of Major. After a year, when the moment of my second medical was approaching, I had the courage to call on the General and beg him not to "recommend me" again. I was ready to face the probable risk that, even if the General acceded to my wishes, he would later tell everything to my mother. I made veiled hints to the effect that it would be better not to do this. He was delighted, and didn't hesitate to promise that he would say nothing. His double chin shook, and his voice seemed to be coming from it, cavernous and strangled. "That's all right. As far as your mother's concerned, we'll put the blame on fate. We'll say that the Major happened to be away that morning, and that there was another army doctor." I can remember how, while he was talking, his cheeks, covered with a spider's web of veins, grew purple with delight over his snowy mustache. That absurd, old-world face was for me a mirage, but a mirage full of security: the symbol of a reality that couldn't be missed, though it was still far away. I had no other reason for wanting to join the army. And a year after I had taken my degree, having followed the officers' training course at Bra, and while I was second lieutenant with the 52nd Infantry at Novara, I reached— with an enormous delay compared with the overwhelming majority of my friends and companions who were not abnormal—the longed-for goal.

I remember perfectly well where it happened: at Villa delle Rose under the bastions. It was a brothel with nothing squalid or dreary about it, either outside or inside. It was a small, middle-class, modern villa, moderately chic, with floral cretonnes, rosy lights, and blond wood furniture.

But I can't remember exactly the first girl. I can only remember a girl who, if she wasn't the first, was certainly one of the first. Her name was Yvonne.

Yvonne heads a long list. They all gave me joy. With all, as I have explained, I was quickly disillusioned. As I thought, from the beginning or almost, that this disillusion was linked up with the surroundings, the procedure, and the short time that was allowed me in the "houses," I began as soon as possible to invite girls to the *pied-à-terre* which, without my mother's knowing, I had rented in Via Pasquirolo. I tried dancers, singers, variety actresses, maids, working girls, clerks, and occasionally women or girls from good families. The outcome was always the same. And in this way I reached the age of forty without ever desiring anything more or different; without ever experiencing the pleasure even of an emotional relationship, which might have lasted slightly longer than sensual pleasure. Every time I was embittered and as though humiliated by this state of things, which I viewed as a grave defect on my part. But, within certain limits, I was also satisfied: for I knew that in this way I was avoiding much worry.

During the war in Africa I was called up and so was away from home for some time. Then I resumed my usual life between Milan and Levo. I saw my brother and my mother regularly: I spent two or three days every week with them. And the affection I felt for him, if not for her, possibly sufficed me. In a word, I was content this way.

It was in Rome in the summer of 1943 that I thought for the first time of the possibility of marrying. Even Meris was a girl whom I had got to know in a "house." It oughtn't to seem strange: for the very simple reason that it didn't seem strange to me. But it would have been absurd had I married her in anything but absolute secrecy: I could not cause such great pain to my mother, who was now old and ill.

I was again in the army. My mother had immediately gone into action and written to one of her old friends, the sister of his excellency General D., begging for a very high recommendation. This time I didn't escape! And that was why I found myself in Rome. For the first months of the war, when they called up my class, I was a Captain in the reserve attached to an office in the Ministry. If I had been in the regular army, under no circumstances would I have had permission to marry Meris, short of resigning my commission: army regulations prescribe "good moral qualifications for the fiancée and her family." But even as an officer in the reserve, I needed to overcome infinite complications if I was to keep the marriage hidden from my mother and therefore from everyone else: even if all went well, there would be a delay of some months.

I bravely began making the practical arrangements: I

had confided in Colonel B., my immediate superior, and he had promised to help me.

I had decided to take this step, which hitherto I had always excluded from my future, in the course of a few days. How had I done so? It's a question I still ask myself, and I believe that I wouldn't be able to give a really satisfactory answer without the help of a psychiatrist.

MERIS WAS my type. Physically, she recalled Pierina, Yvonne, the Tobacconist, all the girls I'd liked best, and (though at that time I never thought of it) my mother as a young woman.

She was tall, dark, plump, with thin wrists and small, well-made hands and feet. She had an ample bust, and a high, large, and pronounced rump. Her eyes were brown, but light brown.

She came from "lower" Emilia, from a family of workers on the land and small artisans. Probably as a girl she had worked in a factory, or in service with some upper-class family in Bologna or Milan. She was fairly cultivated and fairly well brought-up, as is not unusual with the girls of those regions. But above all she was extremely intelligent. She showed this in the mischievous light in her eyes, and in her smile: a light that she could control at will, extinguishing it when she wanted to put on a torpid, tired expression. And this last was precisely her usual expression, one that she never abandoned, but absolutely never, when she showed herself to the clients or moved around in the waiting rooms. So that in the bedroom, while we were making love for the first time, I had the unexpected sensation of finding myself in the arms of a very different woman from the one I'd chosen. Suddenly a spark, as it were, burst into flames. For the first time in my life I was discovering a girl who seemed to understand my inner being, and who revealed to me my own deep feelings, of which I had hitherto been unaware, and who gave me in exchange the revelation of her feelings, which, as it happened, were complementary to my own.

All this happened in one look, one word.

"I," she said, staring me in the eyes while we were making love. "Remember that here it is only I who matter. I. You count for nothing." And the gentle Emilian accent seemed, I don't know why, to complete and make concrete this mysterious statement, freeing it from any mercenary conventionality, from any suspicion of professional rhetoric.

From the moment of that revelation, our love relationship was set free, and very soon became daily. Luckily, I was always dressed in civilian clothes, and was always free in the evening. With immediate mutual understanding, and without any need for reciprocal warnings, we invented a quantity of propitiatory and preparatory rites, always different and always equal, because they all sprang spontaneously from our initial accord. Perhaps I found in her, at last, what I had long dreamed of during the forced chastity of adolescence: finally, I was making love with the Tobacconist.

Yet so far this was nothing.

During all the first month, June, my relationship with Meris was, yes, infinitely happier and more assiduous but not substantially different from my previous relations with other girls. Even with Meris I always felt disillusioned immediately afterward—repentant, avid only for solitude and freedom. I never wanted to prolong my visit, to stay with her for a while, chatting. Meris wasn't only intelligent: beyond her strictly erotic talents, she proved to be witty, full of feeling, delicate, and even tender. She began to ask me to go with her to Fregene on Thursday afternoons, her free day: I said no, on the pretext that I had now been living in Rome for three years and was too well known. In a word, during the whole of the first month, the idea of marriage never even entered my mind.

Until, one evening early in July, when we had only just gone into the room, Meris stopped me with a gesture.

"This time," she said slowly, "this time I'll make love with you on one condition only."

I thought she wanted more money than the agreed-on sum. This was a very common custom with all the prostitutes in "houses": the appeal for something extra that didn't have to be shared with Madame. But until that evening Meris had never hinted at anything of the kind. Hence I remained speechless, somewhat surprised, and also disillusioned: I had imagined that she was fond of me.

She saw what I was thinking in my eyes.

"No, it's not what you think, Carlo. I don't want anything extra, from you. It's just a little sacrifice that I'm asking of you."

"Little? What sacrifice and of what kind, if it isn't financial?" I asked, thinking of something amusing.

"No, don't laugh. Because it will cost you something: not much, but something. That's why it's a serious thing for me, and for you too. I want to test whether you really love me, as you say you do every time when you come in, and then you can hardly wait for the time to go. I've prepared a little punishment for you. . . . Don't be frightened, it's nothing, nothing terrible. But you must promise, now, that you'll do whatever I tell you, after. And if you don't keep your promise, I'll never go with you again. Never, however much you give me, even a hundred thousand lire. Do you understand?"

I hadn't yet made love, I'd come there to do so, and I thought for a moment that the purpose of Meris's strange speech was solely to increase my desire: I thought it was a new preparatory rite. So I smiled and said yes, I agreed.

"No, I don't want that kind of yes. Let me repeat that it's a small thing, but it isn't a joke. You must look me straight in the eyes and say yes without smiling."

While she was talking, Meris's eyes were certainly not smiling. They fixed me darkly, intently, seriously, with that very force that at other moments was enchanting, but now frightened me and made me hesitate.

"Meris! Tell me what it's about. How in the world can I promise something I don't know?"

"Yet you've got to promise me precisely like that, without knowing. If you don't want to, then good-by. We'll never see each other again."

She walked away from me. She hadn't yet taken off her clothes. She was wearing a dark blue velvet dress, very low at the back. She walked slowly toward the little dressing table which, in the half-light of the large low room, sparkled with mirrors and small lamps. Was Meris aware that, in thus showing me her body slowly moving, she was using the strongest argument of all?

She sat in front of the dressing table and began combing her hair. I hadn't moved, and couldn't make up my mind. I wanted with all my soul to make love with her, and to do so at once, and I wanted to agree to her mysterious request, but I was afraid of a trick, of some sort of machination. I watched her from my corner in silence, my heart pounding.

"Well, what are you going to do?" said Meris without turning around and perhaps eying me in one of the three mirrors. "Carlo? Are you still there? Make up your mind.

Be good, and promise. It's for your own good, really. Do you promise? Because, if not, you can go. I've said that already. Good-by. Pay Madame Teresa downstairs."

"Tell me at least whether it's a thing that will hurt me."

"Yes, it will hurt you. But not much, very little; don't worry." She turned around on the stool and, without getting up, added very gently: "Look, if the hurt is really as great as all that, and you're so weak that you can't even bear it for love of me, well then, I'll forgive you even if you don't keep your promise. Is that all right?"

"That's all right," I said, trembling.

"But you mustn't pretend and you mustn't exaggerate. I'm not so stupid that I won't know if you're really being hurt, or just pretending. Are we agreed on that too?"

"Yes," I said impatiently. "So tell me what this sacrifice is quickly. Now, quickly. I'm ready."

"No. Not now. I know perfectly well that you're ready now. You're ready for anything now, hmm?"

She got up and slipped off her dress. She came slowly toward me, naked. She put her hands on my shoulders and scrutinized me at length in silence. Then she said:

"You must promise for afterward, Carlo. Do you promise?"

"I promise."

MERIS's idea was very simple. When she disclosed it to me half an hour later, unwrapping a little tissue-paper parcel already prepared on the dressing table, and showed me a small bronze chain with a little padlock and key, the first thing that struck me was the absurdity of the idea.

Did keeping my promise mean that I should wear two

circles of chain around my waist under my shirt, that is to say in contact with my skin, that the padlock would be kept shut, with Meris holding the key?

I weighed the chain: it was really very light. I tried it on immediately, laughing, while Meris, rather cross, repeated:

"Don't laugh. Why are you laughing? You're spoiling everything."

I would find the chain an irritation after a while, but a minimal irritation.

"And how long must I wear it?"

"How long?" This time it was her turn to laugh. "But for ever, my dear!"

"For ever! Are you mad?"

"I assure you, I've never had my head screwed on so well. You must wear the chain for ever: when you are away from me, when you are not in my company. As soon as we're together, don't worry, I'll set you free. I'll take it off, open the padlock."

I wasn't yet quite sure that the whole thing wasn't intended as a joke:

"And how about if I go to a locksmith, or, better, if I buy a file and break the chain?"

"Fine. You know what awaits you: I'll never go with you again. You don't know me yet. And you be careful, because I'm not joking. Look me straight in the eyes. There, that's right. Do I seem to be joking? I don't, do I? So we understand each other. Clear understandings make long friends."

Her Emilian accent was perhaps not so markedly sweet as it had been that other time, but nevertheless it fascinated me. This was the first time, with her, that I had wanted to make love within minutes of having already made it. To be frank, it hadn't happened to me very often even with other women.

"And supposing I found a little key that fitted?" I whispered as I put my arm around her and slowly went toward the bed.

"You won't find one, my darling. Because it's a very special lock, and there are only two keys in the world that fit it, and both of them are in my possession. Do you understand? And anyway, even if, by some impossible chance, you did succeed in finding a key that fitted, I'd notice at once."

"How, my darling?"

"My darling, it would be the easiest thing: I would just have to look you in the eyes. Didn't you know I'm something of a medium? I can thought-read: the thoughts of someone who interests me, of course. And you interest me not because you're worth anything, but for the very opposite reason: because I have a feeling that as regards other people, as regards the world, you must be worth a lot, but as regards me you're worth nothing whatsoever. You're a nonentity, as I've already told you. And it's just this that interests me about you, it's just this that I like. And I'll tell you something else: if you cheat me, if you find a key that fits, if you take off the chain without telling me and then put it on again . . . if you do anything like that . . ." She suddenly stopped and turned her head away, as if for a moment she didn't want to see me.

Perhaps she didn't want to see me so as to feel me better. And what we were saying had no sense for me, no sense at all: our words were provisional, interchangeable, words that composers of popular songs call *mascherone,* a metrical schema that has to adapt itself to the rhythm of the music. Gently and mechanically I repeated her last phrase where she had broken off:

". . . If I do anything like that?"

I was asking a question but not requiring an answer.

However, Meris gave me an answer. Again turning away her face and looking at a corner of the floor, she said harshly:

"If you do anything like that, some misfortune will befall you."

The way she said "misfortune" gave more weight to the meaning and tone of her words, which had something sorrowful about them, and at the same time sinister.

THEN what in fact happened was this: that evening, as soon as I'd left Meris and got back home—in the disillusion habitual to me after making love, and in the equally habitual craving for solitude and freedom—that chain became much more than an irritation to me, it became real torture. Not a physical torture, but a psychological torture, because the gentle weight on my hips, and the slight coldness of the metal, were enough to remind me continually that a little earlier I'd been making love, and with whom, whereas usually I forgot this immediately, and didn't think of it again until I was again taken with desire.

For my body the discomfort of the chain was easy to bear, but in effect, it was hellish: it chained me down, good and proper, to the image of the person who had given me pleasure, even after this pleasure was completely exhausted. Of course I told myself that I was now experiencing what I had long and vainly desired, that is, to go on thinking of the woman with whom I had made love, after love-making was over: except that it was a topsy-turvy and mocking experience.

My misfortune had always been to feel, immediately afterward, contempt and hatred for the woman whom up to that moment I had adored. Precisely so as not to despise her, not to hate her, I fled and forgot her. With the chain, this wasn't possible.

I began to repent furiously of my weakness, and to curse Meris. On my way home (a good three quarters of an hour on foot; the war had begun making itself felt: I was living in an apartment house outside Ponte Milvio, my car was being repaired, I hadn't found a taxi, and the last streetcar had left its terminus a while ago), I'd noticed that cold and that hindrance around my body at every step, and had become increasingly annoyed with myself: weak, not only weak but soft in the head, that's what I'd been! And with every step I saw, as if in a nightmare, Meris's face, her eyes fixed upon me: it was the gaze of a madwoman, now I realized it, had no more doubts about it: a madwoman; and her mouth, her protruding lips, the flashing of her teeth as she said, "As regards me, you're worth nothing whatsoever!"

"Nothing? You'll soon see, you wretched woman, whether I count for nothing!" While walking, I was talking to myself in a low voice, and imagining that Meris could hear. "Now, as soon as I get home, I'll find some way of taking the chain off, and then I'll have a good sleep, and tomorrow I won't even come and find you, not tomorrow, nor the next day, nor ever again, so it's all finished and done with. Or else, no: I'll come and throw the chain in your face, and if you don't make love, that's all right. What does it matter? There are thousands of c . . . . ."

I walked faster and sang as the soldiers do:

> *Vorrei morire—per non soffrire,*
> *ma il cuore si ribella:*
> *dimmi perchè—tante ce n'è,*
> *la troverai più bella.**

I was certain, certain, I say, that I would get back my fine independence, my beloved freedom, without delay.

* I'd like to die—so as not to suffer, / but the heart rebels: / tell me why—there are so many, / you'll find the next one better.

But when I got home past one in the morning, I couldn't find a file. I thought I'd seen one in the nail drawer, but either I'd been mistaken or someone had taken it. On the other hand I didn't want to wake up the orderly. Probably there wasn't a file in the house, or else he wouldn't be able to find it either. And what excuse could I make for wanting a file at that time of night? So then I tried, with the strength of my hands, to twist one of the links and wrench it loose. But I only managed to chafe my skin, for when I pulled on one of the two circles of chain, obviously the other gripped my waist more tightly. In the end I realized I was being unreasonable. After all, the irritation the chain caused me was perfectly bearable. Next day I'd leave home a bit early, stop the car in Piazza Propaganda Fide, go to Cantini's, the hardware shop, just around the corner, buy a good file, and then file off the chain in the lavatory at the Ministry. Now I was sleepy, really quite tired, and could sleep perfectly well with that slight irritation. Whereas, if I persisted, I was simply playing Meris's game, mad wretch that she was!

I calmed down, had a shower, slowly drank a whisky with a lot of water, and went to bed. While I was under the shower I had forgotten Meris at last; now, in bed, she came back to my mind through the chain: not owing to its heaviness, which was minimal, but because it had got rather wet under the shower.

I fell into a deep sleep almost at once.

WHEN the orderly woke me up at half past seven next morning, I was already thinking of Meris in another way: desire had begun again during sleep. It was not until a few moments after waking that I noticed the little welts, smooth and hard, around my waist: I remembered the chain. I must confess, though not without an element of shame, that I was pleased: the slight discomfort increased desire, and the pleasure of feeling desire.

I would have liked to go to Meris immediately. But I knew she slept until eleven. When the time came, I telephoned her from the Ministry to say good morning.

"How are you?" she asked. I could detect a shade of malice in her voice. "Did you sleep well?"

"Very well."

"Did you think of me?"

"Continually. I'll tell you . . ."

"I already know what you want to tell me, Carlo."

"All right, what is it that I want to tell you?"

"That last night you hated me, but that this morning you love me again. Am I right?"

"Yes, Meris."

"So you see, I know everything about you without your even telling me. And I also know that that's the way it will be at first, and until you get used to it, until you can't do without me, until I become for you like the very air you breathe. . . ."

There was nothing inappropriate in these phrases. On the contrary, their tone was romantic and literary: a direct echo of *Novella* and *Eva* as well as of the novels of Liala and Flavia Steno. But, unlike the magazines and novels that she read so assiduously, Meris was being very sincere: her voice, if not her choice of words, revealed genuine emotion.

Nothing inappropriate. But there was a war on. The Ministry telephones were tapped by an internal office set up for the purpose: if someone had had the whim to check the address of the number I'd just called, I might have incurred grave censure. So I cut short the call and told Meris that I'd visit her at the first possible moment that evening.

In this way the decisive weeks of my life began. It so

happened that the same weeks were equally decisive for the fate of Italy and the war. . . . To tell the truth, the view that this was pure coincidence was the one I held both at the time and for many years afterward; but it was a short-sighted view due to a lack of time perspective and above all to the confusing selfishness of my feelings. Today, with a mind—alas—detached and cold, I realize that it was precisely the great political and military events of those weeks, bizarrely interweaving themselves with my private little erotic affairs, that upset the modest nature of the latter and made them tragic and irreversible, that essentially modified the psychological reflexes which such affairs would otherwise have caused in me, and which would have been, as always, habitual, mechanical, and harmless. In other words, if I had met Meris at any other moment except in the summer of 1943, almost certainly I would have tired of her only a fraction less quickly than I'd tired of all the other girls I'd known up till then, and the chain would in no way have served to bind me to her.

Hardly had I entered the room when Meris, with half-serious, half-joking ceremony, opened the padlock and set me free. Before I went away she put it on me again. And I passed another evening of hell, cursing Meris and cursing myself, and went to bed promising myself yet again that the next day I would stop at Cantini's and buy a file. But when I woke in the morning I no longer felt the same. Each morning when I awoke I found I was—I don't know whether it would be accurate to say more in love but certainly more invaded by her. On the third day, Meris replaced the first chain with another, also of bronze and in every way similar to the first, but a bit thicker and heavier, and after some days with another heavier still; then she reverted to the light one, and so on, alternating the three chains as chance or fancy took her, according to her mood of the moment.

"You must wear the chain: about this there's no possible discussion. But in this way I can accustom you to obeying my decisions, which may change each time, depending on what comes into my head. I saw you, you know, a little while ago on the stairs, and I saw the way you looked at that blonde, Pupy. For a moment you thought you would like to go with her, instead of me. Deny it if you dare!"

It was true, and I didn't deny it. That was why, from the very beginning—that is, from a month before she produced the chain—Meris had instructed me always to have her called "from the door." And if she wasn't free when I arrived, to wait for her patiently in a little private room where her colleagues would never have even looked in: in such cases there was a general habit of professional loyalty among the girls. Meris had become jealous almost immediately: she wouldn't accept my going with the other girls of the house, or, after the first days, my even seeing them.

I began suspecting, though belatedly, that the device of the chain concealed another aim: perhaps her real one. She was showing herself less mad than I thought, she had understood the short duration of my sensual desire and my inability to be faithful, and also the pleasure I experienced in continually changing girls. If I had gone to bed with other girls, I would have had to show them the chain around my body: plainly not impossible for my part, but unquestionably rather embarrassing, and for them and for me the gymnastics of love would have become tiresome and disagreeable.

Finally, the girls whom I would have liked to choose were, out of a natural instinct of compensation, of the opposite type to Meris: thin, pink, blonde, evanescent; and how I would have liked to put the chain on them!

Thursday afternoon came around again. And again with great sweetness, and in a tone of natural supplication which revealed, at least in this desire, her sincerity, Meris asked me to take her to Fregene. This time I agreed.

In the bathing hut on the private beach she took off the chain. A slight reddish furrow was visible on my skin all around my waist. I was beginning to have enough of it. But at the same time I didn't want to lose Meris. Was she really serious? Was it true that she wouldn't have gone with me again if I'd cut through the chain? Well, I wasn't a hundred per cent convinced. Yet I felt there was an element of risk: Meris would have been capable of putting her threat into effect if only out of punctilio and pride. Perhaps money would have been able to persuade her to forgive me? Perhaps. But then I hadn't all that much at my disposal. And then, for the first time in my life, though motivated more by curiosity and caprice than by real emotional need, I wanted to put a girl to the test: to see whether she would cling to me independently of financial interest. Every day I protested and complained about the chain. If Meris's only, or main, aim was to worm money out of me, she would have given me to understand with some ambiguous word that if I took off the chain I could still make up for it by paying. But so far she had never alluded in the remotest way to this solution.

All girls, including those who do not sell themselves professionally, want at a certain moment to test the extent of a man's attachment, and the means they usually choose is very simple, a request for money. Ambiguous means: for money is not only a proof of the man's attachment but of the woman's selfish greed. But, when it's a question of girls who earn their living by prostitution, one also must ask: What other means have they, poor things, of convincing themselves that a man loves them, or doesn't? Little attentions, pretty words, romantic thoughts have their importance, it's true; but it is so easy to feign them, and they cost so little! What man is averse to offering a bit of flattery when he's sure that such flattery will save him a little money?

Now, my case was different and new. I had to consider seriously the probability that Meris was fond of me and intended, with the chain, to make sure of me. She knew that I liked her, that I liked her very much more than any other woman I had met. And perhaps she had decided to measure the real value that my sensual fancy could have for her: in other words, to discover whether this fancy was capable, or not, of being transformed one day into a regular, complete, and lasting affection. Meris was no longer all that young. It was natural that she should begin to think about organizing her life. The girls who work in houses have to retire in time, if they don't they lose their health and the fruit of their labors. And for Meris I was a good bargain. I was a "gentleman," and not only from the social point of view: I had private means and didn't have to work. True, I had made the mistake of telling her this, and hence I couldn't be all that sure of her disinterestedness. This doubt was compensated for by an opposite doubt: what proofs had I given her of my life of ease? It was possible that I could have lied out of vanity: there was no reason why Meris should have unconditional faith in what I'd said to her. But then, it was not out of the question that interest and affection could go hand in hand. There was nothing strange if, in planning how to organize her life, she should try to reconcile the one with the other.

"It's going to end," I said crossly in the half-light of the bathing hut, having shown her the little red furrow, "it's going to end with my having a sore."

She knelt down in front of me and began kissing me and

licking me, with the tip of her tongue, all around the little furrow.

"If it makes a sore, then I'll leave it off for a few days. Then I'll put it on again. And so, little by little, you'll see that you'll get used to it and won't be able to get on without it, and it'll be you who'll beg me to put the thicker one on."

"I don't believe it," I said with mocking certainty. "That, I don't believe!"

"I don't like that naughty laugh, Carlo. Do you know what I'm doing this moment?"

"No," I said impatiently, and I thought that what she was doing was to excite me, and excite herself, to get me ready, and get herself ready for making love. She, however, explained:

"I'm kissing the proof that you give me, every day, of your love."

"What nonsense. If all men who love a woman had to wear a chain . . ."

Meris's answer was ready, and surprised me with its intelligence:

"It's true, all men who love do wear a chain. The only thing is, that for all of them it's a chain that can't be seen, a chain of money, of time, of worries, of thoughts, of everything. It's a chain that women wear, too. Women and men wear it, and make each other wear it, when they love each other. Whereas for you it's a real chain. I could also tell you that . . . about you, about you, I'm very doubtful . . . but I, personally, would perhaps prefer the other, the usual chain of all people who love each other. But how can I contrive to put that chain on? How can I control you, how can I be sure that you'll wear it? Our lives are so separate! No, no, look, let's leave things as they are. It's only this way that I can be sure if you love me."

She was still on her knees. I knelt down in my turn in front of her and, gazing into her eyes, I said:

"But I adore you, you know it."

She smiled ironically:

"Yes, at the moment you adore me: you say it and you believe it. Then, as soon as we've made love, you say it again but in another way, and it's perfectly clear then that you don't believe it any more. And I want you to believe it, you understand? I want you to believe it always, always, always. I want it to be true always, always, always. You must adore me, but in a serious way. You must adore me . . . as you adore your mother."

It was under my breath, because we were in the bathing hut, but my answer was almost a guffaw:

"I . . . my mother—but I don't adore her at all. Quite the opposite!"

She looked at me, terrified:

"What are you saying, you stupid?"

"The truth. I'll tell you everything one day, I'll explain to you."

"All right then, you must adore me . . . as if I were the Madonna."

"But I don't adore the Madonna either. It's years since I've been to church. Long ago, when I was small . . ."

"Very well, then: you must adore me as you adored the Madonna when you were small. You remember it, don't you? Tell me you remember."

I said I remembered. And she got to her feet. I stayed on my knees, and, almost without knowing it, joined my hands in front of her. She gazed down at me from her height for a long time in silence. Then she looked at herself in the mirror which was above me on the bathing-hut wall. She raised her arms and coiled her thick, long, shining black hair around her head, then slowly began to draw on a rubber bathing cap. I was still kneeling. I could see her armpits, carefully shaven. Usually I preferred "natural" armpits. But, in her, I liked everything. I saw that pale circle of skin, barely, barely pale, and I dreamed of the moment when I would brush it with my lips and know it to be barely, barely rough. Once more Meris looked down at me, and whispered:

"And if you want me to be good with you, you ought to pray to me: just as you used to pray to the Madonna. With the same words. In any case, though I've never told you this, my real name is Maria."

"BUT what'll people say?" My bathing trunks just didn't cover the reddish circle around my waist, and I hesitated before going out of our hut to lie on the sand with Meris. It was the usual trouble: in a matter of a few minutes the whole world seemed to me to have changed. I regretted everything, and was furious with both myself and her. Had I been able to disappear, even at the cost of paying an enormous sum, and never see Meris again, I would have done so. I went on, crossly: "I'm ashamed to show myself to everyone with this red mark. . . ."

"You're an idiot. Here, catch, put this around your waist," she said, and threw me a towel. "Then, the moment you're ready to dive in, take it off and run. And when you come out, put it back on again as if to dry yourself. That way you'll be fine."

As I walked over the burning sand beside her, I told myself again that all was useless. What Meris had foretold with such certainty just wasn't true. I didn't feel even the tiniest hint of tenderness toward her, nor the tiniest little hint that I was beginning to get used to that idiotic slavery of the chain; yes, by now that's all I thought: idiotic slavery.

As if she were reading my thought, Meris said:

"Come along, Carlo, come with me. I feel like a walk. Let's take a good walk along the edge of the sea, where the sand is hard. You see, I know that at this moment you hate me. . . . No, it's pointless to deny it. It's pointless for you to say anything. I know it, I feel it. And anyway it's obvious; it's enough to look at you. You'd like to be miles from here, wouldn't you, and never see me again? But listen to this: for me, this is my finest moment. . . ."

I was thinking of what we'd been doing, quickly and violently, a few minutes earlier:

"Why? Wasn't it nice for you, too, in the hut? Do you mean that you were pretending?"

She took my hand. I confess that the mere touch of her hand now got on my nerves. But still, I didn't take mine away: I knew I would have humiliated her. She said:

"Just imagine me pretending! But that's only a part of love, it isn't love. That's what you don't understand, and I don't know whether you'll ever come to understand it. I'm proud, now, to be walking by your side. Proud that everyone should see us together. Were you happy? This time, answer. Don't go on saying nothing. You were happy, weren't you?"

"Yes, dearest, you know I was happy, very happy."

"And don't you want to reward me for the happiness I gave you? I've never asked you for anything. I've never asked you for presents, in all this month and more that we've known each other and seen each other every day. Just the fixed price. And you must believe that if I knew that you couldn't pay, that you were in a tight spot, I'd pay the money for you. Madame Teresa's money. Don't you believe me? Answer: don't you believe me?"

"Yes, I believe you, Meris."

"So, don't you think that I have a right to a reward for the joy you feel with me?"

"But the chain . . ."

"But you don't understand anything," she said, laughing. "The chain isn't a reward for me! I'd like to be able to do without it, as I've told you, haven't I? The chain is of use to me, that's all: it serves to make me sure that I've got you, that you're mine. That's all. No, the reward I want is this: that you should stay with me a little while afterward, and even in public. Am I asking too much? You see, now it's I who am happy. And I want to come back next Sunday, too, when the beach is crowded. You'll bring me, won't you, Carlo? You'll give me that present?"

Once again she asked me with such simplicity that I couldn't but agree, though with a heavy heart.

"Dearest! You don't know how happy I am! If only you knew: Sunday in the house is so dreary."

"But will Madame Teresa give you permission?"

"She wouldn't give it to the others for all the gold in the world. But to me, yes, she will give it." And she explained, laughing, and not without pride: "I'm number one. It's enough if I get back in the evening."

That same week Madame Teresa also gave her permission to spend the night away. I fetched her by car and took her to my apartment. Making love in my house, in my bed, achieved the great, the unheard-of miracle; afterward, I didn't feel my usual disillusion, nor my usual impatience to be alone. I finally experienced what so many other men say they experience and perhaps really do: a sweet gratitude, a tenderness full of respect for the woman with whom they've made love.

We stayed awake a long time that night, talking. Meris told me the story of her life in detail. She confessed her real age: she was thirty-two. And that she'd set aside enough money to be able to retire. This she would do, very probably, in a few months: as soon as she'd finished paying the last instalment for an apartment she'd bought, a lovely apartment with seven rooms. She'd even bought the furniture, and it was already in place, with the refrigerator, an electric and gas kitchen, nothing missing. It was that night while we were in bed, our legs entangled, and chatting in this calm tender way, like a husband and wife who love each other—it was that night that, for the first time in my life, I thought of the possibility of marriage. I didn't say anything to her: but probably, as usual, she intuited my thought. Perhaps it was also hers, who knows. I asked where her apartment was. Strangely enough, before answering, she blushed, then said, laughing:

"How inquisitive you are! No, I've told you everything. But I'm not telling you that."

"Tell me at least whether it's in Rome."

"No, it isn't in Rome. Unfortunately, I've worked only in Roman houses for years: in Rome it wouldn't have done, I'm too well known. . . ."

I was thinking that I, too, was too well known in Rome. The idea of marriage had flashed into my mind, in a concrete way, while imagining that I, too, would change towns, would be born again in a new life hidden from everyone, in Meris's place, in a city where no one knew me. What man doesn't have aspirations of the kind at a given moment? A few days before, there'd been the bombardment of San Lorenzo in Rome. It seemed absurd to think of marriage at that moment. But even the war would end. And if, when the war was over, we were still safe and sound, then we'd even travel. We'd go to Paris and London. At regular intervals I'd go to Levo to join my mother and Costantino. And when the day came that my mother was no longer there, our marriage would become public! I'd introduce all my friends to Maria, my wife. But I couldn't begin this new life in Rome or Milan or Turin.

I ended up the swift silent thread of my reasoning out loud:

"Perhaps in Bologna?"

"I won't tell you," Meris answered, and blushed again. It was a blush that continued to surprise me and that I couldn't explain to myself. Evidently in Meris's life there was a fact that she hadn't yet confessed to me, and that in some way linked up with her new apartment and her future: what she'd decided would be her future.

"And will you be able to live on the money you've saved? Will it be enough?"

"Certainly not. I'll have to work. But calm work, clean work, work that can be seen by the world."

"What sort of thing are you thinking of?"

"I haven't decided yet. At first, I shan't have to worry. When I've finished paying for the apartment, I've calculated that I shan't have to work for a couple of years. So I'll have plenty of time to find something suitable. For instance, I might open a lingerie shop. Of course I would need a loan to start with. But once I'd paid off the loan on the apartment, I could raise another loan for the shop, and pay it off gradually out of my profits. Don't think I have any illusions. I'm perfectly aware that it won't be easy; and in any case I'll have to wait for the end of the war. But one thing is certain: I'll never live this life again. I want to be respected by everyone, and I will be, you may be sure."

"And have you ever thought of getting married?"

"Why not? All women think of it. It's the most natural thing. I don't know whether I want children, that's different. But to marry, yes. If I find a man who I know loves me as much as I love him, and who works, too, of course . . . I've always been ready for this. I'm not like almost all my poor unfortunate colleagues who work in the houses and have a man living off them too. That sort of wretch has never been my sort. I despise them. But I've told you that, haven't I?"

Among other things, she'd told me how she'd decided to go and work in the houses precisely so as to escape from some overbearing wretch. From that time on, she'd never wanted to hear about protectors.

"And why do you call yourself Meris?"

"It really ought to be Amneris, the one in *Aïda*. But it's too difficult. So everyone says Meris."

It was true. Meris, Mneris. La Mneris! When Madame Teresa said, "Do you want Meris? I'll send you Meris," she really pronounced it "Mneris," slurring the first syllable; and in this way, perhaps through the influence of the more easily pronounced "Mary," the original name in Verdi's opera had gradually become corrupted.

"Do you love me?" she said suddenly turning toward me and fixing me with her serious gaze, this time without immediate erotic intentions: a serious gaze and anything but a mad one; indeed, I would have said an extremely reasonable one.

"I love you," I said in some perplexity: I was still thinking of marriage.

"No, you don't love me," she said, her gaze still on me and gently shaking her head.

"I tell you I do," I insisted; but, deep down, I was convinced of the truth of her denial, and I felt this truth like a weight, like a dull pain, the humiliating admission of my final incapacity. It was an unpleasant, an unendurable sensation. I reacted, slipped my arm under her warm soft waist; caressed her skin like fine silk, and holding her to me with all the strength in my power, I repeated over and over again: "I love you, Meris, I love you, I love you . . ."

"Right, but let's put it this way," she said slowly, and without looking away from me, "let's put it this way: you love me, yes, but you love me in your fashion."

THE FOLLOWING Sunday, July 25, we had decided to make an early start for Fregene: for once, Meris wanted to enjoy a whole day by the sea. I was to call for her as early as nine, an exceptionally early hour for her. Though it was Sunday, my orderly was to wake me at half past seven as on weekdays.

But at six o'clock the telephone rang: it was my Colonel.

To begin with, he asked me whether my car was working all right. The difficult period for private cars had already begun, and old cars couldn't easily be exchanged and were in frequent need of repair. Moreover, new tires had become a rarity. But as I'd had my Augusta serviced with a view to the Fregene trip, it was in fine trim.

The Colonel ordered me to call on him immediately: not at the Ministry; at home. He had urgent and important things to communicate, and not by telephone.

My mind immediately flew to the rumor that had been circulating in Rome the night before about a meeting of the Fascist Grand Council sponsored by Scorza. In the last few days the Allies' progress had brought reality home even to those who had never wanted to face it. The Axis had lost the war. Mussolini, if he wanted to save himself, would have to make a separate peace. . . .

The Colonel was waiting for me downstairs, ready to go out. As always, he was dressed in civilian clothes; but, contrary to the usual thing, there was no sign of his car with an army license plate and a driver in military uniform. My car had a Rome license plate of the usual civilian kind. I realized at once that this was the main reason, if not the only one, why my Colonel needed me.

Just before calling me, he had in his turn been waked up by a personal call from the Chief of the General Staff. Nothing was yet known of what had happened during the night, but it was known very well that something had happened. In a matter of minutes the General was to have a complete and detailed account, and my Colonel was to go to him immediately: not at the Ministry, and not even at home, but at an address that the General had given him by word of mouth the day before, foreseeing the eventuality of a very secret meeting: no telephone number was immune from the possibility of being checked by German espionage.

It was in Parioli, on the ground floor of a villa surrounded by a garden. I wasn't admitted to the meeting. During the moment in which the door opened to let my Colonel in, I recognized the Commander of the Army Police, the Chief of Staff, and another General.

I waited in an adjoining room. There were various offices and aides-de-camp, like me, and all, like me, in civilian dress. We sat around on sofas or in armchairs, and looked at each other without speaking. We didn't dare speak, even with each other. It was something if we even dared smoke, or offer each other cigarettes or lighters.

Seven, half past seven, eight. It didn't seem possible that the meeting could last much longer. I began nervously looking at the time, and was worried to see that it was getting on toward nine, when Meris was expecting to meet me and the car, according to arrangement, in Piazza Fontanella Borghese. I slipped my hand under my jacket and under my shirt and touched the chain—more as a talisman than as a memento, of which I had no need. At least I must find a way of telephoning her, so as to warn her. By chance there was a telephone in that very room where I was waiting with the other aides-de-camp. And it happened to be near my chair. All I needed to do was raise my arm, take off the receiver, and dial the number: but I realized that this was out of the question owing to the presence of my colleagues.

The telephone was white and stood obliquely on a little table painted in eighteenth-century Venetian style.

I looked at the time and my heart began pounding furiously: the need to talk to Meris and warn her, before she set out, was becoming imperative. I again began gazing at the white telephone as if I were fascinated by it, and as if by lifting the receiver I could free myself without risk from my duty as "a serving officer in time of war." No, I'd never joined the Fascist Party because I'd had the luck to have private means and thus hadn't needed to work. As the author of occasional articles of musical criticism which I'd published in the magazines and the dailies, I'd belonged to the category of "contributors" who, unlike "editors," hadn't needed a Party card. And from February 11, 1929, I'd been resolutely anti-Fascist—if only because on that day, with the Reconciliation between Church and State, my mother had become an ardent Fascist and an ardent admirer of Mussolini. I was determined in my anti-Fascism; but I was as inactive as I was determined: that is to say, my attitude was purely theoretical, even capricious. I wanted to see the end of the dictatorship, but I wasn't prepared to lift a finger to hasten it. My political ideas were known to my acquaintances, and all my friends, including Alessandro, were in exactly the same position as myself. But I had always hedged when overtures were made to me to join clandestine organizations (more or less active), distribute literature, join in meetings, or get to know the heads of the movements. After women, I loved my brother and music. All the same, I was fully aware that during those days, and especially on this morning, something infinitely more serious and more important was at stake: I felt that at last a decisive moment had come for the history of our country, and that, for me, it was no longer merely a matter of carrying out my duty as "an officer called to service in time of war": it was a matter of involving myself in events which, in one way or another, could not fail to have an influence on my private life.

By now I had decided to talk to Meris about marriage, and I had come to a private decision to talk to her about it on this very Sunday, quite calmly, and explain to her that if she agreed to marry me, our union—though in every way regular from the civil and religious points of view—would have to remain secret as long as my mother was alive.

Now, everything was possible. But the new events, whatever their nature—a separate peace, war against the Germans, a quick invasion by the Allies—might modify even our plan to marry; this could be hindered, or even perhaps prevented, by events; or, for all one knew, it might be just the opposite, and our plans might be furthered.

I looked at the time: eight thirty-five. I looked at the telephone. What, basically, could happen? These were extraordinary times, and everyone was allowed to make telephone calls for family or personal reasons. I touched the chain again and made up my mind to telephone in exactly five minutes. But then . . . the door opened. We jumped to attention. The Generals were coming out.

My Colonel, to whom I had briefly sketched my Sunday program on the way from his house to here, came straight up to me:

"You can consider yourself free," he said. "Go wherever you like, even to the sea. But telephone me at midday, at three, and at six: every three hours. If I'm not at home I'll leave word for you with the orderly. I'll probably need you this evening and tonight. Now I'll tell you what you mustn't tell anyone. It's a military secret, under oath. The Fascist Grand Council has passed a vote of no confidence in Mussolini. For the moment, nothing more is known. Anything could happen. Good-by."

"Don't you want me to take you home?"

"No, I'm staying here for the moment. Then I'll walk home. I prefer that."

My heart leapt into my mouth with relief: I'd arrive in time for the rendezvous. I'd be seeing Meris in a few minutes. Nevertheless I found the strength to make suitable protests:

"Are you quite sure, sir? Otherwise, I could just make a telephone call and be at your disposal."

"No, Captain, you be off, and do what I've told you."

I sprang to attention again and saluted: with this sharp movement I felt the chain slipping down a little around my hips. I ran out.

I SPOKE to Meris at once, in the car, on our way to Fregene. I couldn't wait for the afternoon. There was also the possibility that when I put through that call at midday I would find an order for me to return to Rome. I told Meris everything: except for the Grand Council. But she knew it all already. She knew about me, and my mother, and my family situation; about Costantino who was ill, and about how I had enough money to live without working. She confessed frankly that there was a police official who went to the house almost every day for the inspection, and who was also her client; and how for some time, in fact since the beginning of our relationship, she had gleaned information about me from him. She appeared happy and moved at my proposal to marry her, but not surprised. And she didn't feel very confident that, in view of the present situation, we would be able to get married soon. She seemed to want it, yes; and yet she also wanted to delay it. I thought of the instalment for the apartment. If it was because of that, I said, I would provide it, and I asked her what the exact sum was. I didn't hide from her that now I had one desire above all others: that she should give up her profession at once, and for ever. Then I realized that she was silently weeping.

"Why? Don't you believe what I'm saying? Don't you believe that I'm serious? It looks as though you don't believe me. I swear to you, but I've already sworn to you, that I've never thought of marriage until the other night, much less ever spoken to any woman about it."

"We don't know what may happen," she murmured, still in tears. "That means that if they're roses, they will bloom."

"But meanwhile, let's do some accounts. Tell me what you need, to finish off paying for the apartment. And at the same time you must leave Madame Teresa. . . . But if you don't trust me . . ."

"Of course I trust you!"

". . . And if you don't feel confident about what may happen, tell her that you need a short rest . . . surely you can tell her that? She's a good friend, isn't she?"

"Of course I can tell her. It's just the suddenness. . . ."

"But it's better to do it suddenly. Leave there, and come and stay with me. Or at Fregene, if you like, at the Albergo dei Pini. The expense will be my affair, naturally. Take a rest and go to the beach every day, and every evening I'll come to you."

"You're very kind; but I'm so unlucky. . . ."

"These are stupid nothings!" But the unexpected word "unlucky" had wounded me; it was a confirmation of what I'd suspected when I'd seen her blush the other night: Meris was concealing something from me. I said nastily: "I haven't got friends in the police. I don't know anything about you except what you've told me. Why aren't you truthful? Why? Why don't you tell me what's the matter?"

"But there's nothing . . ."

"There's the fact that you don't want to marry, that's what it is!"

Between tears and anger, she protested:

"But of course I do! Now let's not talk about it any more."

"What do you mean, not talk about it any more? If we're going to get married, we must certainly talk about it!"

"Don't let's talk about it any more today, my darling. . . . Please! I was so looking forward to spending today with you on the beach! You promised to take me in a little boat. Don't spoil everything, Carlo."

When we got there, the beach was still deserted. The sea was smooth. The air was windless, but fresh with an almost imperceptible breeze. The sun shone radiantly. We went straight to a boat. I rowed out to the open sea, and Meris threw off all her clothes. But she didn't bathe. That day, precisely from that very morning, she couldn't, she said, and she added jokingly: "I told you I was unlucky. So you, too, will have to make a little sacrifice today." I had imagined down to the last detail how we would make love in the boat on the open sea. I gave up the idea unwillingly, but also, I noticed, with a strange pleasure. Every time I'd been with Meris, every time I'd seen her naked in front of me—so that I could caress her and kiss her as long as I wanted to, and as I wanted to—my desire had quickly sharpened to the point of a spasm, both painful and voluptuous, that I was all stretched out to satisfy. This time Meris said she couldn't, or wouldn't; and it seemed that I discovered in renunciation a subtler and deeper pleasure. When I think it over, now as I write years later, I would call it nothing less than the maximum of pleasure. If, indeed, the disaster of my sensual relationships was the lightning-swift and inevitable disillusion that I experienced after pleasure, then the nonsatisfaction of pleasure, and hence the prolonging of it to an infinite point, could be a remedy. It was rather like Pierina's legs glimpsed on the balcony through the wisteria, and her feet and her dusty patent-leather shoes; or the hands of the Tobacconist as she deposited a pack of cigarettes and the change on the counter, those beautiful hands with dark skin, white nails, and those monstrous little nests of soft, dark folds on her knuckles: hallucinating, everlasting visions, almost enough to produce a cruel and exquisite drunkenness in me.

For this reason I put up no resistance when, as the sun went down and before we left the bathing place, Meris put the chain on me once more: on the contrary, I was glad.

It was only at six, that is to say at my third call, that I got the Colonel: he would be waiting for me (with my car) at ten, and before that I was to go home and pack a suitcase. I knew that I mustn't ask for explanations over the telephone. All I asked was how long he envisaged our being away from Rome—so as to get an idea of what I should pack. "A few days," he said. I said nothing to Meris. Until, having arrived back in Rome after dark, we were halted at a crossing in Prati by a disorderly procession of demonstrators waving the Italian three-colored flag and shouting: "Long live Italy! Long live freedom! Long live Badoglio! Long live the King!" One of them, passing near us, saw our astonishment and cried out in glee to the others:

"They don't know anything about it yet!" And then to us, still in high glee: "What? Don't you know? It's just been announced on the radio. They've arrested Mussolini. Badoglio is head of the government!"

It was a big thing, certainly. It was a great moment. But as I put the car back into gear, I turned toward Meris and saw that she was not sharing my joy.

"And now what'll happen? Will we make peace?" she asked, worried.

"I don't know, but they're bound to make it . . ." I muttered, and in a moment or two all the turmoil of possibilities poured into my mind. Obviously, getting out of the clutches of the German alliance would be no easy matter. . . . Meanwhile I was realizing that my journey with the Colonel might turn out to be much more important and longer than I'd first thought: I recollected that there'd been a slight hesitation in the Colonel's voice when he said "a few days." I told Meris this, and as soon as we reached Piazza Fontanella, before saying good-by to her, I took out my checkbook to give her some money. It was still my idea that she should leave Madame Teresa at once. The sum I gave her was ample enough to keep her in a hotel for a few months. But she was unwilling to accept it, and I had to insist: she must accept it in any case, even without promising to leave the brothel. She folded up the check and put it in her handbag and at the same time extracted the key to the padlock:

"This way, when you get fed up, and when you want to

go with another girl, you can take off your chain. But don't start forgetting me at once."

"Forgetting you? But what are you thinking of? Do you think I've been joking? We must get married. For my part, I shall start taking the necessary steps, and you should do the same. Write home and ask for your papers and tell them to send them as quickly as possible. You must promise me this."

She promised. But I realized that she wouldn't do it, at least not right away. She would wait at least till I got back. She put the little key in my hand. It was now my turn to be unwilling, and hers to insist.

"Otherwise, you'll have to go to the locksmith, it's all too complicated," she said laughing, and I saw, again, that she was moved.

That night I went with the Colonel to Florence. And from Florence we immediately pushed on in another, faster car, with a Florentine license plate and driven by a policeman in civilian dress. Our job was to inspect the arms and munitions dumps in Northern and Central Italy. The Colonel had to confer with the commanding officer of each.

The post was slow and irregular, and I had neither the time nor the calm to write to Meris as I would have liked. I sent her a telegram every so often, and several times I telephoned her. But the best times for me would have been in the early morning, when the house could not be disturbed save for exceptional reasons. So I telephoned rarely, and late at night. There were hours of frenzied and frustrated waiting in the darkening lounge of some provincial hotel in stifling heat; or, if the hotel had telephones in the bedrooms, there were equally long hours of waiting in desperate agitation between waking and sleep. At last my call would come through, but the line was always bad.

And Meris's voice, however much she tried to shout, came through far away and blurred; and her tone seemed to me tired, indifferent, almost bored by my telephoning her. Or perhaps, I told myself, it was the natural impossibility of bellowing words of love, all the more when there are people around listening: in her case the mistress of the house and all her colleagues. As I feared, Meris didn't leave Madame Teresa, and for the moment had no intention of doing so; at least, that's how things seemed. And I, in my turn, was unable to assure her of the date when I'd be back. The Colonel told me it was on the cards that we'd still be on our travels all through September. Of course I didn't repeat this to Meris so as not to alarm her sooner than necessary. But I was terribly worried that I mightn't find her in Rome when I got back; so my displeasure at knowing that she was still "there" was thus slightly made up for.

I was faithful to her during all those days, and without any difficulty. It was the first time that anything of the kind had happened to me. The chain didn't irk me, and I never took it off except to take a bath or shower. The chain was a constant reminder of my desire, which had remained whole and unsatisfied ever since that Sunday at Fregene: with Meris absent and so far away, the chain itself became a presence, and almost a satisfaction.

ON ORDERS from on high, the tour of inspection was brought to an end at Udine on August 20. We were to return to Rome immediately. There was not even the material possibility of telephoning Meris. And I wasn't sure if she would receive a telegram in time. I preferred to profit by what destiny seemed to have wished on me: a surprise return, with the risk that went with it.

I was anxious, but not out of jealousy. It is difficult, if not impossible, to feel jealousy when one's fancy is taken by a girl who works in brothels. I was anxious because I was afraid that I wouldn't find her: the last time I'd communicated with her was several days before the Assumption, and now the fortnight's holiday might have been changed. Or else I might find her, but in a different mood; no longer—the phrase "in love" didn't occur to my mind; I was afraid of finding her no longer "interested" in me, no longer content to marry me.

We reached Rome in the late afternoon of August 21. I telephoned Meris immediately, and that very night she came to live in my house.

She wouldn't believe that I had never taken off the chain, and that I had been faithful to her. She laughed: she was sure I was lying about the chain to please her; at the same time she was pleased about my lie. She laughed and cried: she was happy and, above all, surprised. After we'd been together for a while, talking between embraces, kisses, and caresses, I discovered that, despite my telegrams and telephone calls, she'd had no hope whatever that I'd return, and even less that I would still want to be with her. She was certain that when I'd spent some time without seeing her, I'd have quickly forgotten her, and that my very journey had been an excuse for forgetting her, for removing all value and seriousness from my intentions and promises about marriage. She confessed to me that she'd cut me out of her life. In her surprise and delight, even her face seemed changed, as though by some enchantment it had become fresher and younger. The light brown eyes seemed almost golden, and in her laughter there was a spontaneity which I'd never seen before, something countrified and childlike. From that evening, the chain became merely a joking memory between Meris and me. I took it off and threw it away, so as never to put it on again. We no longer needed it. We were sure of our mutual love.

We were happy for nine days. When I had telephoned Meris, she had obtained leave beginning from that evening and going on until September 1. In exchange, she had been obliged to promise a fortnight from September 1 to 16. But the morning after I got back, she had gone straight around to Madame Teresa and canceled this absurd obligation. Of course there was a penalty provided for in the contract, and increased by a certain sum for the days of August that Madame had "given her as a present" on condition that she return on September 1. I was happy to pay the whole of it.

We decided to get married at the first possible moment and to overcome all difficulties. At the beginning of September Meris was to go on holiday to her home so as to get her papers in order. After that, she was to go and get the apartment ready.

"What's the name of your village?"

"It's a tiny, tiny village. I'm sure you've never heard of it. I'm ashamed to tell you."

"Is that where you were born?"

"Yes."

"Then I'll see it on your papers when we get married."

"Yes, you'll see it on my papers. But before that, I'm not telling you."

"And what about the apartment? Surely you can tell me that now. Where is it?"

"You'll see that on the papers, too."

She answered laughingly, calm and serene as she had never been a month earlier. And I didn't give too much importance to the fact that she still wanted to keep so many secrets.

"At least tell me the province where your village is. . . ."

"The province of Reggio Emilia. Are you satisfied?"

I thought that the reason she didn't want to tell me the name was perhaps that she was ashamed of her family, when with me; certainly her family must have been very poor.

As for the apartment, I thought that perhaps some other man was acting as a go-between: someone who, in the past, had had a relationship with her, and this relationship had not yet been definitively broken. Perhaps an old flame who had guaranteed the loan for her, at least in part, and from whom she intended to free herself for ever, but she thought it best not to speak of him to me until she had done so.

And I had taken action on my side. I had written to Berardo, my old friend and lawyer in Turin, and asked him to deal with the papers in absolute secrecy. I had obtained from my Colonel a "special leave for grave family reasons," a leave of which I could take advantage whenever it was most convenient for me to have time and liberty at my disposal. My Colonel was a Neapolitan. During our trip together we had finally become real friends, and he had shown himself to be very human. I had told him everything, except for one detail: I had told him that Meris modeled clothes. But it's probable that he didn't believe me. "My dear Captain," he said, "this is really not the moment to marry. And I don't know whether, for all your good will, events will allow you to realize your dream as soon as that. On the other hand, I fully understand that at your age, if you've decided to start a family, you don't want to be held up for time. . . ."

Nine days of happiness. How can happiness be described? I don't even remember it, except that it was something in the sky, in the air. I lived with Meris, I slept with her, I ate with her at a trattoria at midday and in the evening, I went to the cinema with her and sometimes even to friends' houses. I spent all my time with her outside of office hours; and during office hours she waited for me at home, and did bits of shopping in the Ponte Milvio district. She only went into town a couple of times or so. I was happy. I felt only one sorrow that prevented my happiness from being complete: the thought of Costantino. I knew, and it did not escape my thoughts, that Costantino was suffering always and for ever, every day and every hour. I knew, and it didn't escape my thoughts, that my presence would have brought some comfort to him. It goes without saying that I wasn't in Rome of my own free will; I was in Rome because I was called up. But I was happy in Rome, whereas he was extremely unhappy at Levo.

I never gave my mother a thought. She had been seriously ill for several months. But I hadn't forgiven my mother. Of course I wasn't glad that she was ill and suffering; absolutely not. Indeed, in my heart I wished her a long and painless life. But I hadn't forgiven her, and my hardness, my ruthlessness toward her simply took this form: I never gave her a thought.

Obviously, it was neither prudent nor correct for an officer, even though in the reserve, but nevertheless in the secret service of the War Ministry, to live publicly with a woman who was "registered" as living in a brothel. But I, who had courageously decided to take this step a month before when I'd asked Meris to come and live with me, could now confront this situation boldly, and without even thinking myself courageous. It was a moment of extreme social confusion, at least in Rome. Everybody felt, even if they didn't say it, that the armistice was going to come, as well as something like the capitulation of the army. We had the Germans with us, and we felt that they were preparing a terrible time for us; but, perhaps just because we felt it, we all irrationally tried not to think of it, to eat, drink, and be merry, even with a frenzied and childish merriment, and to enjoy freedom, as if the end of the dictatorship were also the end of the war. In the evenings we met in the trattorias, or in friends' houses, for long dinners and talks that lasted till dawn. From Milan and all the towns of Italy, old friends turned up, and one also made new friends. Events and conjecture, good and bad, marvelous and catastrophic, became convulsedly, absurdly interwoven. That was the atmosphere of Rome in those days. And it is only too easy to understand that gossip about somebody's love-making was hardly a matter for scandal, or even interest, in such an atmosphere; nor was it a matter for scandal or interest when, in the nightly hurly-burly of some bourgeois or intellectual drawing room, a beautiful girl whom nobody knew arrived on the arm of an officer in the secret service. We were enjoying, in all senses, a freedom that we felt we were bound soon to lose.

Our happiness, mine and Meris's, was composed of nothing and everything. At night we walked through the darkened city or through Villa Borghese, we went long distances on foot to reach the car, we went up or down the steps of the Piazza di Spagna. . . . We talked about our future, however uncertain it seemed to us because of the great uncertainty of the general situation. Or else we were silent, and the light weight of her naked arm on mine was for me as sweet and expressive as a long talk filled with confidences. And I felt it was like that for her, too; that is to say, when she took my arm, she truly found and felt the total support that I was giving her, and that I intended to give her for life: for life and death. And at last there was no longer any question, none whatsoever, of a more or less artificial prolongation of desire, a prolongation that put off to infinity the disillusion that followed satisfied pleasure, and that thus created a mirage of amorous felicity. It was the thing itself, the real thing, consistent, living, about which I'd read in the novels and poetry of great authors as a boy. It was the first movement of Beethoven's Concerto for Violin and Orchestra, it was Chopin: but in real life. It was love. And I recognized it as such for this reason if for no other: because it was so utterly different from how, idiotically, I had always imagined it. I had imagined it as made up of unheard-of violences and long stupors, an alternation of humiliations and exaltations, intoxications, singularities, refinements, cruelties, disciplines. Whereas this was just the opposite: it was something very simple and almost bourgeois, an idyl full of little things, of deep silences without a moment of boredom, of simultaneous sighs and simultaneous thoughts. This, perhaps, was our basic impression: it seemed to me, it seemed to us (I was sure that she experienced exactly what I experienced) that we breathed together. And the true and precise act of possession, the pleasure of love, in a word, bed, no longer consisted of a certain number of minutes (whether few or many), extreme and detached from the remainder of our hours, but merely of a deeper sinking into our happiness, into our continuous mutual belonging, even when I was at the office and therefore we were materially apart, momentarily invisible to each other.

When we were not alone together, but in the company of friends or acquaintances, in a restaurant or at the evening gatherings to which I have referred, we never stayed long apart: we arranged things so that at least we could see each other, and we spoke clearly with our eyes across the confusion of all the chatter that was going on around us, and the smile we gave each other with our eyes was more living than the laughter resounding in our ears. I knew that Meris's every glance, smile, gesture, movement, was never for others, but only for me. I knew that she never forgot me, even for an instant, just as I never forgot her, even if our awareness of being near might, perhaps, have been able to favor such forgetfulness. But of all the memories I have of those nine days, perhaps the loveliest and most dazzling was this: a memory for whose sake I will never feel that I have lived in vain. It was a picture of Meris in the drawing room of an apartment on the top floor in Via Porta Pinciana, in half-darkness because the windows were open, full of smoke and noise, full of people holding forth and arguing, many of them standing with glasses in their hands. A picture of Meris. Before sitting down on a round stool which a young man had risen from so as to give her, she turned around to look for me with her glance. I was not far away but separated by a low table and by the crowd, and she smiled at me. Her bright eyes, in the half-darkness, seemed to be shining with their own light, passionate and mischievous at the same time. Without removing her gaze from me, she sat down on the stool with a movement that was suggestive to me alone, and she seemed, thus cunningly, to be offering me and reserving for me, that night and always, her body and her whole being. We felt that we were already married, secretly married, and one day soon we would be married before everyone.

On the evening of August 30, at eight o'clock precisely as on every other evening, I emerged from my room in the Ministry and set out along the corridor to appear before my Colonel, two doors farther along, and ask him "if I could dismiss."

Messengers at times ignorant of serious news, casual and unexpected apparitions that contain the announcement of a change in our destiny, perhaps communicate to us some magic suspicion of the truth even before we know it . . . or, in the flashingly immediate nostalgia for a whole happy period that has been lost for ever, even if it has been snatched from us only a moment ago, perhaps we unwittingly endow these messengers with a solemnity they didn't possess, perhaps we load those apparitions with a sad vitality that they lacked. . . .

The telegram came from Stresa and was signed by our doctor, Dr. Bargellesi: "Mother desperately ill attack nephritis deep concern heart condition come at once," or something of the sort.

Though it was only a few days before the catastrophe of September 8, in Ministry circles this was a moment of calm, almost of euphoria. We were all sure that there would be an Allied landing somewhere near Leghorn; there was talk of a separate peace having been already signed; and someone at the height of optimism gave it out as certain that the Germans had already made up their minds that the best strategy for them was to withdraw to the Brenner! Whereas my Colonel did not conceal, at least from me, that he was pretty pessimistic. "All of us, here, will be blown sky-high at any moment, my fine Captain," he said in a weak voice, and sighed. I handed the telegram over to him: he slowly put on his spectacles and then held it out under his eyes, in absolute immobility, and took three times longer than necessary to read it. Was he distracted, and thinking of something else? Or was he really pondering the decision he had to make about me? Then I had a strange impression: that telegram, perhaps, reminded him of something else, some private worry of his own. Suddenly he gave himself a shake, took off his spectacles, passed his hand over his eyes, and told me to leave immediately for Levo.

"It's better that way. At any moment now a trip from Rome to Milan might become impossible." He signed the passes in my name and that of my orderly. The impression given was that I was going on military duty. I would travel by car, naturally; it was slower but, everything considered, in those days much safer.

Meris was waiting for me at home, ready to go out, as on other evenings. The apartment was on the ground floor, and in front there was a little garden. When she heard the car on the gravel, she came as usual and looked out of the window while my orderly ran to take my place at the wheel and maneuvered the car into the parking place.

In the almost complete darkness, and from a distance, Meris nevertheless saw that something was the matter, or perhaps she guessed it from my step. She came to meet me.

"What's happened, Carlo?"

She wasn't flustered or surprised. Often, later, I remembered the expression on her face as I told her that my mother was seriously ill and that I had to leave immediately: it was one of sudden disconsolate resignation, as if she had always known it. I recalled her words, "I'm unlucky." This time, she didn't say them but I saw them nonetheless in her wide eyes as she looked at me. So much so that I answered her as if she had said them:

"Don't be silly. It's only for a few days. In any case, even if the worst happens, I'll be back immediately. I'm taking my orderly. I'm leaving you alone. Get in someone by the hour to do the cleaning. There's the telephone, and if I can't manage to phone you, I'll wire you, and you'll answer. If I'm held up . . . But I won't be. But if I am, why don't you go and wait for me in your village?" Then, suddenly struck by an idea, I said: "You come too. I have to go through Florence and Bologna: I can drop you off at Reggio."

Her answer was immediate:

"That's impossible."

"Why?"

"I hadn't told you, Carlo. But I'm expecting someone here in Rome. Someone who has to bring me all the receipts for the apartment. With the check you gave me before you went last time, and with what I had in the bank, I've paid off the final instalment. Thanks to you, the apartment is already mine. I'm expecting someone who has to bring me the receipts and the papers proving that the mortgage on the loan has been paid off."

"But why can't you go to him?" I asked, instinctively thinking, as always, that the apartment was in Bologna or anyway somewhere in the north.

"I wish I could. But I don't know where he is at the moment. You see, he's always traveling."

"Who is he?"

"An old friend . . . Carlo, what are you afraid of? He's a very decent person who's fond of me and whom I trust because I know he's trustworthy. Don't ask me anything more now, Carlo. Someday I'll tell you everything. But not just now. Come along, let's go and get your bags packed. I'll pack for you. I'm terribly good at it," and, after a moment's hesitation, she smiled in a melancholy way: "I've been living in suitcases for years."

We had dinner together again under the pergola in the old trattoria called Pallotta, at Ponte Milvio. Between us we must have drunk about two liters of Frascati wine, as if from a natural desire to stupefy ourselves and resist the agony of separation.

Then I took her back home. I handed the keys over to her. I took my bags. I explained to the porter that Signorina Maria Ferrari was my fiancée and was staying in my apartment during my absence, and that I'd be away at most a week.

She came out onto the road to say good-by and to give me a last kiss; my orderly was already waiting there with the car.

Before I kissed her I took her head between my hands. I gazed straight into her eyes, into those pale sparkling eyes, smiling through their tears, that knew me to my very depths and that I knew to their very depths, and I could have died gazing at them.

It was midnight. I said:

"Tomorrow evening, from this time on, wait at home for my telephone call. Don't go anywhere, for the call may take hours to come through. You can go to bed and sleep. If I don't call you, it's a sign that the line isn't working. Which could well be the case. But in any case you'll get a telegram the following morning. I'll send it from Stresa as soon as I get there. I count on getting there before night. If the post office is closed, I'll send it from the station."

We went back into the garden, behind the box hedge, and kissed at length, and we felt more and better united in that kiss than in all the countless times we'd made love during rather more than two months.

I ran to the car and told the orderly to start. I turned and leaned out of the window with my hand stretched out in a salutation that was also a vow.

She had dashed out into the middle of the road. She was wearing white, and I could still see her in the distance in the dark tunnel of the plane trees. I could see her until Tor di Quinto Avenue takes a sudden turn toward the north.

WE TOOK turns at the wheel. There was only one roadblock: our own *carabinieri,* on the Futa Pass. But with the far from brief delay caused by four punctures, and the halts needed to repair them—halts we made use of to get some food—the journey lasted all night and all the next day.

We got to Stresa at eight in the evening. Before going up to Levo, I stopped at Bargellesi's house, who by that hour could be expected to be back from his round of calls. I wanted to watch his face while he told me exactly how things stood. I had never before received a telegram like that, above all signed by a doctor; but it wouldn't be the first time that my mother had exaggerated the seriousness of an indisposition for the sole purpose of making me rush to her bedside. I even had a suspicion that it wasn't Bargellesi who'd sent the telegram. . . . That was another reason why I wanted to talk to him at once.

Bargellesi had only just got back from Levo. My mother was in no immediate danger: she would certainly live through the night; but for all that her condition was serious. Her blood pressure was very high, her heart was weak and subject to frightening spasms. She might get worse from one moment to the next, or she might last a long time longer—perhaps weeks, perhaps months. It was clinically impossible that she should recover. Bargellesi agreed with the nursing nuns: if during the night the situation deteriorated, he would go up as soon as he received a telephone call. He had had two containers of oxygen sent up there, but had left orders with the nuns not to use them unless it was absolutely necessary: this, so as not to scare her. I asked Bargellesi whether my mother realized how serious her condition was. He said that it depended; sometimes yes, sometimes no. This evening she was very agitated, he said, because she'd been expecting me to arrive several hours ago.

I called in at the station and sent the telegram to Meris as I had promised. And a quarter of an hour later I went into my mother's bedroom.

Bargellesi had told me to be careful not to tire her or let her talk; she had lost her voice and talking wore her out. Nevertheless, she must have heard the car, for as I was on my way upstairs she managed to shout my name! Giopa had come out to meet me. Costantino, erect at the foot of the bed, turned around, and was astonished and deeply moved at seeing me: I realized that they hadn't warned him of my arrival, so as not to disturb him unnecessarily. Two nursing sisters of Notre Dame de Montpellier were kneeling as if in prayer. They had come from the convent at Intra when she had become dangerously ill, and had never left her side.

"Carlo," my mother yelled when she saw me; and then, louder still, though her words emerged slurred and as though stuck together: "Lord God, I thank you!"

She was almost sitting up in bed, leaning against a mountain of pillows. With obvious effort, and forestalling by a fraction of a second the nun who had guessed her desire and got up to carry it out, she suddenly stretched out her arm toward a blue foulard shading the lamp on the bedside table, and pulled it off so as to make some light. She wanted to see me better, she wanted to scrutinize me, as had been her habit when I came home late at night as a boy, or, as a man, returned from a journey or a particularly long absence. She wanted to discern the traces on my face, or read the confession in my eyes, of the sins that I'd committed and that caused her so much pain: in fact, though she thought they caused her pain as sins, they really caused her pain as betrayals. I was reassured that the end was anything but near, less by the promptness of the gesture with which she had torn away the foulard than by the strenuous persistence of her jealous will to probe and investigate. But in the sudden, stronger light, it wasn't she who saw something new this time; it was I.

The fine, serene, harmonious face appeared enormous, monstrously swollen and distorted, and all covered with tears.

"Carlo, I was afraid I'd never see you again." And she seized me, hugged me, and held me close.

I leaned over the bed with my eyes closed, buried my head in the pillows, said nothing, and let her have her way. She held the back of my neck with one hand, my shoulder with the other. I could feel against my left ear the irksome hardness of the rosary beads which must have been clasped around her fingers.

"*Mère Saint-Charles, Soeur Thérèse, continuez,*" she said in a voice that had suddenly become much weaker, and so slurred that it was quite an effort to understand. "*Et toi aussi,* Carlo, pray with us. Stay here, Carlo. *Continuez. Prions tous ensemble!*"

Mère Saint-Charles resumed the rosary at the point where she had been interrupted by my arrival. I knelt down and leaned my elbows on the bed and began mumbling, partly in French and partly in Latin, taking care only to follow the rhythm of the two nuns who were reciting alternately. My mother held her hand, the one without the rosary, on my head, and feverishly caressed my hair. Now and again I opened my eyes and looked to the side without moving my head, and I saw Costantino. He was pale, erect, at the foot of the bed, as though eaten up with that inarticulate sorrow that never left him. I hadn't seen him for over a year and he seemed thinner, paler, but—strangely—younger too. He seemed to have reverted to boyhood even, to some extent, physically; he stared fixedly at my mother, and his eyes, which were blue and gentle like my father's, looked disconcertingly bright behind his glasses. He wasn't praying: he held his lips tightly closed and seemed to be positively smiling. Whereas Giopa had knelt down and was answering the prayers in a loud voice; his forehead was hidden by his knobbly hand, so that the top of his bald, reddish head was much in evidence.

Giopa's mother and her lover had never married; so Giopa, as the only child of a widowed mother, had never done his military service and hadn't been called up when war broke out.

When the rosary was finished, I exchanged a glance of understanding with Mère Saint-Charles, whom I had known since I was a child. She followed me out, while the other nun ministered to my mother.

Mère Saint-Charles repeated more or less exactly what Bargellesi had told me. I said I was going to get something to eat, and would then be back.

While I was dining with my orderly in the servants' room next to the kitchen, Costantino and Giopa came in. Costantino hugged and kissed me, as he always did when it was time for him to go to bed. His illness lay in the fact that in every way he had remained like a child and, like children, he had to lead a monotonous life and follow a very regular timetable. That evening was exceptional; he was still up at half past nine. But he seemed very calm. And he still seemed to have that trace of a strange fixed smile that I had noticed during the rosary. He said to me:

"Let's hope she dies tonight."

I couldn't help looking at my orderly; though trying to control himself, he betrayed his astonishment. During our journey I'd explained about Costantino and warned him not to pay attention to anything he might say.

Giopa thought it necessary to reprove him. When Costantino said things of this kind, especially, as now, in the presence of strangers, he always reproved him, even though the doctors had advised him not to because it was useless, and even harmful to his nerves. But Giopa confined himself to muttering in his calm and good-natured native lake dialect; and I'm convinced that he was right, not the doctors. For Costantino wasn't so stupid as not to feel humiliated by other people's invariable permissiveness about his remarks: he understood perfectly well that he was treated more as if he were mad when he was not reproved than when he was.

"Costantin . . . you mustn't be saying that sort of thing . . . Your mother's still there!"

"Why not?" answered Costantino, who always said, to everyone, everything that came into his head: "That way, she'd suffer less, so would we. I've already had enough."

"Good night, Costantino," I said, and kissed him again. He responded with all the tenderness that I had put into my kiss. He still had his smell, the smell which I found so moving; ever so slightly sweaty, but clean and healthy as a boy who has not yet reached puberty. The smell of a puppy.

When I went upstairs again, my mother seemed calmer. As if there had been a previous agreement, a few minutes after I'd entered the room the good nuns withdrew into the adjoining room, though they left the door open.

"Come here, Carlo. Come close. I can't talk in a loud voice."

I got a chair and put it beside the bed. I sat down and bent over, with my ear almost touching her mouth.

"Carlo . . . Promise me something." She spoke in a whisper, panting breathlessly.

"Yes, Mamma, I promise. What is it?"

"Promise you'll never go away again!"

"No, Mamma. I won't go away again. But . . ."

"Promise me on this. Swear." She had lifted up her hand with the rosary, from which hung a little silver crucifix. "Kiss it. And repeat what I say."

I kissed the crucifix. Then my mother began:

"I promise I won't go away again . . ."

I repeated:

"I promise I won't go away again . . ."

My mother went on:

". . . I won't go away until my mother is better."

"Yes, Mamma, but I must go back to Rome. I'm under military orders, you see. There's a war on. I obtained leave. As soon as you're a little better, I think I shall have to go. . . . You must understand."

"No, no, no! Promise. There's no problem about a leave. I've had a telegram sent to the General's sister. Promise."

I could visualize my Colonel as he'd been the evening before, motionless, staring at the telegram I'd given him to read. Was it possible that he'd been forewarned, that he had received a direct communication from higher authority, a recommendation that he let me go at once?

"Promise, Carlo," insisted my mother. She was beginning to get agitated. "Repeat it: I won't go away until my mother is better."

I repeated it:

"I won't go away until my mother is better."

"And now kiss this again," she said, putting the crucifix beneath my mouth. I kissed it.

Then she gave a deep sigh of relief. She closed her eyes. And with the hand that held the rosary she clasped my left hand and held it fast.

We stayed like that for a long time. Her eyes shut, her mouth half open, her breathing quick and shallow.

At a certain moment it seemed to me that her hand was loosening its grip. I realized that midnight was approaching and that I must telephone Meris. I tried gently to draw my hand away. My mother noticed at once.

"There's something else I want to tell you, Carlo."

"Tell me, Mamma."

"Open the drawer in the bedside table."

"Now?" I asked, hesitating. I remembered what Bargellesi had said: that she mustn't be agitated. "Why don't you take a little rest now, Mamma?"

Her eyebrows, unlike her hair, which was now more white than gray, were still wholly black, and she drew them together in a light frown: it was only thus, in the expression of her face, and no longer in her voice, that she still revealed her authoritarian character.

"Do what I say. Open it."

I opened the drawer.

"Look inside."

I looked inside. There was one of those orange envelopes which, ever since I was a child, I'd been used to seeing about the house, and above all on her writing desk in the appropriate pigeonhole, one of those envelopes that was both inheritance and symbol of generations of higher army officers and civil servants.

"Is there an envelope?"

"Yes, Mamma."

"Read what's written on the envelope, nothing else. Then close the drawer."

Without removing the envelope from the drawer, I read: "For my son Carlo Felice. To be opened immediately after my death."

As soon as she heard me close the drawer, she said:

"Have you read the envelope?"

"Yes, Mamma. But you shouldn't be thinking of things like that. Bargellesi said that you must keep calm, that there's no danger, none whatever. But you must keep calm and try to sleep. . . ."

"Now that you're here and I know you're not going away . . . if the Lord has decided to take me . . . You understand? I'm more ready."

"Mamma, don't talk nonsense."

"Repeat with me: Sacred Heart of Jesus, I'm entirely thine!"

"Sacred Heart of Jesus, I'm entirely thine!"

"Jesus, Mary, and Joseph, I give you my heart and my soul!"

"Jesus, Mary, and Joseph, I give you my heart and my soul!"

And I was thinking of Meris, and wondering if I'd manage to hear her voice that night. Two lines of Baudelaire came into my mind:

> *Son haleine fait la musique,*
> *Comme sa voix fait le parfum!* *

Certainly I couldn't telephone from the house. The only telephone was unfortunately in the hall on the first floor, between the door into the drawing room and the door into my mother's room. The Rome line was always very bad,

* Her breath spreads music / As her voice spreads scent.

and I would certainly have to shout if Meris was to hear me.

After Soeur Thérèse had given her an injection, she became rather drowsy, though still holding my hand firmly. I had given her the right hand instead of the left, so as to be able to look at my watch now and again.

Toward half past eleven, just as I was raising my eyes from my watch, I saw that her eyes were open and that she was gazing at me intently. I plucked up my courage. I murmured to her that I had been traveling all the previous night, that I hadn't slept since the night before, and that I was going to get a little rest.

"Be off," she said, less in words than by her expression, and, finally, with a gentle smile. But directly afterward I made a mistake: I got up too quickly. She grasped my hand again. As before, she frowned with her eyebrows, scrutinizing me as though suspicious of something, then breathed: "But if I feel bad, I'll have you called immediately, and you'll come right away, won't you? Promise?"

"Yes, Mamma, I promise." I kissed her forehead, which was damp and cold, and went out slowly, not without giving a long look at Mère Saint-Charles.

I went, and waited outside. I was sure that Mère Saint-Charles had understood. But to avoid arousing my mother's suspicions, she waited ten minutes before coming out into the hall.

"Elle entend tout," she whispered to me as soon as she joined me. We moved away to the end of the hall on tiptoe. I explained to her that I had to telephone Rome that night on my Colonel's orders, and that my orders were to do so from the *carabinieri* barracks in Stresa, because the call would get through quicker, and the line was better.

Mère Saint-Charles listened to me in silence, looking at

me sternly, without contradicting or approving. Beneath the high starched coif binding her forehead, she too brought her thin eyebrows together in a frown; but her eyes showed no more than cold incredulity, unlike my mother's, which showed passionate distrust, and hatred for that part of my life that remained unknown to her.

"Et si Madame la Comtesse vous appelle? Si elle nous dit de vous réveiller?"

I implored her to raise objections, to persuade my mother that it was better to let me sleep, on the grounds that I was really extremely tired. . . .

She said she would do what she could, but that she couldn't guarantee anything as she knew "Madame la Comtesse's" character. It would be best if I tried to get back as soon as possible. As soon as I was back I must let her know by switching the hall light on and off three times. Either she or Soeur Thérèse—for one of them was always awake—would see. And I must take great care to make no sound with the car, either leaving or returning.

Giopa and my orderly pushed the car by hand as far as the top of the new road leading down to the village piazza; once in the piazza, I could start up the engine. On my return I could leave the car in the piazza for the night and come up the hill on foot. I told my orderly to go to bed. Giopa insisted on waiting up for me fully dressed, dozing in an armchair outside his room. His room was also Costantino's; it was on the ground floor and enormous, with two beds, and a fine adjoining bathroom.

Giopa showed no surprise that I should be going to Stresa at that hour of the night, and when I had only just arrived. His faith and devotion were total and without flaw: they excluded any impulse to curiosity or any attempt to examine my actions. For him to make a distinction between my whim and my duty was a physical impossibility. I have often wondered whether this, and nothing else, is true love.

I found the Grand Hôtel des Îles Borromées partly requisitioned by a detachment of Germans. The night porter was an old acquaintance of mine, and he quickly put through an urgent call to Rome.

The lounge was plunged in darkness. I selected a corner of a divan and gave myself over to the delight and torture of waiting.

The French windows giving onto the lake were closed and carefully sealed by blue paper. The darkness of the lounge was broken here and there by the mysterious brilliance of invisible mirrors. I had chosen that corner so as to be able to keep my eyes on the switchboard, which was behind the porter's desk: here there was the green opalescent dome of a lamp—the only source of light in all that darkness.

I was worn out but completely wakeful: I felt that the telephone call I was waiting for was extremely important, but I wouldn't have been able to say why, and anyway I didn't even ask myself. I was now certain of Meris's affection. And if a friend had suddenly appeared at my side and asked me to search my soul for the reasons why this telephone call seemed so important to me, I would simply have said: Because I need to hear Meris's voice at the first possible moment. Every minute's delay caused an agonized increase in this need. I could see her in my bed in her filmy pink nightdress. She had gone to sleep with the light on, a magazine in her hands, just as I had found her one night when I'd had to report to the Ministry instead of going out with her; one of the nights of our nine days, on which I sometimes looked back as though they'd been nine years, so many different delights had I experienced, and sometimes as though they'd been nine minutes, or even less: as though they'd never existed, as though they'd flashed across my mind in an indulgent and fleeting dalliance of the imagination. I saw her. I saw her hands holding the magazine: she had small hands, not thin, not nervous, but delicate, hands which immediately showed her intelligence, her natural wit. I saw her black loosened hair spread over the pillow. And the full and delicate shape of her face, closed in sleep; her high convex forehead, her generous lips, all her marked and generous curves, like a sixteenth-century Madonna. And nearby, on the bedside table, I saw the telephone which was shortly, at any moment now, going to ring. Then she would wake up, stretch out her naked arm, and make me happy merely with the sound of her voice.

How long would I have to wait?

Now and again, in the halo of the green dome of light over there, the ivory bald head of the old porter nodded.

Suddenly a group of German officers came in, with a clatter of boots and guttural accents; they passed under the arch of the entrance in a stiff black mass, got between me and the green light for a moment, then disappeared in the direction of the corridor where the elevators were.

How long would I have to wait?

At last the call came through. When I heard the telephone ringing I leaped to my feet. The porter came toward me and showed me which booth I should enter. I dashed into it and shut myself inside it as if for the most delicious of love meetings.

The number didn't answer.

"Impossible!" I shouted. I protested, to the annoyance of the telephone operator. Then I begged him to forgive me, but implored him to make sure that he'd got the right number.

Yes, he had got the right number. But he'd try it again. There was no answer.

I looked at the time, hoping that in my impatience I'd made some mistake, and it wasn't the time I knew it to be. I emerged from the booth and checked my watch with the porter's. I had no choice but to accept the reality. It was half past two in the morning.

I WENT back up to Levo, leaving the car in the piazza as arranged; I went up on foot as far as the gates of the villa, but I could see at once that all my precautions had been vain, as vain, alas, though in the opposite sense, as the imprudence of which I'd been guilty in keeping my promise to telephone Meris. Bargellesi's car was standing in front of the gates.

The only person asleep was Costantino. Everyone else was in a great state of agitation. Toward one o'clock my mother had taken a turn for the worse and had so insisted on having me called that the nuns had pretended to come and awaken me and, when they couldn't find me, had gathered from Giopa that I had gone out because I was under orders to report to the *carabinieri* at Stresa. My mother hadn't believed them; it was an attempt to deceive her; I had gone off for good, to return to Rome! She said they must telephone the *carabinieri* immediately. Mère Saint-Charles had enough good sense to oppose her and, as she was afraid of a collapse, had summoned Bargellesi instead.

Either owing to the shock of not finding me, or through the inevitable progress of her illness, she had indeed had a collapse. I found her under oxygen.

As soon as she saw me she made a desperate sign that she wanted to talk to me. Bargellesi bent over her and urged her to calm down, but in a loud voice, as doctors and priests do when they want to be sure that a sick person in agony can hear them.

"Here he is, Signora, your Carlo. He's here and he won't stir again. But you must promise to keep calm, otherwise I'll tell him to leave the room."

My mother removed the glass mouthpiece, looked at me, and said: "Where were you?"

"With the *carabinieri*, Mamma."

Her face was more swollen and distorted than ever. A contraction, which was intended to be a smile of sarcasm, deformed it horribly: "Yes, with the *carabinieri!*"

I was suffering more than I would ever have thought possible, I was suffering because I hadn't talked to Meris, and because Meris hadn't been at home to wait for my call as we arranged. I thought my mother was the cause of everything, this time too. My mother who, by her illness, had forced me to leave Meris too soon: perhaps we had been living together for too short a time to break off without paying a price. What had happened to Meris? Perhaps she'd left me: perhaps the friend she'd mentioned had arrived in Rome and she'd gone off with him for ever. I'd lost her for ever, perhaps. Or perhaps it was merely that she hadn't got back home. Perhaps she'd had to quarrel and fight with her friend, and it was really out of her delicate feelings for me that she had preferred not to do so in my house. I had been tormenting myself with these conjectures during the fifteen minutes' drive from Stresa to Levo. In either case, whether I'd lost Meris for ever or not, the fault was my mother's, and now I felt a pain, a laceration, a need to hate her which was greater by far than the hate I'd been feeling for years. I saw her greenish, swollen, sweaty face, and her eyes full of tears. And, with a cruelty which made no distinction between me and her, I was almost glad that she should be suffering and dying. She too, at that moment, seemed to be paying back hate with hate.

"Carlo, if I'm so ill, it's your fault. Isn't that right, Doctor, it's his fault?"

"No, really not, Signora . . ." Bargellesi was old. I couldn't remember any time in my life when I hadn't seen Bargellesi: he was our family doctor when we used to come to Levo for the holidays and I was a child; my father was still alive and my mother hadn't yet started calling herself Contessa. But since then nearly everyone had taken to calling her Contessa, and Bargellesi's "Signora" must have sounded to her a bit rough and almost offensive, even at a moment like this. "No, really not, Signora . . . your Carlo has had work to do, he's wearing civilian clothes but he's in the army. It isn't his fault at all. Your Carlo loves you and is here at your side and isn't going away again. Be good, now . . . be good . . . and rest."

Bargellesi signed to the nun, and she drew near again with the oxygen. But my mother pushed away the mouthpiece with a gesture which seemed extremely violent, even though, in view of her condition, it could only have been weak. Soeur Thérèse was alarmed. My mother sought me out.

"Carlo!"

Bargellesi patiently pushed me forward, so that I could bend over her and not tire her by making her talk in a loud voice.

My mother took hold of one of my hands and, looking at me and weeping desperately, said:

"Carlo, I'm afraid!"

I answered pitilessly, and without worrying about the doctor and the nuns' hearing what I said.

"That's enough for now, Mamma. Have a bit of dignity.

What good does all your religion do you? There's nothing extraordinary. This happens to everyone, at a given moment, absolutely everyone. . . ."

"Yes, but this time it's happening to me."

And those were her only words of resignation during her agony, which went on for six long days: the last three almost without consciousness, at least apparently.

THAT NIGHT I got only two hours' rest. I was awake at seven and put a call through to Rome. I'd made up my mind to make my call from there, from the house. I would keep it down to a few words, and wouldn't let the nuns know that it was a woman.

The call came through at nine: the number didn't answer. I made a dash down to Stresa to send an urgent telegram imploring Meris to wire me immediately and tell me what was happening.

The most hopeful hypothesis was always the same: that Meris had found herself obliged to spend a night with her old friend. When she'd wound up her relationship with him once and for all, a relationship complicated by the financial question of the apartment, she would go back to my house, and I would find her again. I telephoned in the afternoon, and again late at night: no result. Then I sent a reply-paid telegram to my porter. What else could I do?

The next day a telegram arrived. I was in my mother's room. She was still conscious, but rapidly deteriorating. I had heard the bell of the garden gate. I went slowly over to the window and, from the darkness around me, saw Giopa going to open the gates, with his long shambling peasant's step, and then I waited, and at last I saw him coming back. He was holding a small yellow square in his hand. It was doubtless the porter's answer. But I hoped, and wanted to hope, that it was a telegram from Meris.

I went down to meet Giopa. I took the telegram and went out into the garden.

It was about eleven in the morning. The sun was hot, the air still. A light high mist veiled the mountaintops and the shores of the deep lake. I walked down the chestnut avenue. I could see the dense shadow on the gravel, broken here and there by rare splashes of sunshine, and by the first leaves that had fallen as a result of a storm a week earlier, before I arrived: that's what they'd told me. When I was sufficiently removed from the villa, I stopped. I looked at the yellow square in my hands, which I was about to open. I listened to the familiar sounds of my mountain: the song of the birds, the clucking of the hens from the hen-run, a dog barking, the distant bells of Campino or Baveno . . .

It was from the porter. It said more or less the following: "Morning immediately after your departure Signorina Ferrari left without message and taking own luggage."

I thought I was prepared even for this news; but I wasn't. I can't remember ever experiencing in my whole life, which by now isn't a short one, a pain as acute as that. I suddenly felt breathless; and everything around me, the trunks and leaves of the chestnut trees, the sky, the colors, the shadows, the lights, the noises, the heat of the sun— everything had become like a show which my senses went on watching by a miracle, while I myself was harshly, physically, excluded. I sat down on the old stone bench at the end of the avenue, and stayed there motionless, without thoughts save for one which wasn't even a thought, but the inarticulate perception of a condemnation: I had lost Meris.

I came to myself with Giopa's footsteps on the gravel: he had come to summon me in for lunch.

In the afternoon I telephoned Madame Teresa. I hadn't thought of this earlier. And I wasn't at all sure that Meris had seen her and had said anything to her. But the truth was that this was my last hope. I didn't know the name of Meris's village in the province of Reggio Emilia, nor the place or town where the apartment was that she had bought, if it was true that she had bought it; I now doubted everything. I telephoned from the public telephone at Levo in the Dopolavoro bar. I had told Giopa that that's where I would be should my mother want me.

Madame Teresa said that Meris had gone to Naples. I was dumfounded.

"To Naples! But what for?"

"She's gone to her house, to have a rest."

"And the address, please?"

"I'm sorry but I don't know the address," said Madame Teresa, immediately and kindly. By an instinct which I'm unable to explain, I was sure she was lying. I insisted, beseeched, implored. But in the end, either because she really didn't know or had promised Meris not to tell me, I had to give up. But then why had she said Naples? Was it because she was caught off her guard? Or because the name of the city wasn't a sufficient postal address and, on the other hand, for her not to know where Meris had gone might seem to me unnatural and thus arouse my suspicions? I asked: "But when did you last see her?"

"The other day. She came to call on me. She said she was going to her house. That's all."

"To her house in Naples?"

"To her house in Naples, I've already said."

"But . . . has anything happened?" I tried; it was a long shot.

"What do you mean, has anything happened?"

"I mean anything . . . serious?"

"No, absolutely nothing."

"She didn't tell me she was going to do that . . ." and I explained in a few words why and how I had left Meris in Rome in my apartment. Madame Teresa said she knew nothing of all that: when Meris came to my apartment, she (Madame Teresa) had thought it was for a day or two. She ended up: ". . . Anyway, she'd been telling me for some time that she intended to have a rest."

"Was she worried? Did she look peculiar? How was she?"

"No, absolutely nothing of that kind: everything was as normal as could be. I'm sorry, I can't tell you anything more because I don't know anything more."

"She'll write to you, she'll send you her address."

"If she sends it to me, I'll let you have it, don't worry. But she'll write to you, too. . . ."

This tiny thread of hope ended the telephone call; and I had a clue, though a very tenuous one: Naples.

My mother died in the night between the fifth and sixth of September. She had been unconscious for three days. A certain Father Attanasio, a Franciscan from the friary at Mesmo, came to give her the last rites; and up to the end, and above all at the end, he shouted obstinately:

"Signora Contessa! Signora Contessa, do it for Jesus, who died on the cross for us! You, too, repeat what Jesus said on the cross: *Fiat voluntas tua!* Signora Contessa, you are in the best position to offer up the *fiat* for us! For us, for your sons, for us all! Signora Contessa, *fiat!*"

And the stentorian voice, and the equally ridiculous use of the inaccurate title, did their best to deprive death of its inevitable solemnity; and at moments they succeeded, but only at moments.

Ah, the spectacle of her death agony, at least during the last endless nights and days, was enough to cure me of all hatred. Whatever the wrongs and faults of my mother, her suffering began to seem a disproportionate punishment: a punishment that everyone gets and no one deserves. My mother, in the final nights and days of her agony, seemed to me at last to be a human being. I contemplated her there on her bed, gripped by her atrocious torture, and there were hours when I forgot myself and my pain, Meris, and all my other infinitely lesser griefs, I forgot the acts of violence, the jealousies, the abuses of power of my mother, which had caused me so much pain, and remembered only the pleasant hours, the sweet hours she had given me. Hours of long ago: I had to take my mind back to my childhood: but hours no less real for that: walks with her in the city, trips when she had taken me with her, or perhaps she had made them for my sake, when she wanted to show me Genoa, Florence, or Venice; and, in the summer, trips to the mountains, or by boat on the sea; when, at Alassio, she had wanted me to learn to swim. I saw her once again during my father's lifetime, when she was still young, really very beautiful and perhaps fairly happy: I saw her strong, ample body, her black flashing eyes, her open, loving smile: she had been a human being in the distant years of her early marriage, too.

The two nuns were used to death agonies. But for me and Giopa, and, though in a lesser degree, for Costantino, after those sleepless nights and those lightless days, shut up in that room with the stench of medicaments and the scent of the eau de Cologne continually sprayed by the nuns to counteract the stench of medicaments, and the ever-changing death rattle, now suffocating, now gurgling, now groaning, which we seemed to hear as if within ourselves, and the hope of the end which advanced and receded alternately . . . after all that, the end, when it came, was, as the saying goes, a liberation.

I looked questioningly at Bargellesi. He replied by staring at me and nodding. I knelt down. I prayed in silence, or believed I prayed, reciting a requiem in my mind. Then I got up and kissed her already icy forehead: someone had closed her eyes. I went out into the hall. But I immediately heard the heavy rustle of a nun's habit coming after me: it was Mère Saint-Charles.

"Vous oubliez! Tenez, vous lirez après." She was holding the orange envelope in her hand, the one I'd seen in the drawer of the bedside table.

Though the writing on it said clearly that I should open it immediately after her death, I felt an irresistible temptation not to do so. I felt stunned, at the end of my tether, and curiously light-headed. Yes, I would disobey my mother. I wouldn't open the envelope "immediately." What else important could she say to me now she was dead? I knew she loved me too much to make any modification to her will, which the lawyer, Emprin, had communicated to me years ago in Turin. Costantino was legally incompetent. Perhaps there would be "legacies" for friends, for acquaintances, for the Cottolengo Institute, or for other pious works—even for the nursing sisters of Notre Dame de Montpellier? Well, I would deal with the "legacies" in due course. The envelope might well contain no more than what is called a "spiritual testament": final counsels, solemn recommendations, sentimental souvenirs which my mother had collected and prepared for me who knows how long ago. No, for the time being, I wasn't going to open it. I folded it and put it in my wallet in the inside pocket of my jacket. If I'd opened it . . . I confess that at that moment I was thinking of Meris. I invented for myself a sort of superstitious test: yes, I would open the envelope when I'd found Meris's address in Naples, not before; or when I'd discovered that I no longer had any reasonable likelihood of finding it.

I was committing an extreme and posthumous act of spite against my mother's will power. A sort of revenge; a harmless and symbolic revenge that could no longer hurt her. I told myself that if Meris had gone away, it was certainly a sign that she didn't love me enough and that, after all, she had no intention of marrying me; perhaps her courage had failed her at the thought of confessing this to me, and she'd chosen to disappear mysteriously and in silence. But my mother, though she hadn't willed it and thus was not really culpable, had favored Meris's flight by her death, and brought about the conditions that made it possible.

She was buried on the seventh day in the Levo cemetery, and I and my orderly left that same evening. On this occasion, too, we traveled without a stop. On the afternoon of the next day, in a bar at Viterbo, we heard Badoglio's voice on the radio, announcing the armistice. We reached Rome toward sunset: the city looked calm. I left my orderly at home, telling him I was dashing to the Ministry to see if I could pick up any news. Instead, I went to Via Fontanella Borghese.

As I expected, it was shut up: precautionary measures. I rang the bell, but no one came to open. I went on ringing, at intervals, obstinately, for ten minutes or more. At last I heard dragging footsteps. The door, closed on the inside with a chain, was a chink open. I peered through and saw in the darkness of the vestibule an old woman-servant who pretended not to recognize me though she knew me perfectly well. She told me to be off, or she would telephone the barracks of the nearby *carabinieri*—of San Lorenzo in Lucina; we were both of us unaware that in all probability, already by that evening, the *carabinieri* wouldn't have replied to a call of that kind.

I slipped through the chink a tip which was more than

persuasive, and told her I wasn't asking to come in, but that I was in urgent need of information: the address of Meris's house.

"Wait a moment," said the woman and closed the door.

She was away for what seemed to me an enormous time, but I didn't dare ring again for fear of ruining everything.

At last I heard the dragging steps again, she opened the door its chink, and with a clawlike hand pushed through a piece of paper. It was an outside edge torn from a newspaper and on it was written in pencil: "Via Silvio Spaventa, 2."

With this address, which I would remember for ever without any need to copy it out, I went straight to the Ministry. I wanted to see my Colonel, hear from him what was happening, and find out if there was a possibility of an immediate journey to Naples.

The Ministry was deserted.

I telephoned the Colonel's home number. The cook answered and told me that the master had left with the mistress that very morning, with endless luggage, and hadn't left an address. Her orders had been to close the apartment and go back to her village.

I went home. Here my orderly, in his turn, asked leave to do what clearly all the military were doing: go home. He came from near Spoleto, and so would be home in a few hours.

But before I'd seen my orderly, I'd already spoken with the porter by the main door, and made him tell me in minute detail the manner of Meris's going.

Toward twelve noon on the day following my departure, he said, a gentleman had arrived and asked what floor I lived on. The porter had replied that I was away. Then the gentleman had said that, in view of my absence, perhaps he could have a word with the lady who had been living for a few days in my apartment, Signorina Maria Ferrari.

I asked: "Did the gentleman know the Signorina's name, or did you tell him?"

"He knew it already, he knew it perfectly well," he answered, and he couldn't help a gleam of malicious delight showing fleetingly in his eyes.

"What was the gentleman like?"

"Young."

"Very young?"

"No, about thirty-five. He was a tall, thin, dark gentleman, with glasses. Ordinary clothes. I wouldn't say smart, but not old rags either. I went with him as far as the stairs to show him the door, and then . . . and then because . . ." He stopped, hesitating.

The porter was a small, thin, anemic, and nervous man who spoke without looking you in the eye; his wife had been for some time in the clinic and he never stopped complaining about overwork. When he hestitated, I grew suspicious.

"Why did you go with him as far as the stairs?"

"I wanted to see whether the gentleman really knew the Signorina or not."

"Well then, did he know her?"

"I couldn't tell you, Captain, sir, because I went with him to the foot of the stairs, and at that very moment I heard someone calling me: it was the Administrator who'd come into the garden with his car and was in a hurry, so I only pointed out the door to that gentleman, 'Look, it's there,' I said and I didn't see him again. After not even half an hour, but no it must have been even less, twenty minutes, the Signorina comes into the lodge and says, 'I'm going, look, here are the keys.' 'Should I say something to the Captain when he comes back?' 'No, nothing,' she said, 'the Captain knows everything already. Thank you and good day.' And off she went."

"Did she go with the gentleman?"

"Yes, that gentleman had already gone on with the luggage. And they had a car outside waiting here in front in the road with another gentleman. They loaded up and all three made off."

"You didn't see the car's number, by any chance?"

"No, to tell the truth I didn't bother about it, Captain, sir. . . ." Once again I seemed to detect something ironical in his expression, or something worse: as if he'd seen the license plate clearly enough and was taking malicious pleasure in telling me that he hadn't bothered.

"But you saw the car," I insisted, "and you saw that there was another gentleman sitting inside. . . ."

"That I did. I didn't move from here, look, from here, just where we are now. . . ." We were on the threshold of the porter's windowed lodge. The porter ended up with a frank laugh, now, and apparently kindly. "And you'll appreciate, Captain, sir, with the distance, a car over there on the road, you can see from here if there's someone inside, but you couldn't read the license plate." We both remained silent for a moment. I was staring at him in anguish, and he was avoiding my eye and looking at the road over there as if the car that had taken Meris away was still there. With his last statement the porter had partly contradicted his preceding one: it wasn't true, then, that he hadn't bothered about the license plate; in any case, he wouldn't have been able to see it because of the distance. But in that moment of silence he realized from my anxious stare that the contradiction hadn't escaped me; and that seemed to me to be precisely his intention—to insinuate a doubt in me, wound me.

While my orderly was packing his suitcase, I had my last

surprise, my final blow. Though I was exhausted and starving, I needed still more to have a shower and change. Then I'd go out and have a snack at Pallotta's: it was a way of going on thinking about Meris. The bad side, or, if we prefer, the good side about the sufferings of love is this: that at least at first one doesn't want to forget, one doesn't look for distraction, but takes pleasure in suffering. I'd be eating alone at the same table where I'd been happy with her for the last time. . . . It seemed to me almost impossible, almost unreal, that I'd lost her in such a stupid way; and I blamed myself for not having had the strength of mind to follow my instinct to the very end. I shouldn't have admitted defeat, I should have insisted on taking Meris with me and leaving her at Stresa, at the Îles Borromées, for all the period of my stay at Levo. I would have gone to see her every day, several times a day. In a word, we should never have separated. I wouldn't have lost her. As I was dressing after my shower, and transferring my wallet and papers from one jacket to another, I saw the orange envelope, my mother's "spiritual testament," which up till then I hadn't opened, and indeed had forgotten. Right, now that I knew Meris's address I could open the envelope without breaking the promise I'd made myself.

It wasn't easy to go to Naples in those days. Besides, now I had the address, I could even put the journey off for a week or two and try to organize it properly. The situation seemed so uncertain that my first thoughts went to Costantino; it would be better to return to Levo immediately and reassure myself that Costantino wasn't having to suffer. I'd already had the idea of sending him and Giopa across the frontier into Switzerland.

There were a few old family friends in Locarno, Bellinzona, and Lugano, and we had a certain amount of free currency in the Vallugano bank. Once the villa at Levo had been closed down, Costantino safely lodged in Switzerland, and the Turin house sold to pay off the big loan I'd arranged with a Milan bank without my mother's knowledge, I'd be able to go to Naples. Meris had wanted to leave me; I couldn't have any lingering doubts about that; if I went on deluding myself about it, I would be being not only pig-headed but silly. Hence all I wanted was to see her once more; for her to say a proper good-by to me, with her own voice and looking into my eyes.

I opened the orange envelope.

The thing that first astounded me was the date: August 28, 1943! So it wasn't, as I had supposed, a letter my mother had prepared long in advance. She'd written it only the day before Bargellesi had sent me the telegram summoning me to Levo and taking me away from Meris.

The letter is still in front of me on my desk here in Auckland. I slip it out of its envelope, of an orange which seems to have retained its gloss over a whole sixteen years. My mother's handwriting, always hard, clear, bold, with the t's crossed with short precise strokes, and never a stroke forgotten, was now for the first time shaky and unsure. It was certainly her handwriting, but as if reflected in a liquid and moving mirror.

I copy:

Darling Carlo,

You've been the only true and great love of my life. That is why I forgive you everything. And I forgive you, too, for the harm you've done me in these last days: the harm which I know my poor heart, pierced by the dreadful news, will not hold out against. Bargellesi came to see me *afterward,* and found me terribly low. He hasn't said so, but I know my condition is grave.

Through very reliable information, which came directly to General D., the brother of my dear Clotilde, it has come to my knowledge that for some time you, in your apartment in Rome, 147 Viale Tor di Quinto, have been living with a depraved woman, with a shameful and unspeakable past. Take care, Carlo! This is a crime that you are committing: a crime, first of all, against God; and then against your Country, against the honor of your Family, against yourself and against me. I put myself last although, when *I knew,* my state of health, which was already causing anxiety, unexpectedly deteriorated. I have to make a superhuman effort to hold the pen in my hand and finish this letter: but I want to finish it before Mère Saint-Charles arrives from Intra to help me in this, my last (I feel it!) illness, for she certainly wouldn't allow me to tire myself by writing.

I forgive you. And I pray God that He, too, will forgive you.

I willingly offer up my poor life, filled, as you know, with trials and sorrows, I offer up the suffering that has torn at me from the moment *I knew* about that filthy person who is with you, I offer up my death, I offer up everything as a sacrifice, so that you may be saved: and so that one day I may see you again where I hope that Our Lord, in His infinite mercy, will welcome me in saecula saeculorum.

I kiss you as I did when you were small, and as you can't have forgotten. . . . My Carlo, you have been the only true and great love of my life.

Your Mamma

At Gurro, in the Val Cannobina, I knew an old and experienced smuggler. Years before, he had taught me the tunes of the old local songs, melodies of ancient Scottish origin. With him as guide, all went well. But the crossing was no joke, especially for Costantino, who had slight resistance for walking along mule tracks and goat tracks up in the mountains.

I went with them, introduced Giopa to the manager of the Vallugano bank at Lugano, and obtained authorization for him to cash checks; then, once again making use of the guide, my friend from Gurro, I returned to Italy, where, meanwhile, our army had collapsed; Mussolini, who had been set free, was founding the Social Republic; and the Allies, who had landed at Salerno, entered Naples on October 4.

I stopped off for a few days in Milan and Turin: everything had been prepared for the sale of the house in Piazza Bodoni; with the money derived from this, I paid off the bank loan and bought a *pied-à-terre* in Via Borgonuovo. And I got back to Rome at last.

Without admitting to anyone what my real aim was, I searched around for contacts among friends and colleagues who were preparing to cross the lines and get to the Allied armies. I knew English well enough, and hoped to be taken on as a liaison officer. I don't want to boast of a warrior's impulse, which I never had. And I can't honestly say that my bid to serve patriotic and political ideals—in which, for better or worse, I believed—or my dash toward Naples, would have taken this form if I hadn't hoped to find Meris. But my desperate and disillusioned state of mind in those days did favor such a decision: I wanted to take a more active part in the war so as to find an outlet, so as to forget and fill the great emptiness within me. So much so that, having crossed the lines with a small group of colleagues, and not without risks and adventures, and having arrived in Naples, unlike the others I didn't call at once on the Committee of Liberation in Piazza Carità, but went straight to number 2 Via Silvio Spaventa!

This street is very near the Central Station, and runs into the main piazza on the left when you arrive. Many houses in that part of the city, and in that street, had been bombed and destroyed, or half destroyed. Number 2 Via Spaventa was still standing. It was a sizable building of five or six stories, put up toward the end of the last century or the beginning of this one, like all the buildings of the nearby main thoroughfare, the Rettifilo. It had a dirty, proletarian air, with shops on the ground floor, offices on the entresol and first floor: I could see by the name plates beside the door.

I asked the porter for Signorina Ferrari. No tenant of that name existed or had ever existed. It then occurred to me that Meris might have been married for some time and never have told me, so she might have another surname. So I tried to describe her physical appearance to the porter, but without result. Then, a little higher, I saw other name plates, of pensions and rooms to let; perhaps Meris lived there. I won over the porter with a tip, and went up and down the four staircases of the building, ringing every bell, not just those of the pensions and the apartments with rooms to let, and I asked everywhere.

Via Spaventa was short; there were five buildings in all, two on the right, three on the left, all detached, between the main piazza of the station and Via San Cosmo fuori Porta Nolana. Number 2. That was what was written on the scrap of paper the old woman had given me, but for all I knew it might be wrong. So I tried the other buildings in the street, every single one that hadn't been abandoned because it had been destroyed. With each house, and every door, my hope waned. In the end I had to give up. Why, I asked myself, why had I been given a false address? Perhaps it was Madame Teresa's fault—she had thought this up to get rid of me, and in accordance with Meris's express orders. I was becoming more and more convinced that Meris wanted to disappear from my life, and to disappear in such a way that I would never find her again.

In Piazza Carità there were days of waiting and uncertainty: examinations, interrogations, ordeals, humiliations, and great patience. Finally I had the good fortune to get the backing of old General Pavone, a friend of my Colonel's. He remembered me and knew perfectly well who I was. Pavone was trusted by the Allied military command, and he stood as guarantor for me. I was taken on as liaison officer with the American Fifth Army, and was in regular service until several months after the end of the war.

In vain I asked General Pavone for news of my Colonel; and in vain I looked for my Colonel in Naples at the house of one of his brothers, an engineer. He must have hidden himself away in the country, and there was no knowing where: perhaps in the north, as his wife was Piedmontese.

My mother's "spiritual testament," combined with the recollection of how my Colonel had behaved when I showed him Bargellesi's telegram, insinuated into my mind the suspicion that he'd known about the absurd police inquiry my mother had started up through General D.'s sister. If there was any truth in this suspicion, then my Colonel shared the blame in my regard. He was a decent man, and may have been on the point of telling me everything; possibly that was why he'd hesitated like that, and stared at the telegram in his hand. But he was altogether too conformist to "face the music." And perhaps he was annoyed at being deceived by me—for I had withheld from him Meris's real profession. . . . In any case fate prevented me from reaching any certainty, anything more than suspicion. After the end of the war I discovered that my Colonel had retired to Ceva, where his wife came from, that he had been arrested by the Germans in March 1944, deported to Germany, and had died in a concentration camp.

And the same applied to the wrong address I'd been given in Naples. When, eight months later, I reached Rome in the wake of the Fifth Army, it can well be imagined where I paid my first visit. But in the meanwhile Madame Teresa had "retired" too, and the old servant who had given me the piece of paper pretended she couldn't remember anything; she was obstinate and, for once, unbribable, though this incorruptibility was both mysterious and sinister.

THIRTEEN years passed. Though I certainly hadn't become a woman-hater, the idea of marrying had never again entered my mind. I had gradually come to the conviction that this endless craving to make love was almost a bad joke, if not of nature in general, at least of my nature. Ever increasingly, and ever more rapidly, I had the sensation after making love that Dante felt on meeting Casella: empty shadows. The hug I gave Costantino when he came to wish me good night was more real: there were his touching boyish smell, even though he was now forty-five, his thin shoulders, his pale hollow face, with the skin cut here and there from his Gillette razor: he insisted on shaving himself, and had never learned how to do so properly.

I concentrated on work with more application than I'd ever done in the past. I was putting together a book on Puccini. As I now did signed music criticism for a Milan daily paper, I had assumed for the first time an obligation to work regularly, though admittedly the work wasn't very burdensome.

I spent half the week at Levo and half in Milan. The building housing my former _garçonnière_ in Via Pasquirolo had been destroyed by bombardment, but I had now established myself in the _pied-à-terre_ in Via Borgonuovo; and there I received my girl friends, though I took care that their vists alternated—according to a rhythm which was only apparently a whim—with the visits

I myself paid to other girls in the brothels. As I have already said, those houses were closed in 1958, some time before I ran into Alessandro at Brignole Station.

By now I was resigned to this life, with a touch of sadness and a certain serenity: I viewed myself as arid, but not abnormal. Sometimes I tried out—why not confess it?—the game, the trick, the expedient of the chain, the expedient that Meris had taught me and that had made me fall in love with her; but the result was not comparable, not even remotely! After a few minutes I just laughed, and the irritation of the chain around my waist became unbearable in almost no time. This made me realize that I wasn't—what for a time I'd thought myself to be—a pervert, a masochist. Before I made love I sometimes liked to imagine that my partner was making me suffer: that was all. It was imagination, not real suffering, and always in different forms, physical or spiritual, and on the whole mild.

THREE MONTHS after the meeting at Brignole Station, that is, on a September afternoon of that same year, I was sitting at the Cellerino Café on the lakeside at Stresa. It was a Saturday. I had just come back from Milan and had stopped to take an apéritif before going up to Levo. Every Saturday, unless there was some concert or first night in Milan, I went back to Levo and spent Sunday and Monday with Costantino. I didn't stop at the café every Saturday. Indeed, I would say that it was a rather rare occurrence. An unlucky inspiration had persuaded me to stop, one time too many, at this occasional halting place. But what inspiration?

I don't even remember very well. As I was running out of gasoline, and as the following morning early I wanted to take Costantino and Giopa on a trip to the Simplon Pass, I had stopped at the filling station opposite the café. While the man was filling up the tank and checking the oil, I absent-mindedly watched the tourists strolling along on the other side of the road just where the tables of the Cellerino Café were arranged along the pavement: the wicker chairs were already occupied—by tourists: many of them were foreign, Germans, Swiss and French. In the good season of the year, and when the weather is fine, the Cellerino Café is always like that; it has a cheerful and good-humoredly adventurous air, as if for a holiday in which passing foreigners can take part without commitment. Or pershaps a darting image had attracted me, from among the people sitting at the café, an image that had flashed before my eyes without reaching my consciousness. The fact remains that I felt a desire, which I couldn't see as anything but neutral and harmless, to sit down there too, and drink a quiet port. I asked the garage attendant to park the car, and I crossed the road.

I sat down in such a way that my back was to the café and my face to the lake. I ordered my port. After a few minutes, as the waiter hadn't returned, I turned to look for him, and I saw . . . I saw something I hadn't seen at first: two tables behind me a large, dark woman, with big sunglasses, wearing a white cotton dress, her arms bare, her breast full and very décolleté, very sunburnt, leaning over and talking to a little girl of six or seven sitting at the same table; both were eating ices. The shape of her back and her arms, the way her black hair fell to her shoulders, and what I could see of her face notwithstanding the dark glasses and the fact that, by leaning toward the little girl, she turned her profile away from me—these things reminded me of Meris. But how often I had seen women who looked like Meris, in the streets of Milan or elsewhere! How often had I doggedly followed them until I'd convinced myself of the absurdity of my impression, and scrupulously eliminated the faintest possibility of hope. And every time I'd felt more tormented than ever by the question that I'd never been able to ask her: "Meris, why did you want to disappear?" One winter's night, in my car I followed a streetcar as far as the terminus, until I saw the woman alight who, through the frost-misted glass, had seemed to be she!

But this time I had a thought that should have calmed me at once: if the dark woman in the sun-glasses were Meris, she couldn't look so firm and young, her skin couldn't look so smooth and healthy. I made a rapid calculation: by now Meris would be at least forty-five.

So there could be no question of its being she.

Anyway, as if she were aware of my interest and found it tiresome, or, on the contrary, wanted to encourage it, the dark woman now changed her position in her chair in such a way as to turn her full back on me . . . ah, no! A magic act or just a coincidence: she had changed her position the better to rub off with a moist napkin a drop of chocolate ice that had fallen on the child's dress. Supposing, I said to myself, just supposing it were really Meris after all?

As when a distant voice or noise sometimes awakens us from a delightful dream, and we try to seek sleep and the dream again, so now I abandoned myself to the exalting and intoxicating supposition: if she were Meris? And I gazed at that raven-black, thick, shining hair, really identical with Meris's hair, falling over her bare shoulders and hiding the smooth sunburnt skin. I gazed at the soft plump arms, the right arm moving briskly and quivering as it removed the stain, and thereby revealing the clean white circle under the armpit, suggesting an impeccable shave . . . like Meris. Oh, if it were Meris I certainly wouldn't behave as Alessandro behaved when he saw Mumi again, after so many years, under the arcades of Via XX Settembre. The dark woman had no air of having fallen on bad times, like Mumi; her clothes and the little girl's had nothing out-of-the-way about them, but nothing poor either: they were clean, simple clothes. And their hair was tidy. She had now finished removing the stain, but she didn't turn toward me: she placed the napkin on the table and on her wrist I saw a little watch with a white strap. I got the impression of someone enjoying modest ease and secret pride, who, unable to allow herself a really expensive watch, preferred a leather or silk strap to a vulgar gold one. Even this detail fitted in with my memory of Meris. . . .

No, I wouldn't behave like Alessandro. She would weep and beg my forgiveness for having deserted me, and she would explain the reason. And I would offer her everything. I would immediately give her all my possessions. I would again ask her to be my wife. My wife? But in all likelihood she'd already be married and the girl would be her daughter; the little girl was dark, too, with plenty of hair and a round, determined face.

Now the child's eyes turned toward me. They were wide, black, and sad. She stared at me a long time as if fascinated, perhaps because she'd noticed that I was watching her.

The waiter arrived with the port. I paid right away, and drank quickly, so as to be ready to get up as soon as the dark woman did, and follow her.

When she got up, I told myself, of course I'd see at once that she wasn't Meris. But I didn't want to see that. I wanted to prolong the illusion as long as possible.

Now the dark woman extracted cigarettes from her handbag, a big white straw handbag, and lit up. Then slowly, and as if without realizing it, perhaps prompted by the child's gaze, which was still resting on me, she turned around: she looked toward the lake, and perhaps she looked at me. I couldn't see her eyes, hidden behind the huge sun-glasses. But I saw her face.

She wasn't Meris. Meris had a full, oval face, with soft, delicate curves. This was a hard face, with pronounced cheekbones, and lips, without lipstick, closed in a sorrowful, severe fold, with down-turned corners. A German face, I told myself.

She slowly inhaled her cigarette. She made no movement. And now, perhaps because she, too, had noticed the insistence of my gaze, she seemed in some way to be responding to it: she seemed to be looking, not at the lake, but straight at me. The child was behind her, and was now no longer concerned with me but only with meticulously finishing her ice.

Something extraordinary then happened: my heart suddenly began beating furiously: the dark woman was smiling at me.

I swung around to make sure that she wasn't smiling at someone else, a passer-by. No, I saw no one. I looked at her again, and again she smiled at me, more plainly now than before, as if to tell me that she'd appreciated my doubt and wanted to dispel it.

My heart still beating furiously, I gave a little bow. She replied with a brief nod of the head and another smile; then, her mind made up, she turned toward the little girl, bent over her, talked to her, and, at last, as though continuing the same conversation, turned toward me again and said to me—yes, to me—gaily and in a loud voice:

"How are you? What a pleasure it is to meet you again. Come and join us, Doctor, come and sit here," and she motioned to an empty wicker chair at her table. The accent was strange: the "r" of Doctor was slightly guttural.

I got up and went to her table. I could feel my legs shaking: I don't believe I would have been more moved if the Tobacconist of the Via Carlo Alberto had suddenly asked me, at the age of eighteen, to go with her into the back room of her shop. . . . She held out her hand. It was very different from Meris's hand—a large, nervous, almost masculine hand. Once again she invited me to sit down. Smiling, she said:

"This is my daughter, Ilse. . . . You remember, I talked to you about her at Santa Marinella. I'm so sorry, Doctor, that I didn't recognize you at once. Ilse was looking at you, but I didn't see her. Forgive me!"

"I wasn't sure . . ." I murmured, flabbergasted by all this. I was mathematically certain that I had never made her acquaintance. Santa Marinella? I'd been there from Rome to go bathing, three or four times all told, and I would never have forgotten a woman like that. And then, Santa Marinella . . . it was absurd. Yes, I'd been there, but fifteen or sixteen years ago when she would have been a mere child. I thought confusedly of two possibilities: either she was mistaking me for someone else, or this was a game so that the little girl wouldn't notice that she was making advances to someone she didn't know. She wasn't wrong in calling me Doctor: in Italy you're on pretty safe ground if you call a well-dressed person Doctor. She spoke Italian fluently, but her accent was slightly foreign and with something German about it—that was it—which went with her face. Anyway, whether it was a mistake or a ruse I would have to wait till later to know. For the time being, I couldn't not back her up. So, "I wasn't sure," I said; "the sun-glasses . . ."

"There you are," she said, and took them off with a lively, sweeping gesture, and with a good smile that showed her very white, strong teeth. Yet her eyes didn't seem to share the smile: they were strangely large, black, and, so to say, lifeless; like a second pair of glasses more mysterious than the ones she had taken off. "Do you recognize me now? I'm Sandra, Alessandra Bulài. You remember, at the Pirgus Hotel in Santa Marinella. It must be about . . ."

"It must be about . . ." and I stared at her in an effort to communicate to her with my eyes more clearly than I was able to the certainty that we had never seen or known one another, and that this was why I couldn't remember when.

Her enormous extinguished eyes showed no sign of having received the message. She said:

"It must be . . . It *is* exactly two years ago; the summer of 1956. What brings you to Stresa, Doctor? Are you on a trip?"

"No, I live here. In a village high up on the hillside, at Levo; an old family villa. I live here and in Milan; I commute . . ."

"Oh yes, now I remember you come from here. I wasn't really thinking . . ." and as she said these phrases she was looking toward the child—in fact almost pointing her out to me with her chin, and with the way she put on her sunglasses again, and with her tone of voice that seemed to suggest that I shouldn't say anything embarrassing. Finally she gave me to understand that we were, indeed, playing a game.

All the same I thought I could ask: "And what in the world brings you here?"

"Oh, we have been living at Pallanza for nearly a year, in a nice little house; today we came to Stresa in the bus for a change of scene. Two years ago, when I was at Santa Marinella, Ilse was staying with her grandparents at Merano. But now she's with me. In a few days . . ." she hesitated an instant, as if to adjust her sun-glasses better, and she lowered them a moment, but merely to look at me fixedly over them, as if she had no other way of giving life to her own eyes, so large and anyway so lacking in light, ". . . in a few days she's going to school."

"Really?" I said, turning to the child. "And what class are you in?"

"She's in the *prima elementare*," answered the young mother vivaciously. "She looks big, but she's only six."

"And are you glad to be going to school?"

"Yes," said the little girl loudly, "because I don't want to go to prison."

"Ilse, what are you talking about?"

"Yes, Uncle Tommaso says that little boys and girls who don't go to school end up in prison."

The mother gave another laugh, but it was a little too long to be natural. It didn't even cross my mind to ask who this Uncle Tommaso was, but I would have liked to know. As if she had guessed my thought, and as if she wanted to prevent me from asking about Uncle Tommaso, she drew nearer to me, still laughing. A cigarette was between her lips, and she asked me for a light; while I was lighting it, she deliberately rested her hand on mine. The contact had an immediate and magic power over me. I looked at her: she took in a deep breath of cigarette smoke, then breathed it out through her nose. She was an extremely lovely woman, strange, unique. I said:

"And are you going back to Pallanza by bus this evening?"

She looked at the time. The watch strap was made of leather. She was wearing no bracelets, rings, earrings, or necklaces; nothing. Only that little watch. Her wrist, like her hand, was rather strong for a woman.

"Yes; in fact we ought to be leaving right away. We're late. . . ."

"If you'll let me, I'll take you by car."

She thanked me without any hesitation. I paid for the ice creams and we went to the car, which was parked in front of the landing stage, not far from the big newspaper shop. In those days I had a specially made green car, foreign, which caused a sensation.

"What a beautiful car! Isn't it lovely!" she said. "Just think, I was admiring it earlier, when it was at the filling station. Only I didn't know that it was yours. What extraordinary coincidences there are in life!" She took some money out of her purse and gave it to the child. "Here, Ilse, go and buy your little paper."

The child ran off. The woman drew near me. Suddenly I said:

"May I see you sometimes?"

"Of course, thank you," she answered quickly, and added: "But . . ." and she turned toward the newspaper shop. I said:

"Could I telephone?"

Again she answered quickly:

"I haven't got a telephone. I could call you . . . I want to ask you a favor . . ." and, while I was giving her one of my visiting cards, with the Milan and Levo numbers, she went on: "The child is going to school on October 1. Could we meet on the morning of the second or third, if it's not a Sunday . . ."

"Telephone me whenever you like. I'm always in in the mornings. In Milan, or here."

I realized from the child's delight that she had never been in a car of that kind. The mother, I think, had: she was too much at her ease. During the brief journey, she suddenly asked me whether I knew anyone at the Ministry of Justice: she needed a recommendation for an employee. I said I didn't, but that I could surely find someone to take the matter up. I told her she could, anyway, give me the name of the person to be recommended.

"Thank you," she answered, "another time, if . . ."

At the beginning of the Pallanza lakeside, she said we had arrived and I should stop. She explained that it was impossible to go on because she lived up there, beyond the narrow streets of the old town where such a big car couldn't get through. There was no logic in her explanation: at the point where we had stopped, near the first narrow streets of the old town, there was still at least a kilometer of lakeside, and the natural thing would be for me to take her on over that distance. But judging by the determination with which she opened the door, I realized that I mustn't insist: probably she didn't want to be seen getting out of the car.

Sandra, Alessandra. The coincidence of the name was strange, too, which reminded me of my old school friend and hence of an example not to be followed. I wasn't following it, and wouldn't follow it; if the situation arose, I'd throw myself, body and soul, in the opposite direction!

Returning toward Stresa, I looked at the lake rippling with silver and blue, at the black crests of the Mottarone, at the sky, crimson and pink where the sun had set. I felt strong and happy. I hadn't found Meris, but, while thinking of Meris, I had nevertheless found something extraordinary. A love? Perhaps only a passing fancy, a bit more violent than usual—so I was thinking at that moment—a slightly longer adventure. And wasn't that better than a love?

I remember the scent exhaling from Sandra as she sat beside me in the car: not a Franch scent, subtle and refined, but a simple odor of freshness and plain soap, newer and more intoxicating than any of those other scents. And when I entered our old dining room and, in the cone of light above the set table, saw Costantino and Giopa bending over their soup and sad because I was late, I felt my heart bleed. Their life, compared with mine, was so impoverished, bleak, hopeless, and already in decline; whereas, as by a miracle, mine was once more resurrecting into youth.

SHE TELEPHONED next morning. She spoke excitedly. She was in the public telephone booth and, through the glass door, she was keeping an eye on the child as she spoke. She told me the child had no father, and that she was engaged to be married to an employee of the Ministry of Justice. She was supposed to be getting married within the next few months, as soon as her fiancé had reached the prescribed age limit; but the Ministry had to give its permission, and this permission was "subject to the good moral qualifications of the fiancée": that, in so many words, was what the regulation said, and, alas, the fact of the child couldn't be absolutely overcome without a strong recommendation. She'd told her fiancé that she had known me two years ago at Santa Marinella, as a client at the Pirgus Hotel, where she had in fact been working as a maid. She begged me to forgive her, but neither she nor her fiancé had any backing, they knew no one of importance who could help them. She would be so grateful if I could help, and would show her gratitude. When the schools opened again, she would have the mornings free and in this way we could see one another whenever I wanted: but not at Pallanza, of course, and with great caution. I thought quickly, and decided:

"It would be best for me to meet your fiancé."

"*Sie sind ein Schatz* . . . You're a treasure. I didn't like to ask you."

"Would you come with your fiancé and visit me here in the villa? I live with my brother. There'd be no harm in it. And anyway, I'm getting old. . . ."

"What are you saying! Old, you're certainly not that. But serious, yes: in appearance, anyway." And she laughed a low, muffled laugh. I was upset. But I said, nonetheless:

"As for that, you look serious too."

"But you don't know me yet. You'll see. I *am* serious."

"Not too serious, I hope."

"Why? Can't the attraction that two people like us feel for each other at first sight be something serious too? Here's the child. I must fly. When can we come and see you?"

"This afternoon toward six. Is that all right? I'm expecting a visitor, but he's an old friend. . . ."

"That's even better. Everything will seem still more innocent to my fiancé. . . ."

"I'll be expecting you."

"Look, my fiancé is . . . is a very simple person. He's a Sicilian, and a corporal in the *carabinieri* here in the reformatory for minors. He has rough manners, but he's so good, you'll see."

I was surprised to find a hotel maid showing such alertness of mind. Then I remembered that she came from the Alto Adige, that is to say from a very civilized region, and that perhaps the calamity of having a child without being married, and the need to earn money, had obliged her to take a job beneath the standing of her family; just as, now, she was obliged to accept a prison guard as a husband.

I had never of my own free will got to know the fiancés or husbands of the girls with whom I'd had, or wanted to have, a relationship, however fleeting. I had always tried to forget their existence as far as possible, and ignore their physical side. It had always been an instinctive rule with me to maintain a rigorous distinction between social relationships and love relationships. But how could I say no to Sandra? In her determined face, and in her ways of speaking and behaving, there was something aggressive and imperious that alarmed and fascinated me: perhaps I could have resisted, but I didn't want to.

I began anxiously counting the hours that still had to pass before her visit. I sent Giopa to Stresa to buy cakes and ices for tea. The old friend I was expecting was Maestro G., who usually spent September at his villa in Baveno.

I admired and envied G. more than anyone else in the world. When I went to visit him in his little room at the Scala, during intermissions, there was never a time when I didn't ardently want to be him. I said to myself: There goes the only completely happy man I know. In him intellectual and physical activity coincide and fuse. Drenched with music as much as with sweat, he always changed his clothes completely from head to foot after each act. I looked at him and thought: What anxieties, other than those of his art, can touch him? What significance can the paltry, raving, delusive joys of eroticism have for him? From the flickering light crouching in his eyes, from his concentrated and whimsical face, to the short lock of fair disheveled hair falling across his forehead, he was bursting with joy: it was the immaterial fantasy, the mathematical intoxication, the enfolding waters of the music. Conductors like him are the only human beings who, without any pride, indeed with the humility of a boundless gratitude to destiny, can almost feel themselves to be gods.

I was waiting for Sandra; and in the agitation and alarm of waiting, and in my apprehension as to what she, a new and strange woman, might have it in her power to do to my future, I envied G. even more than I'd ever envied him before.

G. arrived a little in advance of Sandra and her fiancé, so I had time to tell him the whole story. He was as amused as if by a fairy tale. He laughed and screwed up his eyes; it seemed as though, behind my words, he was listening to some distant music and never missing a note. If I hadn't known him so well, I might have thought that he was listening to me absent-mindedly, but I knew he wasn't, and indeed at a certain moment he interrupted me vivaciously.

"The Ministry of Justice? But I've a friend there who's Director General! He's from Bergamo, like me," and he said his name. "Your *Histoire Extraordinaire* has taken an unpredictably lucky turn. Now we can assure the lady that the business, if it's do-able, is done!"

The corporal of the guards, Tommaso Vaccaro, native of Sperlinga in the province of Enna, was a strong, sturdy young man, with regular features and almost handsome, except for his low forehead, which was really excessive. His hair was black and thick and compact like steel wool, whereas his face seemed curiously rosy and delicate. Arab, certainly: but such a rosy complexion must indicate some northern cross-breeding, however distant. Then his eyes were of a glowing blue, like those of new-born babies. General impression: exceptional physical health, strength, and cleanliness.

He was dressed in black, his "Sunday best." Whereas Sandra, despite her little blue cotton frock, as simple as the white one of the day before, had all the air of a great lady; he looked like her chauffeur: so obvious was the disparity in manners, education, and class. Yet in a dim way they had something in common; and from the very moment when I saw them coming toward me in the shade of the drive, holding the little girl by the hand between them, I was struck not by the difference between them but by the resemblance.

In the high valleys of the Adige and the Inn, as indeed in those of Susa and Aosta, it is not unusual, even today, to find Saracen types. The famous skier, Tony Sailer, is an example. Traces of the raids which, in the days of the great Arab expansion from Spain and the Tyrrhenian coast, thrust right up into the Alpine valleys. Or are these characteristics inherited from the very ancient Phoenician and Ligurian settlers? Who can say . . .

Sandra's and her fiancé's hair was not only of the same color—black, almost shot with blue—but of the same thickness and strength. The line of their mouths, hard, sad, always tight, was alike. And the shape of the head, which was round and small compared with the shoulders, was very similar. Indeed, the roundness and smallness of her head was, now I came to think of it, a basic difference between Sandra's appearance and that of Meris, whose face was large, placid, and oval. How in the world could I have thought of Meris for even an instant, the day before in the Cellerino Café!

Yet Sandra and her fiancé, the German and the Sicilian, looked like brother and sister. And as I watched them, I gradually discovered that the divergence in manners—she so sophisticated, he so rough—lost its importance, and that the differences—dark or blue eyes, brown or rosy complexion, guttural or aspirated accent—became reduced to physical and superficial details, facts calculated to reinforce that intimate, natural, animal accord between them, which seemed to me absurd, almost monstrous, and caused me considerable irritation.

It must be the result of jealousy, I told myself: that,

perhaps, was the only reason why I never wanted to see the faces of my rivals! And so I tried not to think about it too much, though I found that difficult, with the corporal there in front of me.

He refused to sit down though I pressed him to do so. He remained the whole time standing in the military position of "at ease," and slightly behind Sandra's chaise longue. Whenever I went near him, he drew himself to attention. He kept his extraordinary baby-blue or animal eyes fixed on the person speaking, whether this was me or G.; and if Sandra spoke, he stared fixedly at me as if to observe the effect her words were having on me. He himself remained almost entirely silent; when he spoke it was to answer "yes-sir," "no-sir," or other abrupt and contracted phrases. When G. mentioned his friend at the Ministry, and said he would write to him in the morning:

"Very good thing," said the corporal. He took three steps forward, which grated on the gravel in the general silence, drew himself up to attention in front of G., took from his pocket a sheet of notes he'd prepared, gave it to him, adding: "Need this. Thankyou, Excellency." After which, he returned to his place. I noticed his shoes, which were black boots high over his ankles, and very highly polished. I noticed his lips; in their sad, downward curve they resembled Sandra's, but they were full and red, and, in all his appearance, were probably what most gave an impression of force and decision.

Apart from the long love-hate relationship with my mother, which is obviously an exceptional case, I believe that throughout my life I have only hated people who were, or others who still are, charged with excessive political or financial power: with such people I find it impossible to distinguish between the man and the symbol of violence or abuse with which he is identified—even when these are involuntary. With the exception of these people, I have never hated. I shall go further: I have never found anyone antipathetic; in the worst cases, when I have felt sorely tempted, I have immediately sought to overcome the temptation, and have always done so, realizing, in a flash of pride, that the antipathy born in me for another was the transient, misleading consequence of some stupid accident: my rancor, the result of some small vexation or paltry disappointment. I have always liked everyone, more or less, and have always found everyone agreeable. But the corporal Tommaso Vaccaro was, I felt, something different, and for me, perhaps, unique. I didn't hate him, either. No, it was in no way a question of hatred. It was simply that he struck me as repulsive, impenetrable, eluding every attempt that I made inside myself to feel affection for him; he stood there before me, hard, immobile, with his disciplined stance, his unsmiling face, a creature which I feared I wouldn't be able to explain to myself, and whom I really would have preferred not to exist—or else, as he did exist, at least not to cross my path.

I thought of what I knew, which was little and superficial enough, about the hinterland of Sicily; I thought about the province of Enna, about those mountains and villages which, twenty-eight years ago when the corporal was born, were doubtless infinitely more backward than they were now. Peasants or shepherds, it might be, a very large family. Hunger, poverty, ancient customs and prejudices, and above all the ancestral, terrifying veneration for power in any form: a head of the Mafia, a Sicilian baron, or the government. Merely to get through primary and middle school was an enormous success, and the exams necessary for being accepted as a candidate for the *carabinieri,* or the customs officials, or the traffic police, or the security agents. Veneration for power quickly took on the name of "respect for the constituted authority," but it was always an abstract and inarticulate fidelity to the master who provided the food. Delinquents, smugglers, suspected persons, prisoners thus became, almost automatically, the second—equally abstract and inarticulate—term, of that kind of fidelity: a harsh and ruthless attitude toward them became a necessity, an inevitable consequence; and the spirit of the young security agent was bound, gradually and painfully, to become embittered and harsh with an unconscious rancor against his own destiny, and finally to adopt the habit of the most miserable of all consolations, namely, learning to enjoy the suffering of others. . . .

I was thinking all this while looking at the corporal's impenetrable countenance and trying to form some conception of the reality of his nature, interpreting as best I could his strange, shut-in appearance.

How, for instance, did he behave with the boys in the reformatory? Obviously very differently from the subservient and awkward way he displayed in the presence of G. and myself: probably he was harsh and violent with the prisoners, possibly brutal. The sheet of paper containing his *curriculum vitae*, which he had given to G., said that "Vaccaro Tommaso was in service for five years in the institute at Civitavecchia, and was then transferred to the penal reformatory at Pallanza owing to his exemplary conduct, seriousness, and reliability." And when I saw his red lips, protruding and firmly shut, I could imagine the impression they must make on the unfortunate wretches shut up in their places of punishment, and they seemed to me a sign not so much of strength and decision as of cruelty.

And when my eyes turned from him and alighted on Sandra, a mixture of brown and blue, casually outstretched on the chaise longue, in harmony with the elegant composition of her elongated curves, a creature no less mysterious than the corporal, and yet adorable and eminently caressable, from the tip of her hair to the tip of her toes, with her slender legs, her slim, straight ankles, her graceful hips, her full breasts, her smooth-as-smooth skin, bronzed, it now seemed to me, by nature rather than by the sun, her features well defined and angular but harmonious and refined, her perfect little nose, her huge and fascinating eyes like bottomless and lightless wells, then I suffered at the thought that her companion and husband-to-be should be such an inhuman man, such a black and roseate rock, steep and unscalable.

The child, Ilse, had gone off with Giopa and Costantino to see the hen-runs and rabbit-hutches. The corporal turned to G. and me and said:

"Excellencies must excuse me," and he looked at the time. His wrist was almost as thick as his fist, and the skin was so red that it looked roasted. "On night duty." The funicular railway was stopping here within ten minutes. They had to be off. They called the child.

In saying good-by to him I noticed that his hand was so massive that it was quite difficult to shake it. He bowed to us several times, with the clumsiness of an old laborer toward his master. Whereas Sandra expressed her thanks openly, letting all the visible signs of sincere emotion have full play; in short, she said good-by with that ease of manner that only the well-bred possess, and which seems to compensate in advance for the favor asked, and even to diminish its value a little.

Hence the contrast of her manners with those of the corporal was almost hallucinating. And yet as soon as we were alone, G. said: "Strange: those two are so different, and yet so alike!" He screwed up his eyes as usual, as though listening to distant music that I couldn't hear, but perhaps in reality to get a better look at me in the bluish shadows of the autumnal sunset. Night was coming, with its damp breath and gentle approach, from the north, from the veiled and mysterious distance of the lake, from the lights of the villages that sprang up one after the other along the shores. Up above, on the mountains of Maccagno and Luino, there were still wide slopes of violet. And at water level the two strange white triangles of the rocky promontory of Caldé suggested, even better than usual, the image of a fantastic sailing boat on the point of departure. G. hesitated; he was looking for words; he didn't want to hurt me too much. At last he smiled with the affectionate and open irony of a friend about to goad his friend—that is to say, maliciously but not malignantly: "Different, yet alike. My impression is that the solution of this Hegelian-type antinomy, between the appearance of the secondary figure and that of herself, can be found only in an erotic-type synthesis," and he stopped, laughing, with his eyes half closed, his head a little on one side, his short lock of hair gracefully resting on his forehead, so as to scrutinize the effect on me of his quip.

But even to me, at that moment, it didn't seem a really ferocious quip.

THE GENTLE creak of the communicating door which was slowly opening—perhaps because it hadn't been properly closed, perhaps pushed by its own weight or by a breath of air from the windows giving onto the lake—wouldn't have been audible to me had I not been there in the gray artificial night, alone, motionless, longing, waiting for her, from the other room, to say I could go in.

October had come, school had started. One morning,

as agreed, we had met each other. I had given her a rendez-vous in the safest place of all, not too far from Pallanza: the bar of the Hôtel des Îles Borromées. Perhaps the hour was rather extraordinary. And it was raining cats and dogs: if anyone had discovered us he couldn't possibly have thought that we had a rendezvous for a trip in a motor-boat. On the other hand, there was some advantage in its being so early in the morning: the only witness of our meeting was the barman, someone discreet by profession and completely outside the circle of the corporal's acquaintance.

I had booked a two-room apartment with a communicating door and a view over the lake. We went in. She took a few steps toward the double bed, then looked with jaunty self-satisfaction in the three or four mirrors, which showed her her slim figure still tightly enclosed in her shining white raincoat, and she said the sacramental phrase that all women say in such circumstances:

"My God, how light it is!"

But in fact the rain was beating against the windows. Lake and sky were fused in a dead gray mass. Pallanza and Laveno, the two shores, couldn't even be seen. Even Isola Bella, just outside, was a vague shape, hardly darker than all the rest. But while she was taking off her raincoat, I hurriedly lowered the blinds nonetheless, and closed the shutters and pulled the thick curtains. Then, with all the delicacy that she still awoke in me, and with the respectful yet sincere hesitation that a man of my age is bound in any case to feel when a young and beautiful woman offers her-self to him for the first time, I approached her.

"No," she said, and put out her hand, even though I'd only drawn nearer, but made no gesture. She had thrown her raincoat on the bed. She was wearing a beige cashmere sweater and a tweed skirt. In the silvery ray of light that still came from the adjoining room, through the half-closed door, her face, framed in a mass of black hair, was cadaverous, and her enormous eyes like holes. She smiled. "I want to confess something. It's a long time since I've been able to have a proper bath. At Pallanza we only have a shower. You'll forgive me, won't you?"

"I'll go in there," I said, "and when you've finished you can call me."

"Du bist ein Schatz . . . You are a darling," she said. This time she approached me, and just touched my lips with a hint of a kiss. Yet I could feel the tips of her breasts against me, her light breath, and the fresh smell of soap that came from her whole body.

As night had now fallen in the room next door, I'd stretched myself out in an armchair and was trying to resist the temptation of weaving fantasies around the pleasure to come. But I couldn't stop thinking about her. How in the world did she have such good taste and simple elegance in her way of dressing? Where had she learned it, and from whom? It was possible, I told myself, that she had worked not only in hotels but also with rich families, perhaps with foreigners. It wasn't surprising that she should speak German, for that was her native language. But how about English?

The communicating door creaked and slowly opened, and I got up, thinking it was Sandra. But when I looked toward the other room I realized that, as sometimes happens, it had opened by itself. In the almost total darkness, the bed was a big pale square, like the screen in a dark empty cinema. And a bright line of light showed from the closed bathroom door in the opposite wall. I went back to my chair, then realized, as I looked in a mirror in front of me, that I had forgotten to close the communicating door. The mirror was in front of me, and beside the door: through the opening I could see the darkness of the other room, and, in the background, the strip of light filtering through from the bathroom.

Without realizing it, and almost without thinking about it, I went on staring at that strip of light for I don't know how many minutes: until the handle moved, the light increased, and Sandra appeared wrapped in a big bath towel. She lit the lamp on the bedside table, then pulled back the covers as if she was going to slip into bed, then, as if with second thoughts, she turned toward the large mirror in the wardrobe, which was not in my line of vision but parallel to the bed between the bathroom and the window. She let the towel slip from her body to the floor, and she looked at herself, naked, in the mirror, slowly turning around. As she turned, and before she reached the stage of contemplating her side view, her eye fell on the communicating door; but owing to the darkness, or because she was too absorbed in her beauty, she perhaps didn't see that it was open, and perhaps didn't see the mirror in the next room which would have had my reflection in it. I thought about what she had said a little earlier: "It's a long time since I've been able to have a proper bath." In her little house in Pallanza, she almost certainly didn't have a big mirror, either, in which she could look at herself right down to her feet. Or perhaps . . . Slowly she went on turning around, went on looking at herself; now she was stroking her hips with a satisfaction, I thought, that could not be more justified.

I had leaned forward in my chair so as to get up, but then decided to remain seated, as I didn't want to make a noise. Suddenly, without turning toward me, she said softly:

"You see, I know you're there. Don't imagine that I haven't seen you. *Do you like me?*"

"Stay there," I said, trembling. "Stay there, it's lovelier like that, now. I can see you."

"And I can see you . . . *ich sehe dich, aber . . . aber es ist als ob du nicht existieren würdest* . . . I can see you but it's as if you didn't exist . . ."

At these words I felt as though something were breaking within me, and my heart beat wildly: a sudden and immense hope, which I hadn't experienced since the time with Meris: a final happiness, which perhaps had begun in these very moments, which would go on for ever, and which I would lose only with my death.

Had Sandra understood this without realizing it?

No, it was impossible. "*Als ob du nicht existieren würdest*," she'd said, laughing, and, precisely so as to give it less weight, in the language most familiar to her. So, for her, it had been a joke. Whereas for me it had been a sudden and unforeseen sounding, reaching a depth usually unattainable.

Oh, to find a woman like Meris again, a woman in whose company, and when looking at her, I could at certain moments feel I was forgetting myself, freeing myself at last from all responsibility, as though the weight of my own body had been lifted from me: feel, in a word, nonexistent, save for that delicious sensation of nonexistence that alone remained to me! Nonexistent, because at such moments I seemed to count for nothing, as compared with her. Total rest! Limitless freedom! Almost a game, yes, almost a fiction, almost a comedy between Meris and me, which didn't last, or not very long each time. But it was a passionate game, a poetic fiction, a comedy performed with the whole being; and, miraculously, we could repeat the performance without any diminution of its effectiveness, on every blessed night. . . . Could the same thing happen with Sandra?

"Sandra," I said, and my voice couldn't fail to betray my confusion: "Sandra, I'm happy."

"For so little?"

"I've never been so happy."

"You're mad!" she said, laughing. She picked up the towel and wrapped it around her naked body, then let it fall again. With something like a leap, she got into bed and pulled the sheet up as far as her chin.

I undressed quickly. As soon as I reached the bed, she switched off the light. I pulled at the sheet, but she held it tight, preventing me from getting in.

"I don't want to," she murmured in the darkness, as though the darkness had suddenly been enough to change her mood. And until the moment before she'd been laughing! But I wasn't surprised by her refusal: women find these games amusing. What did surprise me was the sudden change in her tone of voice, which had become sad, agitated. "No . . . I don't want to!"

"What do you mean, you don't want to?"

"This time, no. Please forgive me. But I have to tell you something, something important, something serious . . . something I didn't tell you the other day, and now you'll see why. . . ." She talked without pause, quickly, like a child who's made up his mind to confess a misdeed. And she broke off to get the better of a sob. She went on with obvious effort: "I'm so ashamed . . . it might have been better if I'd explained everything and told you everything right away . . . but it's so difficult. Now you'll have to know, and your friend, too. He'll understand why I couldn't say anything before, too. He'll forgive me. He seems so kind and intelligent. And you'll forgive me too. No, I couldn't say it right away. But now he'll have to write another letter to his friend in the Ministry. I'm so sorry to cause him so much trouble. You'll tell him to write, won't you? You'll do that for me, *mein Schatz?*"

"What is it, Sandra?"

"Don't put on the light, please. I feel it's easier in the dark. Are you cold? No, please don't get into the bed. Please." And now she seemed to be becoming overwhelmed by emotion. Her hand groped for mine, took it, raised it to her lips, kissed it over and over again, bathed it with tears. "Are you cold? Look, there's the blanket at the bottom of the bed. Put it around you. *Schätzelein*, let me tell you everything like this . . ." But she couldn't go on, she broke into desperate tears. "I've always been so unlucky, always, always. . . ."

Then, without calming down, and with short disconnected sentences, she began telling me the story of her life. She was twenty-five. Her father was a chemist in a small village near Merano. Her mother, too, was of a good family. Sandra had been through primary and secondary schools, always getting high marks; but she had refused to go to Vienna to study chemistry, which was what her father wanted so as to have her with him in the shop one day. She herself had a strong bent for languages, so she enrolled at the interpreters' school and embarked on a thorough study of French and English; she already knew German and Italian. Subsequently she had decided to follow a course for hotel secretaries. Only, during the summer between her first and second years at the interpreters' school, she had thought it a good idea to take a job in England. This had been the first of her misfortunes. When she came back she realized she was pregnant. Yes, she knew who the father was: he was a Mexican, a kind of playboy who had been a weekend guest in the country house of the rich industrial people whose children she was looking after. Sandra was then just over eighteen, but it wasn't the first time she'd had relations with a man. She had, alas, every reason to dismiss the idea that the Mexican would behave honorably and generously. Moreover, she could give him only her word. She knew she wouldn't be believed, and didn't want to humiliate herself to no purpose. So, proudly and courageously, declaring that she alone was responsible, she told her family what had happened and confronted fate. Little Ilse was born.

But it was two years later, when she was legally of age, that her most serious misfortune befell her. She didn't want to tell me how, with whom, or exactly where. Unfortunately, she said, it was in Italy, and in a provincial town. Once again she found herself pregnant, and decided, though the idea was deeply repugnant to her, to terminate the pregnancy. She went to a doctor in that little town, who had for some time been courting her without success. He was an ignoble individual. At a suitable moment he demanded, first, to make love to her. Sandra lost her temper, insulted him, and fled. She then had recourse to a woman, a nurse, who had been recommended to her. But the thing was found out, by means of an anonymous denunciation, and a whole series of clues showed that the author could be none other than the rejected doctor. The nurse had to go to prison for four years, and Sandra for a year and a half. After an appeal, her sentence was reduced, but she had to do ten months. And it had been there, in the Civitavecchia prison, that one of the sisters attached to the women's branch had spoken to her about Tommaso, and had spoken to Tommaso about her. The sister was a Sicilian too, and came from the same place as Tommaso, Sperlinga.

Tommaso seemed a harsh man, and was certainly so when carrying out his duties. But for Sandra he was the kindest and most generous man she had ever known. He adored her, tried to please her in all things, and was ready to marry her and give the child his name. It would be a blow to him if he were obliged to give up his career, because within a year he would be promoted to the rank of sergeant, and three years later to warrant officer. With a warrant officer's rank, he would be entitled to a separate residence even outside the prison or reformatory, and a whole number of other advantages. But if unfortunately the Ministry didn't grant him permission to marry Sandra, then he'd resign and look for a job as a guard in some industrial establishment. It wouldn't be easy to find such a job immediately. At the early stages the pay would be low. This alarmed Tommaso: not for himself, but for Sandra and the child, for he would like to keep them in comfort.

That was why Maestro G. would have to be kind enough to write again to his friend in the Ministry: so as to tell him that she hadn't been deliberately deceitful but had merely lacked the courage to tell the whole truth there and then. Sandra went on telling me about the regulations. She knew by heart the phrases of the marriage section, article 49. "Guards cannot contract matrimony without permission of the Ministry. Such permission is granted to guards of good conduct, and is subject to the good moral qualifications of the fiancée and her family." The sentence of appeal which had curtailed her time in prison had recognized her misfortune, her good faith, and her exemplary conduct in prison. She had a copy of it, and would give it to me, so that G. could send it to the Ministry with his second letter.

When Sandra left the Civitavecchia prison, she hadn't the courage to go back to Merano. Moreover, she needed to find work immediately so as to earn money. It was Tommaso himself who had found her the job of maid in the Pirgus Hotel in Santa Marinella. Then, when he'd been transferred to Pallanza, he'd suggested that she should come up north too, and await the day when they could get married.

For Tommaso, Pallanza was a paradise compared with Civitavecchia. Prisons are never happy places. But reformatories for minors are certainly less sad than full-blown prisons. For one thing, none of the boys stay for more than a year or two, and none are faced with a future without hope.

Until they reach warrant officer's rank, guards are obliged to live inside the establishment. But Tommaso had managed to rent modest accommodations, with a bit of garden, in a small house in the old town, at the foot of one of the narrow streets that mount the hill behind the reformatory. He went to see her there every day, and spent all his free time with her.

At Santa Marinella, the manageress of the hotel knew her story, and soon everyone employed there had got to know it too. After Santa Marinella, Pallanza had been a paradise for Sandra, too: especially during the first months. At last she'd been able to get to know her child again, and have her with her.

Sandra had work, and work she could do without leaving Pallanza. At the moment, for instance, she was translating leaflets and brochures into German and English for a tourist agency.

While Sandra was talking, I kept thinking of the very intimate and complete understanding that G. and I had thought we'd detected between her and the corporal.

"And you, do you love Tommaso?" was the question I almost involuntarily put to her after I'd heard her story, without throwing any doubt on its authenticity.

"Do I love Tommaso? It depends on what you mean by

love," said Sandra, still in darkness, but in a voice that was calmer at last. "Look at it this way. If love is what he feels for me—he'd be ready to die for me, yes, I'm sure he would, if it was necessary—then no, I don't love him like that. But I'm fond of him, I'm grateful to him, and I respect him. I don't love him."

"And does he know this?"

"Yes, he knows it. He once said to me, 'I know you don't really care for me, but it's enough for me that you'll always stay with me and be faithful to me: I'm satisfied with that.' "

By now it was after eleven. Sandra had only just time to put her clothes on again, and catch the bus back to Pallanza, before the child came out of school.

I let her go without a word. But I promised to speak to G. and give him the copy of the sentence: Sandra didn't forget to give it to me, in spite of the furious haste with which she said good-by and went off.

I stayed for a while longer among the mirrors gleaming sinisterly in the semidarkness. I wandered back and forth between the two deserted rooms. I was thinking about the corporal, about Sandra, about myself, and about what the outcome would be.

THE Îles Borromées hotel was irreplaceable: no other in the area could guarantee the necessary secrecy. But the hotel closed down in the middle of the month and wouldn't reopen till Easter. I had only a few days left, and they passed without my being able to see Sandra again.

She telephoned to make sure that I'd talked to G. She telephoned again a week later: she was thinking of me, and felt she was fond of me, but, until there was a new schedule, we must give up the idea of a rendezvous. Tommaso was on night duty, and came to her, regularly, every morning, which was the only time she was free from little Ilse.

There then began for me a period of solitude and growing infatuation. I won't say that I tried to foster this infatuation and really wanted it. I'll only say that I made no attempt to resist, and that I gave myself over to it with extreme pleasure. Sandra was my first thought in the morning, and the last just as I was going to sleep. If I woke up in the middle of the night, I immediately imagined that she was beside me; and it was the same during the day, whenever I was alone. October, November: the Scala was still shut, and I went to Milan for my work very rarely. And when December came, I deliberately slowed down on the job: I gave my newspaper the excuse that I had to finish my book on Puccini, which was true, but only in part, because I was working at it pretty half-heartedly and had enlisted the help of a ghost writer. In fact, I wouldn't have slept in Milan for anything in the world, and so exposed myself to the risk of not being at Levo early in the morning when she might telephone or even want to see me at once. I loved solitude, I sought it out, precisely so as to detach myself as little as possible from thinking about Sandra.

I took long walks in the beech woods and chestnut woods, whose greenness had by now disappeared to make way for red and rust, and gradually for yellow, becoming each day brighter, shriller. I lost myself as I trudged the soft earthy paths deep in leaves. I tramped as far as the gorges of the Erno, and stood on the bridge suspended over the ravine. I stared and stared in fascination at the thundering, foaming torrent. By a curious yet spontaneous mechanism, I saw her in everything. The slender trunks of the birches were like her body. But the clear sepia of her skin more resembled the color of certain distant open fields. The sudden, deep, frightening darkness that I saw beneath the fir trees, when I passed alongside the wood of the Villa Riva, was the mysterious darkness of her eyes. And sometimes, on misty mornings, as I walked between the trees in a damp, thick, pearly whiteness, following a path visible only a step or two in front of me, I found myself madly shouting her name, not only for the joy of hearing it but as though to stop her and have her wait for me, as if she were just ahead, hidden in that whiteness, from which at a given moment I would see her emerge.

From my study window, without getting up from my desk, I could see the lights of Pallanza as they came on at night. I looked at them for a long time, and while I looked at them I thought of nothing but the day, the hour, the moment in which I would see her again.

Of course I often re-evoked her body in the mirror, or rather her dark gaze when she saw me in the mirror "as if I didn't exist." And I didn't exclude an infinitude of other complicated fantasies, but not as necessary conditions of our being together, not as a need, not as a vice. I thought of the mirror only as of the loveliest moment that I had had with her. I remembered Meris's chain; now I knew that even the chain hadn't been a vice, but a game. And there was something else more important still: I didn't frequent other girls any more. One of them telephoned me from Milan in astonishment that I'd made no sign of life. Giopa had orders to answer that I was away traveling. This experience of not wanting the company of any other girl except one had only happened to me twice before: with the Tobacconist, when I was a boy, and then with Meris. I would have been ready to wager that it would never happen again.

And then at last, toward the end of November, I saw her again.

I waited for her at the Feriolo crossroad, halfway between Pallanza and Stresa. Sandra arrived with the bus. So as not to be conspicuous, I didn't get out of the car. She got in after making sure that there was no one around who could note her movements. I took the Simplon motor road as far as Gravellona, and then the high circular road of Lake Orta, up beyond Nonio and Césara.

It was one of the last sweet days of an Indian summer, a warm, limpid morning such as happens sometimes at that period on the lake.

I knew a hidden byway, not paved, winding up through a huge chestnut wood toward the top of Civiasco. I stopped in a totally deserted spot. The mild sun shone brightly through the leafless branches. You could hear all around, in the distance, the lost autumnal cries of the migrating birds. I don't remember how Sandra was dressed that morning. All I remember is my possession by a sudden certainty: she was the loveliest girl I had ever known.

I hesitated, then put an arm around her waist, which was both soft and firm. Without saying anything, I looked at her huge deep, dark eyes, and at her pale lips, closed in their sad curve.

She seemed to respond to my kiss passionately and at length, as if she, too, would have liked it never to end. But as soon as I sought for something more, she freed herself, opened the car door impetuously, and threw herself out.

I followed her. She had gone only a few steps. She wasn't angry. She seemed sad, that was all.

"Why don't you want to, Sandra?"

"Because I'm afraid."

"What are you afraid of?"

"What's more, you said it yourself, that other time. It's better like this, you said."

"It's better like this, for a moment. Even, perhaps, for a long moment. And perhaps on some occasions. But not for ever. For two months now, ever since I met you, I've thought only of you. . . ."

"You're very kind, Carlo, and I'll never forget what you did for me. You and your friend. Let's leave it like that. Don't let's spoil everything. I'm happy to see you now and again. If you don't want that, then we won't see each other again. That'll be sad for me, but it can't be helped. So, I implore you, don't let's spoil everything."

Her expression seemed so sincere that I didn't dare insist.

We went on seeing each other, now and again, but relatively seldom throughout the winter and the beginning of spring. She came out with me in the car for two or three hours in the morning along the wildest and most lonely roads of the mountains around Lake Maggiore and Lake Orta. There were kisses as if between a boy and girl still inexperienced in life. And that was all.

On one of these occasions—it was a few days before Christmas—I gave her a big box of goodies, and some toys for the child. I stupidly hadn't thought of the corporal. Sandra said my presents were too good: Tommaso would be suspicious. She accepted only one doll and one cake: and she begged me, in the interests of not arousing Tommaso's suspicions, to send them to her through the post, with my name as sender clearly written.

At the end of April, G.'s friend wrote to communicate the good news that the matter was now on its way to the desired solution. I informed the corporal of this immediately, telephoning him at the reformatory. They came the following Sunday, with the child, to express their thanks. They were both cheerful, and seemed happy. They said they had already fixed the wedding day for early September. I watched Sandra's face: was her apparent cheerfulness genuine or merely an expression of expediency, so as not to be out of tune with Tommaso's obvious delight? I couldn't make up my mind. I could have sworn that there was something different about her from when I had last seen her, about a month before. Something more lively, clear-cut, decisive.

Two or three times, with the beginning of a smile so slight that I alone could detect it, with her eyes just half closed and a faint tremor at the corners of her mouth, she stared at me and repeated an identical gesture with her brown nervous hand with its well-kept though short, unpolished nails: she carefully arranged her hair over her ear and at the nape of her neck, until I at last observed that she had changed her hair style. That gesture and that look were as much as to say: "But how is it that you haven't noticed? I look nice, don't I?"

Before, her hair had fallen in a great smooth mass all around her face and almost down to her shoulders. Now, it was cut short in a fashion initiated that very year; it was called "duck's tail," the hair forming a compact and slightly swelling helmet, an oblique fringe concealing the forehead, and two graceful curls caressing the cheekbones.

Of course I didn't say anything, but I think my look reflected my admiration clearly enough. Sandra's head was small in relation to the almost athletic tilt of her bust, and the great mass of hair had emphasized this defect and given her a slightly old-fashioned, provincial air. Now, her short hair left her neck free and revealed its harmonious, slender contours, so that her whole person acquired a franker, freer grace.

Costantino and Giopa had appeared from the bottom of the garden with fresh grass for the rabbits; they were on their way to the hutches behind the house. The little girl, remembering the former occasion, took the corporal's hand and insisted on going to watch. So luckily, if only for a very short while, we were alone. For a moment Sandra followed Tommaso and the child with her eye, but when she turned back to me her expression had suddenly become different. I saw at once that it was not just a matter of the hair style. Sandra had suddenly become serious: she seemed positively angry with me, or as if she were asking me something, without speaking. Her gaze, suddenly hard, concentrated, exacting, was above all mysterious: it disturbed and upset me. I saw that the corporal was coming back toward us. I plucked up my courage and said in a low voice

"Telephone me tomorrow morning."

She looked at me as if she hadn't understood. And I was left wondering whether perhaps I had spoken so softly that she really hadn't understood.

She'd understood perfectly. But she telephoned only a few days later. The Îles Borromées was open once more, but I had only the slenderest hope that Sandra would agree to go there again. In an offhand, almost joking manner, so as to be less humiliated by her probable refusal, I suggested that we meet at the bar, as on the first occasion. And she surprised me by saying yes, she would love to come, and she at once stated the day and the time. I was understandably delighted, but I also thought that she was doing it only out of dutiful gratitude. What was she risking, after all? She knew perfectly well that by now I'd become resigned, indeed accustomed, to claiming no more than a kiss.

I waited for her at the bar. I waited till the very end, that is to say until the time when she would have had to leave to fetch her child from school.

She didn't appear. I was exasperated, desperate, and—not as the result of any kind of reasoning, but merely out of instinct—I would have wagered that she hadn't come on purpose: she wanted to torment me, she wanted to put me to the test. But what test, seeing that she would soon be married and everything would be over between us, even that which, truth to tell, hadn't even started?

She called up again the next day. She was humble, she was sorry, and explained that when it was already too late to let me know, there'd been a change of schedule at the reformatory, and Tommaso had spent the morning at home. She implored me to forgive her, and gave me another date.

I ALMOST felt I was dreaming. I was again in the same armchair in the same room at the Îles Borromées. I had darkened the room as on the previous occasion. And I was staring at the strip of bright golden light under the bathroom door at the other end of the darkness of the adjoining room, as reflected in the mirror. I was waiting for Sandra to emerge with the towel.

Everything was like last time.

But I was also thinking: This won't ever happen again, and how can I again indulge in the game, in the pleasure of pretending not to exist (if only for a while), in the luxury of postponing indefinitely the deep and real pleasure? When Sandra appeared, I completely forgot about the other time: I emerged from the mirror and held her in my arms.

I kissed her. I tried, with desperate tenderness, to lead her toward the bed.

"No," she said, "no, no . . ."

"Why, no?"

"Because you don't love me."

"I don't love you! How can you say such a thing, Sandra?"

"You desire me, yes. But you don't love me."

"I desire you and love you."

"Perhaps you think so, Carlo. The truth is that you're deceiving yourself. You don't love me."

"What makes you so certain, dearest?"

"Tommaso loves me, yes. But not you, oh no!"

"Tommaso? But of course Tommaso loves you!" On other occasions, on our rare winter excursions, I'd been on the point of telling her what I thought of the corporal: that he was a decent boy, yes, but too inferior to her, and that I almost hoped the Ministry would end up by refusing the famous permission. But I'd always kept quiet so as not to hurt her. Now, my impulse to speak was irresistible. And I spoke: "Naturally Tommaso loves you! You're so superior to him! I'd like to see him not loving you! That would be a real effort on his part!" Even before finishing what I was saying, I realized how vulgar I was being, horribly vulgar. I shouldn't have thought of saying that! Ashamed of myself, I withdrew from Sandra even more quickly than she withdrew from me, and I murmured: "Forgive me. . . ."

She had turned aside to hide her tears. She said:

"Tommaso, for instance, who is a poor peasant, would never have said anything like that. . . ."

"Forgive me. . . . I ask your forgiveness, I wasn't thinking what I was saying. . . . But it's because I really do love you, Sandra!"

"Now stop it! Stop this about loving me for good and all! You don't even know what love is! Tommaso gives me the whole of himself, the whole of himself, understand? All. And do you know what he asks of me in exchange, do you know that? Nothing. Look, I'll tell you something I've never told you before. . . . Perhaps you'll despise Tommaso for this, and perhaps you'll despise me too. But

I want you to know so that you'll understand, if you're capable of it. Well then, well, if I felt like it, I could even . . . even not stay with Tomasso, ever, you understand? And he'd go on adoring me just the same. He doesn't ask anything from me, not even faithfulness. Yes, I could, without losing him, even go with others if I wanted to: on condition that no one else knew. And this, not on grounds of pride, no, but because he'd be frightened for his career. And he's only frightened of losing his job because of me and the child—if they dismissed him, how could he provide for us? For Tommaso, I'm . . . I'm almost God. Do you understand now when and how someone can say: I love you? Now leave me. I'm too miserable."

She lay full-length on the bed, still wrapped in the towel, and stayed there limp, motionless, and silent, her huge eyes—which I could only just see in the semidarkness —turned toward the ceiling.

I had sat down beside her. She had suddenly twisted my heart as though with an iron vise. What Sandra had said was true. Yes, true! Sometimes it happens in dreams that we suddenly become aware of a terrifying and mortal danger which for a short while, or even a long one, we are facing in our subconscious: for instance, a bottomless chasm, an abyss whose edge we've been walking along for hours, lightly, jokingly, whereas with every step we could fall headlong. Until suddenly we see it and draw back in horror. Perhaps I'd always lived like this, though without realizing it. I thought I loved, but I didn't love. I never gave anything to anyone, except, perhaps, but so little, to Costantino; and except to Meris, for so short a time. And in the last analysis all I could say about Meris was that for a short period "I was prepared to give." I had hated my mother, I hadn't yet forgiven her and still never stopped blaming her; but only now did Sandra's words finally open my eyes: only now did I understand that my mother hadn't really loved me, either, not with true love, because she'd always demanded in exchange that I should live exactly as she wanted me to. And what right had I to think I could condemn Alessandro for his lack of generosity toward Mumi and toward life? Alessandro, too, had in fact behaved as I myself had always behaved: he paid, he didn't give. I, perhaps, had paid rather more, that was all: I'd never given anything. One gives nothing when one doesn't give everything. A little less than everything is already nothing.

"Sandra," I said softly, "Sandra, are you listening to me?"

"Yes, I'm listening. You must forgive me for talking like that. I meant every word of it; but it was ungrateful of me after all you've done for us."

"Sandra," and I still hesitated a moment. I swear I didn't know whether I was falling into the abyss or whether I was saving myself for ever instead. In that moment I coldly measured the two possibilities: they seemed to me identical. "Sandra, supposing I asked you to become my wife?"

Of the two possibilities I'd chosen the one that was new, the one that forced me, for good or ill, to change my life: only for that reason, and perhaps for no other, had I made that choice.

IT WAS I don't know what day in April. From that day until July 19 I lived in a trance, as if the dream of the abyss (headlong fall? salvation?) were continuing without the interruption of even the briefest awakening. The first thing I thought of was to resign from my newspaper: I felt an irresistible need to change everything. I rang up the editor and asked for an appointment.

It so happened that on the very day of the appointment I ran into Alessandro. I was going into the Biffi Scala restaurant for lunch, and he was coming out of it. I hadn't seen him since that time at Brignole Station. He seemed to me to have grown ten years older in one year. Still thinner, more bent, and almost entirely white. He was with his wife. I already knew that his wife didn't much like me. But even if I hadn't known it, the way she greeted me would have enlightened me. Alessandro had come to Milan to be examined by his old doctor. For some time he'd been suffering from liver complaints.

"But I can see you're in very good fettle," she said sharply, sarcastically, as though being well were an offense.

Of course I didn't tell him about Sandra, nor of my intention to marry. Even if I would have liked to confide in him, the presence of his wife made it impossible. But I told him I wanted to resign from the newspaper.

"You're making a mistake," he said. "One must work, one must always be doing something."

"Why?" I asked, laughing. "Is idleness the father of all vices?"

"I'm very much afraid it is," he answered at once, and in his old gray eyes as they scrutinized me I saw again a flash of interest—that is, of affection. Or was I deluding myself?

"Once you gave me some advice with another proverb," I said, still laughing. "Do you remember?"

"No, I don't."

"It was this: A madman knows more about his own house than a sage about someone else's. Do you remember now?"

"No," he answered dryly; and I didn't know whether he

was speaking the truth, or was on edge because his wife obviously wasn't pleased with our encounter, at the restaurant door, being prolonged in this way, with the possible additional danger that we'd arrange a meeting for the afternoon. He was afraid of being reproved. For this reason we said good-by without embracing.

Two months ago I saw his obituary in the *Corriere della Sera,* the only Italian newspaper that finds its way to Auckland. It was loaded with his titles of nobility and fortified by the names of all his children and relatives. Poor Alessandro. But that day at the Biffi Scala he caused me anger rather than pity. And if I still entertained some doubt about my resignation, his opinion was enough to disperse it. In the afternoon I called on the editor and freed myself from every commitment.

When I left the newspaper office and set out for Levo again, I had a very definite feeling that my new life was beginning.

But Sandra changed too. Light, which had hitherto seemed to be denied to her strange dark eyes, now appeared in them.

Now, in our rendezvous, which were still cautious and secret, but ever more frequent, it was she who reiterated: "I love you, I love you." And she went on maintaining that, in spite of everything, I didn't love her, or at least didn't love her yet. On no occasion was she ready to make love. "I'm afraid of losing you," she said.

She organized everything with an intelligence and care for times and details of meeting that overwhelmed and enchanted me. But for all that there was the real difficulty and much more than a difficulty: a disturbing, distressing, and anguishing thought: How and when would she tell Tommaso?

In the middle of June, when the school holidays began,

she had at least a pretext for absenting herself from Pallanza. And Tommaso couldn't go away with her: he had asked for, and obtained, leave for the whole of September. The marriage was still fixed for early that month in Pallanza itself, after which they were to go to Sicily, where he would introduce her to his family in Sperlinga.

The pretext for absenting herself from Pallanza was simple: Sandra was taking the child to a holiday camp at Marina di Massa, as she had done the year before, then she was going to Merano for a few days to persuade her mother to take the child in from July to October.

I joined Sandra at Marina di Massa, directly after she'd left the child at the holiday camp.

We went to Naples. We had to decide where we were going to live after marriage. She didn't want the north, as it would be too near to Pallanza or her family, so Turin and Milan were ruled out. And she didn't want Rome because it had too many unpleasant associations. Her second and graver mishap had occurred in a small town where she'd been looking after the children in a rich family, a small town not far from Rome—she didn't want to tell me its name and I imagined it would have been Perugia or Terni. In any case, her trial, after she'd appealed, had taken place in Rome.

It was she who started talking about Naples. For me, it was true, Naples meant Meris. Meris had lived there, certainly or almost certainly, though not at number 2 Via Silvio Spaventa, during the period that I'd been living there myself, during the months immediately preceding the liberation of Rome; but at that time, despite all my investigations, I'd never found her. By now Naples was even bigger than before; even if I found Meris again, after an interval of sixteen years, what could happen? Nothing. During all those years, Meris had lived in my mind as a sort of image that didn't exclude the wildly improbable eventuality of a resumption of our relationship; but since the advent of Sandra, Meris had become little more than a character about whom I'd read in a novel.

Sandra had a very exact plan. We would buy a house in Naples, not only a house to live in, but one which would provide a revenue from letting apartments which, by itself, would guarantee us a livelihood. We found two large newly built houses up above Posillipo, in Via Orazio; together, they provided twelve very good apartments, six in each house. We could reserve for ourselves one of the best, on the ground floor, with a private garden, tall trees, and a wonderful view of the bay.

The price was such that I had to sell everything I possessed to meet it: my *pied-à-terre* in Via Borgonuovo, the villa at Levo, my shares, everything. I thought about Costantino. It was in thinking of him that I had omitted the shares I still held in Switzerland when telling Sandra the extent of my possessions: not a small sum, but, compared with all the rest, a mere pittance. Even from the strictly legal point of view, it was less than what would have gone to Costantino as his share in my mother's inheritance. Hence I was perfectly aware that I was robbing my brother. I told Sandra of my obligation to take him into consideration. But Sandra persuaded me, and even now I can't explain to myself how she managed to do so, that it would be better for both Costantino and myself if he was put into a nursing home.

I realized what it would mean for Costantino to leave Levo, and to live without Giopa and me. When, today, I think back to my amenability at Sandra's hands, every time the subject of Costantino came up, I simply can't forgive myself. My brother was weak, defenseless, innocent, alone. His only faith, his only love, his only protection against life and the world, both so hostile to him, was myself. To be sure, Tommaso would have given Sandra everything he possessed. And if I really loved Sandra, I should do the same. But I hadn't the right to look on Costantino as a possession; I couldn't, no, dispose of him as an object. Which is why I can't forgive myself or find any peace of mind. I would like to be able to "believe" again, to pray again, as when I was a child, if only to weep better over my vileness and my crime; I'd like to throw myself to the ground and pray to God and ask his pardon. And when I think of the harm I did my brother, and that it could have been much graver and lasted much longer, I thank God, God who is within us or outside us, I thank him with all my soul for having saved me in the end.

As we weren't yet married, the houses in Via Orazio were bought in Sandra's name as absolute proprietor, and in mine as tenant. By now the time of her absence was running out, from Tommaso's point of view. She didn't go to Merano; she reached an agreement with her mother by telephone concerning little Ilse's summer holiday. We spent our last hours in Naples wandering round the boutiques, buying things for her, and ordering some clothes from a dressmaker which would be ready in about a month, when we returned. Sandra had a natural, and apparently very simple, gift for elegance; but her wardrobe, the outcome of infinite patience and subtle cunning, was in fact, and by the force of things, very modest. It was I, therefore, who had encouraged her to make this outlay.

She went back with me by car as far as Milan, and continued alone by train to Pallanza. The time was drawing near for her to talk to Tommaso. She didn't yet know how she was going to do it. In everything, except this, she had displayed assurance, clarity of ideas, decision.

For me it was a month of frenzied activity. I spent it

mostly in Milan and Turin, between banks, and lawyers' and solicitors' offices. In Naples I had merely paid a deposit on behalf of Sandra and myself: all the liquid cash I had. Now I had to pay out vast sums. The villa at Levo was given as guarantee to a bank, with mortgage, and was immediately put up for sale. Yet I cherished a hope that we wouldn't have to vacate it before the end of the summer. One night I told the whole story to Giopa, who listened with terror and consternation. He looked at me with his honest blue eyes full of tears, and went on reiterating: "Master Carlo, Master Carlo! Be careful not to do anything you'll have to regret later!"

I had found a nursing home near Varese for Costantino. Giopa and I decided not to say anything to him yet. Then, when the moment came, we'd tell him that it had to do with some special treatment prescribed by the doctor; this treatment needed to be done in hospital, and we'd chosen this nursing home precisely so as not to have to send him to hospital; in any case, the treatment would only last a few weeks. In my heart of hearts, I really hoped that this might come true: once I was married and installed in Naples, why shouldn't he, as well as Giopa, come and live with Sandra and me, or at least near us in one of the smaller apartments of the houses? I didn't dare raise the subject with Sandra: by now I didn't want to risk her opposition. But I would certainly do so after we were married.

In the middle of July, Sandra again had a pretext for leaving Pallanza: she went to pick up the child at the holiday camp and take her to her mother at Merano, as arranged.

And now, everything was ready: the church was fixed, the day, everything. Berardo, my Turin lawyer, and G. were to come to Naples and be the witnesses. They were my dearest friends: I could no longer count on Alessandro. For the time being, I thought it better not to communicate the news to other people, to acquaintances. Sandra, too, had only taken her parents and her sister into her confidence. The real trouble was that she hadn't yet spoken to the man who should have been the first to know about it.

Sandra said good-by to Tommaso, still without summoning up the required courage. On one of the last evenings, in an effort to begin talking, she had referred to the possibility of postponing their September wedding date. For some time now, whenever Tommaso had mentioned that she seemed preoccupied, Sandra had complained of a vague indisposition. So on this occasion she told him she'd been to the doctor and that the doctor had diagnosed intense exhaustion, with a threat of complications, and had ordered rest, calm, and tranquillity. So Sandra feared she wouldn't be able to face the journey to Sicily. At these words Tommaso had been very upset, but, as always, submissive to her wishes, and he had asked very simply: "When would you like?"

Sandra had murmured that she didn't know, she had no date in mind. Any other answer would have been a worse betrayal! Tommaso had said that there were still two months before September, and without the child she would be able to rest, she would get better, and then if she still didn't feel well in September, well, it couldn't be helped, they must postpone it!

So in the end Sandra decided on a long letter. She had already written it; but she intended to post it only at the last moment, so that Tommaso would receive it two or three days before our wedding, and hence would realize that by then there was nothing to be done.

I went to meet her at Bolzano. The hours of the journey

by car down to Naples were the happiest, the only really happy ones, that I spent with Sandra. Perhaps there was something cruel in her laughter in the Baglioni Hotel, at Bologna, where we stopped for the night, and where, between the two communicating rooms, I tried absurdly and in vain to reconstruct my favorite game. It was a miracle that the huge mirror which I'd unhooked from the wall and tried to hoist onto a table didn't fall shattered to the floor. But it didn't: and this seemed to us a sign of good luck, and redoubled our joy.

"A little more patience," she said, imitating the Neapolitan accent, "and there won't be anything you don't know about mirrors. *Schätzelein!*"

Cruel laughter. But I laughed myself, thinking that now, surely, she'd be generous.

And still laughing she pushed me away.

"Nein, mein Schatz, nein! I know you! You don't love me!" Before getting into bed, she prepared to close the communicating door. "I know you, you're a philanderer, and if I'm weak with you, at the moment of entering the church you'll be all set to run off with the first tart you find. . . ."

"Even if that happened," I said, carrying on the joke, "you'd still be left with the ownership of the houses: I feel that would be a good indemnity!"

"Yes! And with you having perpetual tenancy! They're worth much less. I've been making inquiries, you know. In Merano, I consulted my lawyer. . . ." Perhaps this word "lawyer" was the only Italian word that she never in any circumstances managed to pronounce correctly: she always said something like *affocato* instead of *avocato*. The word would have been sufficient to betray her origins. But she really had consulted the lawyer: and for her that remark was very important.

We reached Naples in the evening of the next day; and as she was—yet again—closing the communicating door, she gave me the letter she'd written to Tommaso. It was Sunday night. We were going to be married the following Saturday. So there were five days to go. While I was reading it, she went back into her own room.

The letter said that, after all the sorrows that she'd undergone, she didn't feel she had the right, now, to refuse this immense, unhoped-for good luck which was being offered her, in other words, to renounce for ever the possibility of giving absolute financial security to her little girl and of making her into a real lady. She begged forgiveness on bended knees. He must never attempt to see her again; it would be better for both of them. But she swore before God that she would, now and till death, regard herself as his humble debtor. And she went into details. Deep down she owed everything to him, even the good luck of meeting me. Without him, who knew what would have become of her? She ended up by saying that she would venerate him for ever as her first, her true savior and protector.

As I read, I instinctively tried to put myself in Tommaso's place. But for me Tommaso was a mystery. I failed in my attempt to imagine his reactions: rage, plans for revenge, or else despair, resignation . . . as I saw it, anything was possible.

I looked up from the letter and saw Sandra coming back toward me: she was naked. She took the letter, and with her other hand caressed my hair, lightly and tenderly. Then she looked me in the eyes, and said slowly that she wouldn't send the letter, and wouldn't marry me, unless I also made over the tenancy to her—by a legal document.

I was struck dumb. I would have expected anything rather than this; yet, when I saw her before me, tall, smooth, with her erect perfect breasts, and when I looked into her dark eyes which were staring intently at me as though to penetrate me, I felt I would surrender with no struggle.

"Why, Sandra?" I said. "You know perfectly well how much the property is worth, even without the tenancy. You'd only have to sell one of the two houses to live for years without worry. . . ."

"This letter," she said, as she folded it carefully, "is a bad action. And I don't want to have remorse."

Perhaps I should have corrected her: it was a painful action, not a bad one. But when I looked into her eyes, which were looking into mine, I realized that she was right.

That night I didn't sleep. I was at last about to do what, deep down, I'd always wanted to do without having had the courage: sacrifice myself entirely to a woman. But was this desire of mine right? Did it really correspond to my nature? I didn't doubt Sandra's love, or, rather, it didn't matter to me if she was, as she seemed to be, self-interested, shrewd, calculating. On the contrary. In all probability what had fascinated me most about her from the very first, when, at the Cellerino Café, she'd promptly and diabolically pretended to know me, was that very coldness, that implacable rationalism. What I doubted was myself. Did I love her? Would I go on loving her even when I was living with her? And how was I to know unless I put myself to the test, once and for all?

Early next morning we went to the solicitor and signed the deed handing over the tenancy. For fiscal reasons, the deed was formally stipulated to be a deed of sale. Afterward we went to the central post office and posted the special-delivery letter to Tommaso.

ON THURSDAY, July 16, the *Stampa* newspaper contained the following news item:

VERBANIA, JULY 15.

A prison guard, Tommaso Vaccaro, aged 28, of Sperlinga (Enna), corporal attached to the reformatory for minors at Pallanza, took his life this morning with a revolver shot in the head. Inquiries are under way to ascertain the causes of the suicide; the authorities carrying out the inquiries, and his colleagues, have made no statement.

Vaccaro came to Verbania some two years ago, transferred from the prison at Civitavecchia. It appears that he shared a small apartment in Via Magnolie at Pallanza with a woman and a girl of about six who was the woman's daughter. The woman seems to have been unmarried. According to rumor, Vaccaro took his life owing to troubles of a sentimental nature. But it has been impossible to obtain confirmation of this hypothesis. Indeed, Vaccaro left a letter, as to the authenticity of which there can be no doubt, addressed to the Governor of the Reformatory. In the letter Vaccaro states specifically that recently he had discovered that he was afflicted with an incurable illness: this is the only motive that urged him to suicide for which he declares that he assumes full and exclusive responsibility.

The corporal carried out his tragic plan this morning at 7:20. He entered the headquarters of the "guards on duty," lay down on the small bed, and fired a shot into his temple with his regulation revolver. The explosion brought several of his colleagues to the scene, who looked after Vaccaro and took him by ambulance to the Intra hospital. The doctors saw immediately that there was nothing to be done. The corporal died shortly before 11.

G. read it before I did. He telephoned me at once from Baveno and it was he who gave me the news. He was to have left that same morning, so as to arrive in Naples within the day; but he naturally assumed that the marriage would be postponed, if nothing else, and had already telephoned the airline to cancel his flight reservation. He remained speechless when I told him that Sandra had never dared inform Tommaso, and that she had only done so on Monday: the special-delivery letter must have reached Pallanza on Tuesday evening, and the tragedy had occurred on Wednesday morning. . . . It was now up to me to tell Sandra. G. wished me luck.

The telephone call had waked me up. Sandra was still asleep. We'd been late the night before getting from Don Vicienzo to Piazza Dante. Paula, Sandra's sister, had reached Naples by car from Merano accompanied by her fiancé and another young man, a friend of theirs. At the last moment, in her joy, Sandra had been unable to say no. The sister and the two young men were profiting by the seasonal feast-days to attend the wedding, and it was also an excuse to see Naples and have a joy ride across Italy.

I went downstairs and bought the *Stampa*. I wanted to read it with my own eyes in the absurd hope that G. had got it wrong. Before going back to Sandra, I telephoned Berardo in Turin to tell him not to come; the secretary, who answered, said that the lawyer had already gone off for the feast-days and, moreover, had already left for Naples, where he would arrive either that evening or the following morning.

The communicating door was shut. But Sandra was awake: as soon as I knocked she came and opened. I was holding the newspaper in my hand.

"Sandra," I said, "a terrible thing has happened. . . ." I hadn't the courage to go on, but she saw my face, and saw the newspaper which I was holding in my hand as if preparatory to handing it to her. She looked at me with wide-open eyes and shouted, but with a stifled and as if voiceless shout:

"Has Tommaso killed himself? With a revolver?"

I gave her the paper. She read. She withdrew, sat on the bed, took her face in her hands, and stayed like that, curled up, silent and still.

I'd thought, when she shouted, that Tommaso had told her that if she left him he would kill himself with his revolver; but she had said nothing of the kind to me. I looked at her, her small head buried in her hands, her neck slim and wiry, its nape elegant with the duck's tail haircut: she was guilty, and I myself was guilty with her guilt. And I felt even rage rising within me, a sudden indignation: after all, I'd given everything to Sandra without asking for anything in return, and my absurd and mad generosity had been every bit as disastrous as Alessandro's avarice and caution when he'd refused a word of comfort to Mumi and thus urged him on to crime. . . . Or else the contradiction was only apparent: perhaps my generosity was selfishness like Alessandro's, only a more subtle form of it.

The telephone rang. Sandra remained motionless, as if she hadn't heard. I took the call:

"No," I said, "just at the moment she can't."

"Who is it?" Sandra asked, jerked back to life and quickly coming toward me.

"The dressmaker. But I said you . . ."

"Give it to me." She took the receiver, and spoke fluently, rapidly, almost angrily: "Yes, yes . . . A quarter of an hour, half an hour at the most . . . I'll come at once. Thank you." And she began dressing with the same fury.

I commented: "Sandra, I feel this haste is pointless, as things are now. . . ." This was the dressmaker who was making her wedding dress.

"What? Pointless? Why? I still have to try it on three times, otherwise it won't be ready: once this morning, once tomorrow morning, and then again in the evening."

"Sandra, you're mad!"

"Mad, why?" she asked, still in a rage as she pulled on her skirt.

"Because . . . I feel we'll have to put it off. . . ."

"Put it off? With my sister and her fiancé who've come here on purpose?"

"All the more reason. When they hear . . ."

"When they hear what? Nothing. They never even knew that Tommaso existed. I never said anything. If I said something now it would be like . . . like admitting it's my fault."

"But you knew . . ."

"I? You're mad, Carlo, you, not I! What do you imagine that I knew?"

"But you shouted, even before I told you."

"Because I guessed, from your face . . . and from the paper in your hand. . . ."

"Then he . . . he never threatened . . . ?"

She leapt up in a fury. She took me by the shoulders and stared straight into my eyes.

"Look at me," she said, "look at me, and never say such a thing again."

I was terrified by her look.

"Sandra," I mumbled, "I was saying . . . all I was saying was . . . that to me it seems difficult for us . . . the day after tomorrow . . ."

"Difficult? Difficult? The truth is something else!" Suddenly her eyes filled with tears. She was still holding me by the shoulders and staring at me. "Do you want to know the truth? Do you want me to tell you? Well, the truth is that, at this moment, you don't want me any more, and you're using this accident to get free of me! Oh no; my child must have your name, you understand? You promised, and after this accident you must keep to it more than ever. Do you understand?" And she flung herself on me and began kissing me with desperate fury. She had never kissed me like that before. But I remained completely cold and unresponsive. Her mouth had a strange and monstrous effect on me, like a leech. She leaned against me, she pushed me, she threw me onto the bed. She went on crying and kissing me with the same fury, saying: "You've never understood me! You've never understood anything! I love you, my love, I love you and I want you . . . you're mine, you're my man, my husband!" And she felt with her hand for my sex, then knelt down, more desperate than ever, and began kissing that. Now she wanted to offer me right away what she had always refused me. But I could see Tommaso stretched out on the narrow bed in the room for "guards on duty": I could see his rosy face, his protruding, fleshy lips, his blue eyes staring but looking at nothing: I saw Tommaso, and I couldn't.

With a short struggle, I rebelled. I disentangled myself from her embrace.

"Now, go to your dressmaker," I said. "Perhaps you're only too right. Perhaps I do want to free myself from you. But as for you, why are you worrying about the child's name? Even if we don't marry, you're rich enough to find a husband, and to pick and choose at that. Now go, go! So that, whatever happens, the dress will be ready. . . ."

I had never before had the experience of a woman wanting me, a lovely young woman, and me refusing her. For the first time, I was distracted by a thought that was stronger.

I went back to my room, and Sandra went out to the dressmaker.

I WAS alone on the balcony of my room at the Excelsior. I was contemplating the glory and the life of the Bay of Naples in the midday summer sun: the complicated and fantastic Castel dell'Ovo on its jetty, so like a building seen in a dream . . . with keeps, and bastions, and little houses and gardens snatched from the high courtyards and enclosed within the parapets of the fortifications . . . the green of citrus fruit trees and the red of geraniums peeping through where once there gleamed the bronze of cannon . . . and the restaurants, the narrow streets, the hovels, and the little carts of the Borgo Marinaro . . . and, in the harbor, the fishing boats and yachts . . . and the packed groups of small floating casks, like lacework or constellations . . . What were they? Buoys for mooring? Supports for the cultivation of mussels? I was asking myself this question without any curiosity as to the answer, with the sole aim of filling, if only for a second, the sudden and total emptiness I felt within me. The whole of my life, from the moment I'd read about Tommaso, had seemed to me pointless, futile. I'd been the unconscious wheel in a vast, dark mechanism of evil intent. I'd collaborated in a crime, in a frightful atrocity. And I'd collaborated free, for nothing: that is to say, without any real usefulness to myself, without any real benefit to my self-interest, nor even to my lowest and most vulgar instincts.

Emptiness. And as it were the apprehension of a last judgment that reduced my existence, already pretty long, to nothingness. In that dead and bottomless sea, the only anchor was the thought of Costantino, the responsibility I felt toward him, the remorse for having betrayed and abandoned him. I had just put in a call for him, and was anxiously waiting for it to come through.

To the left of the bay, the Sorrento peninsula and the island of Capri, hazy on the horizon in ashen similarity owing to the great heat, could scarcely be distinguished from the sea and the sky. To the right, much nearer, was the cape of Posillipo, and its gardens and villas—among which, if I'd searched, I might have been able to make out the two houses in Via Orazio, which were not only the symbol but the proof of my unpardonable folly, the body of my crime, the object that had served me in corrupting Sandra and destroying myself. Now, suddenly, everything was clear to me: I had never loved Sandra, I had never really even desired her. It had been an old man's fancy, an illusion that I'd been able to entertain and cultivate only because Sandra had been clever enough not to yield to my importunings. But even in this the person first and most to blame was myself, not she. It had been I, with my vicious ways and masochistic tendencies, who had suggested that cleverness to her.

I had accustomed myself, over the years, to not being afraid of myself, and to regarding my vice as a harmless game, a voluptuous comedy, an ephemeral infatuation. For years I had amused myself by repeatedly and tirelessly playing with fire. I had amused myself: for I knew that, immediately afterward, every time, and with unfailing regularity, I would return to a sense of real life.

There was no doubt about it. Apart from Meris, I had never loved any of my girl friends. When Sandra had told me I didn't even know what love was about, I'd realized she was right. Only I had believed that I was still in a position to make the great experiment. Too late! And who knows, I now said to myself as I contemplated the loveliest bay in the world and its cruel serenity, who knows whether even in those days, even with Meris, it wouldn't have been the same! True, with Meris I'd had nine days of perfect happiness, I had lived with her for nine days in sublime harmony; but who knows whether, even then, it wasn't a matter of illusion, fostered by the deceptive expectation of freedom with which all of us in Rome in those days intoxicated ourselves! Who knows whether, if I had really married Meris . . . But I didn't want to finish that conjecture, one way or the other. I wanted to reserve for myself at least the posthumous hope of a lost possibility: I wanted to go on believing in a capacity for love that I had never put to the test.

Only one certainty remained: my brother. Costantino had been, was, and would always be, for me, what I had been for my mother. I, too, could calmly repeat the concluding words in the orange envelope: "the only true and great love of my life": Costantino.

The telephone rang. And after a moment or two I heard his dear voice, hesitant and as though veiled, not by distance, but by the sweetness of his nature, by his surrender, by his trust in me.

"I'm coming back almost at once," I said without thinking of anything else, but surrendering myself entirely to him in my turn, as he surrendered himself to me; and, always without reflecting, without calculating the arrangements I'd have to make so as to be able to keep the promise, I added: "Certainly before the end of next week!"— and I didn't remind him of what, alas, would be in store for him after my return: the move to the nursing home at Varese. I didn't remind him of it, but I couldn't help thinking of it all the time I was talking to him on the telephone.

That, unquestionably, at least for the moment, was my worst torment. The immediate future, for my brother and myself, seemed to me an abyss that had suddenly yawned at my feet. I had made myself Sandra's slave even before marrying her. Henceforth I was dependent on her. Whereas I had only one desire: to free myself and flee. But how could I provide for Costantino?

Sandra returned at two. I was lying on the bed, quite still. She came toward me softly, and lightly kissed my forehead. She said:

"Paula and the boys are downstairs waiting for us to go to lunch. If you don't want to come, I've already explained that you're not feeling too well, and that you didn't sleep last night. . . ."

I got up and went down with her. I thought of how life picks up again and continues after great disasters, even to the surprise of the worst sufferer. From now on, nothing mattered to me except Costantino.

I had known Sandra's sister and the two young men since the previous evening. Paula was rather younger and less beautiful than Sandra, but she, too, was dark and slim. Her fiancé was a ski champion, and so was his friend: they were two nice boys, fair, with light eyes and red copper coloring. Walter, the fiancé, was very tall, thin, and freckled. The other, Stefi, was of medium height, but so robust that he seemed stocky, and his face was at one moment shining with tears, and at another contorted with exaggerated, noisy, and childish laughter.

Lunch, in the restaurant of the Excelsior, lasted longer than Sandra and I would have liked. The three of them joked and chatted together. We two were silent, or confined ourselves to answering their questions. At a certain point, Stefi, with one of his bursts of laugher, said perhaps there had been a mistake: it seemed to him that we were preparing for a funeral rather than a wedding. *"Ich bin sehr müde,"* murmured Sandra to her sister, who was also amazed by our behavior. It was only Thursday, and the ceremony was on Saturday morning. There were still forty-eight hours. Fortunately, Paula, Walter, and Stefi had arranged to go on the excursion to Vesuvius and Pompeii the following day, so they would go to bed early tonight, and we would be free of the obligation to take our meals with them until Saturday morning.

In the afternoon Berardo arrived from Turin. He telephoned me from his room to let me know. He knew nothing whatsoever, and hence was very cheerful. I went at once to see him.

If G. was my maestro and my imaginative friend, Berardo was my lawyer and my common-sense friend. Both were very intelligent. But whereas G. seemed to turn his attention to faraway things, Berardo seemed to turn his to things close at hand. Even their faces confirmed this difference. G., with his head tilted on his shoulders, and his eyes half closed as if the better to perceive the most fleeting and delicate sonorities and images. Berardo, with his bald forehead, heavy and bowed, his great protruding eyes, opened fully to the person or object just in front of him, as if he wanted to profit by this presence, to collide with it, to snatch its reality from it, and so to avoid in the future any approximations and deceptions of memory; he also had a grizzled, anticlerical beard, which was an integral part of his ironical expression. Both he and G. had an almost fixed smile of amazement and amusement; but this irony, too, had two different and even contrary meanings. G. seemed amazed and amused because he was continually noticing that reality was more beautiful than he'd thought; Berardo, on the contrary, because it was uglier.

Though buried in an armchair, he appeared to me as he was: tall and corpulent. His bald head bowed toward me, his big protruding eyes scrutinizing me, he began to listen. I had made the mistake of not telling him earlier that Sandra was engaged. If Berardo had known about her and Tommaso, he would by instinct have made me take certain precautions: if only that of postponing the wedding till

Sandra had been gradually assured of Tommaso's reactions; and in this way, perhaps, the worst would have been avoided. While talking, I saw all the ironical amusement extinguished from his face, until only the stillness and pallor of amazement remained. When I reached the point of telling him that I'd ceded the tenancy of the houses to Sandra, he seemed to stop breathing. He was terrified and utterly dismayed. Then he came back to life. And little by little, as he scolded me, he entered into a kind of fury. The deed ceding the tenancy must be annulled: we must go to court at once. We had proof. Sandra hadn't now, and never had had, the money that would have been necessary for a financial transaction of such magnitude: it could be shown that the sale had been "fictitious." Sandra had refused to marry me if I didn't cede the tenancy: "coercion" of my will, and that too could be proved.

I asked Berardo how it could be proved.

"With your collaboration," he snapped.

"And that means . . . ?"

"Telling the truth, letting me say it, then confirming it when the judge interrogates you!"

Did this mean that I would be obliged to reveal the details of my relationship with Sandra? "Of course," Berardo said. And would it be shown that the first contract, by which Sandra had obtained the full ownership of the houses, was also a fiction? All the absurdity, all the shame of that kind of buffoonery came into my mind. I told Berardo that I could never take back my word given to Sandra: for nothing in the world would I debase myself to that extent.

"Then there's only one way!" shouted Berardo, almost beside himself. And this was "to uphold in court my incapacity to understand or to will." That I was mad, Berardo couldn't doubt. Only a madman, a madman fit to be shut up, could have resolved to act as I had acted. Oh, it wouldn't be difficult to obtain expert medical opinion in this sense. In a few days my brother was to go into a nursing home. My brother had been considered legally incompetent for more than twenty years. That meant that I, too, could be so declared. It couldn't be helped. Extreme ills required extreme remedies. There was nothing for me to fear: Berardo would get the magistrate to appoint him as our guardian: his fame for professional integrity in Turin was more than adequate guarantee to that end. So I would get back my inheritance without more ado. . . . I would be declared legally incompetent, but it was worth it, rather than lose everything. . . .

All right, I'd been mad, I said: I couldn't deny it. But I would never lend myself voluntarily to being examined by a doctor who would certify me insane. If Berardo valued our friendship, he would have to abandon his plan.

"If you say that, it's a sign that you're still mad," he shouted.

"Maybe. But I've decided that it's useless for you to insist."

"And what if, for your good, I didn't take your decision into account? What if I telephoned to . . ." and he mentioned the name of the most famous neurologist in Turin, ". . . and told him to get into the first plane and come here?"

"He wouldn't find me. I'm leaving tonight. I was just going to ask you if you'd care to drive up north with me."

Berardo got up to get cigarettes from the bedside table. He came back without having found them. He had them in his pocket. I saw that he was flabbergasted; at the same time I saw that he wanted to say something, but hesitated.

"Why?" he said, leaning toward me and looking me in the eyes as if he himself had suddenly become the psychiatrist by whom he wanted to have me examined, "why? Have you given up the idea of marrying?" He spoke very slowly, separating his words, as if to gain time.

"I was going to leave this morning," I said. "As soon as I saw *La Stampa,* I telephoned your office in Turin to tell you that you needn't come to Naples. But you'd already left. I only stayed on so as to see you."

"So . . . you no longer want . . . to get married?"

"No. And that's that. It was all a mistake."

"Excellent. But in that case, try at least to be logical now. If you admit that it was a mistake, you should try in every possible way to remedy it."

"That's what I'm doing. I am remedying it. I'm not marrying her. I'm going away, and I never want to see her again."

"You're perfectly right. But that is only part of the remedy: the other part, which is far and away the most important, is to obtain the annulment of the deeds ceding the tenancy, as I told you. The ownership will still be hers, and that's already enormous. She'll soon convince herself that at bottom it's also in her interest—rather than facing a legal action. . . . Let me have a word with her."

"No, never."

"And if I summon a doctor and have you examined by force?"

My only answer was to look into his eyes as he had been looking for some moments into mine.

"Oh, as to that, I feel quite at peace," I said. "I know perfectly well that you're my friend, my dearest friend, and that you'll never do a thing like that."

He sighed. "Perhaps I ought to do it precisely because I am your dearest friend."

And he fell back into the armchair, again totally dejected. That sigh and that "I ought to" made it plain enough that henceforth he would make no attempt to implement his threat, conceived in a moment of rage.

"Thank you," I said. "You know perfectly well, just as I do, that of course I have committed an act of madness, but that I am not mad."

"But then . . . seeing that you refuse . . . ," he sighed deeply again, ". . . and perhaps you're right, you refuse to have the lease ceding the tenancy annulled with the means you would have at your disposal and that, I agree, neither the one nor the other course is, let us say, exactly pleasing . . . but then, at the point things have reached, this one of not marrying her is another enormity: it would be a complete disaster!" And he showed me, by quoting the legal code, that for me still to have some chance of not losing all my inheritance, I ought to marry her; because, as a husband "property-less and unemployed," I had a legal right to a percentage of the income to be returned as a "monthly allowance for maintenance"; and I had a special right to it in case of a legal separation. Besides which, when it came to giving an exact evaluation in figures of such a percentage, Sandra couldn't deny the evidence, namely, that the cession of both the ownership and the tenancy had occurred by means of a fictitious sale. If we weighed up loss against loss, I could still get back something by marrying Sandra. And I had an obligation to get it back—at least toward my brother. Berardo felt pretty sure that he would succeed in arranging things so that the allowance that would come to me as Sandra's husband would not, even at the worst, be lower than the revenue of the percentage of the inheritance which was Costantino's due. I would save what was essential. But I would have to marry Sandra.

THE CEREMONY took place, as had been arranged from the start, at Santa Maria di Piedigrotta, an old church on the wide piazza outside the Mergellina Station. Berardo and Walter were the witnesses.

By eleven in the morning the thing was already over. We emerged from the church. With a shout, Stefi stopped us on the steps and made us go back three or four times to take photographs. Sandra, in her white dress, with her bouquet of orange blossoms clasped to her breast, seemed, pale though she was, a model for a glossy cover.

The sun was burning hot. We still had the problem of the ritual lunch, which, alas, couldn't be avoided. But, luckily, Paula and the two young men, very depressed at having to leave for Bolzano that very evening, had decided to swim before lunch. It was a solution. Sandra and Paula went to the hotel to change. Then, all together in the car, we went to the Lícola Lido. Walter and Stefi had brought a case of champagne from Naples—their wedding present. As soon as we got there, they rushed off to the beach with Sandra and Paula. Berardo and I waited for them under the wide pergola of Pascalone's restaurant, where we'd ordered lunch. The champagne was put in the refrigerator.

Pascalone's was still a very rustic restaurant, half a large farm and half a fishermen's house, standing not far from the beach, in that enchanted and wonderfully fertile plain that extends from the Lícola pinewood as far as the first slopes of the Campi Flegrei.

The air was very hot, but clear and with a breeze. From beneath the vine branches of the immense pergola, here and there could be seen the sky of an intense blue. The tables were of simple boards, the chairs of rough wicker, while the farmhouse was washed pink, but a pink all peeling and scratched, with the black rectangles of the doors and windows. And behind the farmhouse, in a corner of the space adjoining the pergola, was the open-air oven: a pink cone with a large black blot in the middle. Two pigs, also pink and black, grubbed about freely in that space and sometimes came up to the tables where the customers were sitting. There was a group of Neapolitans celebrating who knows what family festival: thirty-odd of them, including old people and young, men, women, and children, all at one long table a short distance from us. The men were in striped pajamas and slippers: evidently they had jumped into their truck just as they had tumbled out of bed shortly before, and emerged from their holes. They were shouting, laughing, singing in chorus to the accompaniment of a guitar and a mandolin played by two cart-boys. It was an act by Eduardo, but with something more blatant, more rough and savage: a mixture, one would say, of Mexico and Naples. Even the sulky looks of the men in pajamas were too marked to be appropriately identified with De Filippo's characters, who are basically civilized and shadowy. At first Berardo and I were convinced that they were Italo-Americans on holiday, perhaps returned to their original family home. We didn't want to surrender to the evidence, and we stretched our ears in vain, in that tumult of Neapolitan cadences, so sorrowful even when, as in this case, they wanted to express joy, for the dry gunshot of "Bruccolino" (Brooklyn) slang. But no, they were pure Neapolitans, and perhaps they appeared to be Americans because of the type and speed of their profits: fruit-market gangsters, perhaps, like those in the film *La Sfida*.

> *Ammore, ammore, portame stasera*
> *'ncopp'all'onne chiare 'e Marechiare.*
> *Dint'e vase damme 'a vita,*

tutt'a vita m'he a fa sunnà!
A Marechiare suonno 'e stu core,
a Marechiare stasera io torno ancora a suspirà! *

And the sweetness, the languor, the beatitude of the melody, like warm air yet with a breeze, and of the colors that our eyes could see all around us, blue and green, pink and black, seemed, suddenly, to contradict the idyllic tourist convention about Naples, adapting themselves in deeper and, for contrast, almost funereal ways, to the violence of those gangsters in pajamas.

Basta che c'è stu sole
basta che c'è stu mare
'na nenna core a core
'na canzone p'a cantà:
chi ha avuto, ha avuto, ha avuto,
chi ha dato, ha dato, ha dato:
scurdammoce 'o passato:
simm'a Napule, paisà! †

Life is made up of toil, violence, tyranny, death: when the festive day arrives, we don't even make the effort to get dressed: we enjoy the sun, the sky, the sea, the wine, the food, and we don't think of anything any more:

Simm'a Napule, paisà!

The two sisters and the young men came running back from the beach. From the first I had realized that Sandra

* My love, my love, my love take me tonight / on the crest of Marechiaro clear waves. / By your kisses give me life, / for all my life keep me dreaming! / At Marechiaro, dream of my heart, / tonight at Marechiaro I sigh once more!

† It's enough to have this sun / it's enough to have this sea / a girl heart to heart / a song to sing: / who's had, has had, has had, / who's given, has given, has given: / let's forget the past: / we're in Naples, guy!

had made up her mind to be happy on this day, and to forget everything. The champagne was already chilled. The first bottles were immediately uncorked. Sandra began drinking without restraint. I didn't dare say anything to her: any word of mine to moderate her, even a gesture, would—so it seemed to me—have called up the shade of Tommaso in our midst, and thus have added to our guilt the indignity of hypocrisy.

To be sure, I wasn't like Sandra, who wanted to make a complete break and begin again from the beginning. But I realized that, in a certain sense, she and not I might be right. Now that we had done what we had done, to seek moderation and make a show of sadness would almost be worse. I didn't feel it in me to follow her example, still less encourage her; but neither did I feel it in me to hold her back. I looked at her with a mixture of fear and fascination. And so too, I noted, did Berardo, with his great protruding eyes and his bald head inclined toward her.

Sandra was drunk before the dessert course. She was still wearing her swim suit. She cleared the table of cloth and cutlery, then leapt onto it and began singing and dancing:

Ohi Susanna, ohi Susanna
ist das Leben noch so schön . . .

Walter, Stefi, and Paula acted as chorus and beat their hands in time. The cart-boys played an accompaniment with guitar and mandolin. The gangsters at the big table —silent and motionless—watched as though it were a play, and when it was over they clapped with frenzy. Someone asked for an encore, and Sandra didn't wait to be urged:

Trink ma noch a Flascherl Wein . . .

It was extraordinary how she managed, in her drunkenness, to preserve a certain measure, a certain elegance.

Indeed, I would say that she revealed, at least to me, a quality that was new to me: a sort of antique grace, rustic and childish. Her strong arms waved about, her long legs rose and fell quickly and rhythmically, her heels beat time on the table: she leaned forward, she leaned backward, she pirouetted showing the perfection of her young figure. And her strange face, thin and strong, her straight nose, her small pale mouth, were transformed as though invaded with a new vitality.

It seemed to me, at a certain moment, that her eyes, half closed and laughing in drunkenness, song, and dance, winked at me maliciously, indeed with the joy of cruelty, as if to say: "But yes, my old friend, don't you understand? All's well that ends well! And we two are destined to love each other! And tonight we'll love each other at last! You'll see! You'll see it! *Ist das Leben noch so schön!*"

At no point, not in the café at Stresa where I saw her for the first time, nor at the top of Civiasco or on our other winter trips, nor even through the mirrors and in the hotel bedrooms, had she seemed to me so beautiful. Perhaps things weren't as I'd started thinking they were the other morning, when the news of Tommaso's suicide came. Sandra wasn't really "a near-delinquent" and I "a weak but decent man." Perhaps it was much simpler than that: Sandra was a living person, and I an old man who was afraid and who had never before had to reckon with the tragic side of life. . . . A tragic side perhaps inevitable, but I had always evaded it, and so I lacked the sense . . . *"Il morto giace e il vivo si dà pace"*: this was what Sandra was telling me with her malicious winks. Now that I had, formally, taken the great step of marrying, why shouldn't I profit by it? I desired Sandra. I did indeed desire her. In this explosion, in the ancient dance of her country, I felt I was seeing her for the first time, quite new and different:

stronger, harder, but also truer and more beautiful. I desired her as I had never desired her. But also, for the first time, I was afraid.

Now the gangsters had taken up their favorite song again:

> *Chi ha avuto, ha avuto, ha avuto,*
> *chi ha dato, ha dato, ha dato . . .*

and Sandra, with the coolness of a professional, had switched from her Tyrolese dance to a tarantella. A subtle sweetness, like a drug in the air, persuaded us to accept, to welcome, to resolve in some way, cruelty and death. The gangsters, delirious with enthusiasm, had got up and gathered around our table, singing in chorus and clapping their hands to the beat. Sandra was dancing the Neapolitan tarantella, throwing her head back, shaking her black locks, and singing at the top of her voice:

> *. . . scurdammoce 'o passato,*
> *simm'a Napule, paisà!*

WITH NO SHEET, naked, supine, her legs wide apart, Sandra was still sleeping as when I had lain her on her bed, completely drunk. Now it was two in the morning. I had taken Berardo to the airport and had come back to the Excelsior. This time, the communicating door was open: wide open. I stood in the half-light, looking at her.

Her body was so slim, so youthful. Supposing, after all, Ilse wasn't her daughter? Supposing it had all been a cheat?

No, I told myself: I was obstinately trying to find a mystery in Sandra, almost seeing her as a creature of the devil, whereas she was a terribly simple creature. To what purpose would she pretend that the child was hers? I reflected. In fact, Sandra had found herself in perfect accord with the gangsters in pajamas just as she had found herself in harmony with Tommaso. She was a simple creature, almost an animal, for whom death and life had a very precise and very circumscribed meaning. That was perhaps why her body, despite her motherhood, prison, the years of toil and sorrow, had remained so young. I gazed particularly at her sex: the little black and curly triangle, perfectly in proportion, and slightly convex. My future depended entirely on that.

I felt that, now, it was no longer as it had always been in the past, with all the other women, a joke, a pretense, a comedy. This time I would have to behave seriously. And I was afraid. What would happen to me if I—and I only just avoided reaching that point—overcame my fear? Would I still be in a position to live with Costantino, or even to help him, to see him when and as I wanted? Would I still be free, as I'd always been since my mother's death?

My mistress was there. There, in front of me. She was asleep. She was waiting for me in her sleep, sure that I would come to her, and that I would throw myself at her feet like a slave, afraid of waking her up.

No, it wasn't a game this time. She really was "my mistress." Was she? She would be . . . But I could still win. Or lose. Who knows? In moments like this, one is never really certain whether the decision one is about to make is the best or the worst, the mistaken one or the right one. A subtle and invisible thread holds us suspended. We decide one way or the other, and at that moment we don't know, sometimes we shall continue to live without ever knowing, whether or not we have broken the thread by our decision. What, then, is it that guides us, that impels us to decide? I don't think it's ever a rational process, or an idea. In my case, it was a passionate, lightning-swift calculation of the hours by car that separated me from the joy of seeing Costantino again, and of pressing him to my heart.

Very quietly I packed my bags and departed without Sandra's waking up. I left a couple of lines for her with the hotel porter.

I REACHED Levo the next evening at sunset. On that very day, two bank officials, and various people who were probably the purchasers or their agents, had come to view the house and land. Giopa was devastated: far from staying on for the whole of September, we had to vacate the place within a week! He was crying. "What could I have done alone! What a good thing you've come, Master Carlo!" But the moment he knew that my marriage had gone up in smoke, he almost fainted with joy: I had lost everything and it was terrible, of course, terrible, but it couldn't be helped: "So you see it was fated that all your belongings would end up like that. And thank the Lord!" Yes, we should thank the Lord because the essential had been salvaged! Giopa didn't say this, but in his affectionate face, sad, resigned, not servile, I read his ancient thoughts more clearly than if he had spoken: the essential had been saved because "Master Carlo has got rid of that big tart!"

Oh, I didn't agree with Giopa. Everything considered, perhaps I too was a conservative, but not to his extent; and if I liked a woman, I didn't come later to despise her because I'd noticed that she attached too much importance to money!

No. Not only was I not in agreement with Giopa. But, however absurd my hypothesis may seem, I even admitted the possibility that Sandra was genuinely in love with me. It was I who didn't love her. I who, precisely in accordance with her last words, had profited by Tommaso's death to flee. I had given her everything, but precisely not "the essential." Had I loved her, I would have felt less responsibility toward Tommaso and more responsibility toward her. I would have experienced first and foremost the need to comfort her, to protect her from her remorse, almost to unite myself with her even in guilt. No, I hadn't loved her, and I had lost her, and I was already regretting it. But not for the world would I have gone back.

This was why Giopa's phrase had such a mournful echo, though at the same time sweet and resigned: "So you see it was fated that all your belongings would end up like that. And thank the Lord!" It was like the Levo church bell ringing the Angelus on autumn evenings, when it seems that the chimes reach the immensity of the lake, and the heart is wrung by a sweet melancholy.

I had sold everything "lock, stock, and barrel": Via Borgonuova and Levo. In view of the vastness of my misfortune and my folly, I could view it as a minor piece of good luck: we hadn't got to face moving the furniture! But even so, we still had to pack the piano, the books, the record player, the silver, the linen, and personal belongings. So that Costantino should be spared this painful spectacle, and the agitation and confusion, I decided to take him to Varese at once.

Since his return from England twenty-five years earlier with my mother, and with the exception of a few short trips by car with me to Milan and the Riviera, Costantino had never moved from Levo and the immediate surroundings of Lake Maggiore. This time, Giopa had prepared him very slowly and with due precautions for the great novelty, and he had finished by becoming used, if not resigned, to the idea. But when we'd crossed the park of "Villa Quiete" between dark evergreens and fields with high, uncut grass and when the crunching of the tires on the gravel was followed by the strange silence of all nursing homes, and from somewhere behind the villa, far away yet, alas, only too clear, there came a sound like howling which ended up with a laugh, and was repeated at regular intervals; and when, on raising our eyes, we could see barred windows at the first floor, Costantino said to me: "I don't want to stay here, Carlo. Let's go somewhere else. Let's go to a real hospital."

I explained to him with all possible gentleness that it would be too complicated to change at this stage, that it was for his good, and that soon, very soon, I'd come and take him away. He bent his head meekly and said nothing more to me; but he said nothing more to anyone, and he didn't even answer the falsely cheerful and sinisterly gay greetings of the bearded director and the sisters who received him.

I left him in his room: light, almost cheerful, but with barred windows, which his eyes fell on at once, as soon as we entered. But there was a telephone on the bedside table. I said that I would call him every morning, and the hour for this was arranged in the director's presence.

I went back to Levo. Now it was a matter of storing the piano, the record player, and the books. G. put at my disposal a ground-floor room in the cottage of the caretaker of his Baveno villa.

Giopa, heartbroken, returned to his village on Lake Orta; he was ready to rejoin me anywhere, at any time, just as soon as I'd made my arrangements.

I rented a tiny furnished villa at Lugano Paradiso. We would have possession in October: before that, it was occupied. Besides the kitchen and bathroom, there were only three rooms: a living room, a room for me, and one for Costantino and Giopa. There were heating and all the conveniences, and the rent wasn't even high; yet the sum of money I still retained at the Vallugano bank was only just enough to carry on for a year. I'd have to work. Now, the monthly salary that I used to get from the newspaper, though by no means princely, would have come in handy; but I'd given it up, and my column had been taken over by someone else.

In October, as arranged, I went to fetch Costantino, and, with him and Giopa, settled in at Lugano. The future was more than uncertain. Casual articles in reviews and newspapers brought in paltry sums. I would absolutely have to find something permanent and more remunerative. Throughout the whole winter I commuted, as I had once done to Levo; only now, as I no longer had a home in Milan, I always went back to Lugano to sleep. And the aim of my trips to the city wasn't the Scala, and still less girls. As regards girls, I now suddenly felt old, tired, and disgusted. I renounced them naturally, and I would even say with sensual pleasure: that is, I gave them no more thought. Whereas in another respect I felt young, younger perhaps than I had ever felt before. It was the first time in my life that I'd really needed to work, needed to earn money for myself and for the only people I was sure I loved: Costantino and Giopa. I had to find a job. It wasn't easy. I went to Milan in the morning and returned to Lugano in the afternoon. During the long winter evenings, and on Saturdays and Sundays, I took up again my study on Puccini, not so much because I hoped to make a profit on it as to occupy myself and distract myself from remorse and worry about the future. But one day I got disheartened and chucked it; then, looking back on the strange and disastrous story of my failed marriage and the loss of all my possessions, I jotted down random facts, notes, a disorderly outline of an autobiography. Meanwhile, I'd failed to find any solution to my agonizing problem, no offer of work that I could accept, not the faintest glimmer of light.

I still had a cousin in Turin, slightly younger than me, whom I hadn't seen for thirty years; he was the chairman and chief shareholder of one of the largest vermouth producers in the world. Our two grandfathers were brothers, and equal partners in the firm from the time of its foundation. In 1889 they separated. When my grandfather retired from the firm, ceding his own half to my cousin's grandfather, the capital that fell to my grandfather was equivalent to the capital that remained in the hands of his, but it was equivalent only in appearance and only at that moment, because, as from that moment, the wealth which would later go to my cousin steadily increased, whereas ours did nothing but diminish. Theirs was productive capital, ours wasn't. Nevertheless ours, though too modest today to be compared with theirs, would have been amply sufficient for my brother and myself to lead an easy and tranquil life if what had happened hadn't happened. I had never asked the smallest favor of my cousin. It was impossible that, in all his industrial complex, there shouldn't be a place for me, who bore the same surname as he! So I wrote him a long letter; but, just as I was posting it, family pride and the pride of Turin proved stronger than my need, and I abandoned the idea. And the winter passed, and my position was on the way to becoming desperate, when once again G. came to my aid.

One of his old colleagues and friends, one of the best-known English conductors, in passing through Milan, asked him whether by chance he knew someone suitable for taking over the musical direction of a new record company in Auckland, North Island, New Zealand.

It meant saying good-by to Italy for a number of years, and amounted, practically, to emigrating. But the remuneration was higher than anything I had previously hoped for. Besides my salary, I had free accommodation: judging by the photographs, a marvelous house among very tall trees, close by the establishment, near Papakura, an Auckland suburb in the bay of Manukau. And of course I could take Costantino and Giopa with me. Air fares were paid for all three.

Our departure was fixed for early June. I was filled with a curious delight: an impatience, perhaps, no longer to have before my eyes the images and landscapes which, however dear to me, and however beautiful—and I had no illusion whatever that they would be surpassed by the marvels of New Zealand—were somehow overlaid with the patina of those obsessions and that melancholy which had governed my life since earliest childhood.

Given this state of mind, it can well be imagined how early I started the preparations for the journey! Nothing was overlooked. I drew up a program and followed it meticulously, day by day. I was helped by Giopa and even by Costantino, who as if by a miracle had emerged from his usual apathy and had caught a little of my enthusiasm.

In view of the fact that to obtain the visa on our passports medical certificates were required, I had hurried to get them. Nevertheless the visas were delayed. About halfway through May, when there were not many days to go before our departure, the Consulate informed me that, as a result of some cases of toxoplasmosis found among the immigrants in the last half-year, there was a temporary regulation which also required an oculist's examination, and in particular the result of a dye-test known as that of Sabin and Feldman. It was in this way that, in going to deliver the blood specimens for analysis at the Serotherapeutic Institute in Via Darwin, outside Porta Ticinese, I stumbled by chance on that mystery over which I had never ceased to ponder, although I had for long resigned myself to regarding it as insoluble.

I was in the car with Costantino and Giopa. Costantino, following one of his old habits, was repeating aloud the names of the shops, the names of the streets, the advertising slogans on the posters, and anything else he happened to read along the way; and almost always, and sometimes very rightly, he found in them matter for laughter.

We had stopped at the traffic lights in Via Giuseppe Meda.

"How fearsome!" Costantino said. "I wouldn't at all like to live in this street!"

"Why?" I asked calmly, to pander to him as much as anything, as one always had to. And I raised my eyes to the name of the street, while Costantino read it out in a loud voice, and laughed:

"Via Silvio Spaventa."

How could I ever forget that name?

Three days later, early in the morning, I returned to the Serotherapeutic Institute to fetch the result of the analysis. This time I was alone: Giopa and my brother had stayed behind at Lugano and were busy with the heavy luggage which had to be sent by a plane earlier than our own. On my way back from Via Darwin, I again went along Via Giuseppe Meda, and once more found myself at the corner of Via Silvio Spaventa. It was a whim. A whim which perhaps was also part of the excitement, half exultant, half nostalgic, caused by the imminent separation from all the old things. I turned into this Via Spaventa, so different from the Naples Via Spaventa, and stopped directly in front of number 2.

A woman with spectacles and white hair was cleaning in

the entrance: doubtless the portress. When she saw me staring in her direction, she asked me if I was looking for someone.

"Signora Maria Ferrari," I said, so as to make my escape and without even getting out of the car.

"Ferrari . . . Ferrari . . ." and she knit her brows in painful concentration. Ferrari is a name, especially in Milan, which is so common that the portress's perplexity was only too natural: it was not at all unlikely that a Ferrari lived there.

But after having thought for a moment, the portress shook her head and said:

"I'm sorry, sir . . . But no Ferrari lives here." Then she suddenly added, "At least . . ." and a shadow of uncertainty, an air of suspense, remained in her face between her eyebrows and her spectacles.

"It doesn't matter. I wasn't sure. You mean I'm mistaken. Thank you," I said, and was about to put the car in gear when an old woman with a shopping bag, who had meanwhile appeared in the entrance, approached the portress.

"Wait a moment," the portress said to me, reinforcing her invitation to wait with a lively gesture of the hand, while concentrating on what the old woman was now rapidly whispering into her ear. The portress then answered the old woman, also muttering into her ear. And there began a dialogue in dialect between them, muffled, excited, mysterious, of which I caught only a word or two. Every now and again they glanced at me with curiosity while talking.

"Maria Ferrari . . ." the portress said at last, turning to me with complete satisfaction, and an air of triumph was also on the face of the old woman, who approached the car too, ". . . but, excuse me, but do you know the lady?"

"Yes, indeed I do," I replied.

"But perhaps it's a very long time since you saw her . . ."

"Yes, quite true, many, many years," I said, surprised but still not quite comprehending.

"Because, you see, a lady by the very name you mention used to live here . . . in fact she owned the apartment on the top floor."

"A dark lady?" I said; and meanwhile, in a flash of memory, I saw again that torn-off bit of newspaper that the servant's clawlike hand had pushed at me through the door that was ajar: the street, and the number, were written on it, but not the town. I'd immediately assumed that the town was Naples because Madame Teresa, with the obvious aim of misleading me, had said it was Naples. . . .

"Yes, a dark lady," the portress confirmed.

"A little, well, not exactly thin?" I added, trying to describe Meris with a sweep of my hand.

"Yes, that's it," exclaimed the old woman, unable to resist putting in her oar.

And the portress went on:

"Yes, but she's no longer called Ferrari. Oh, she's been married a long time now. And she doesn't live here any more. Oh, she's been gone for a long time. They sold out directly after the war. Now she's called Colnaghi. They sold so as to buy, just near here—over there, do you see?" and she pointed toward Via Giuseppe Meda. I turned, following the portress's peremptory direction.

"What, there?"

"Yes, there . . . the dry-cleaner's. Colnaghi's Modern Dry-Cleaning. It's written above. You can even see it from here."

I thanked her and went off. Of course I don't mean that I went straight to the dry-cleaner's: while I was maneuvering the car I saw that the two women had stayed in the doorway to watch. I went off toward Porta Ticinese and parked the car three blocks farther on. Then I turned back on foot and walked along the Via Meda in the crowd.

Was it possible, was it really possible? That after so many years I was on the point of finding Meris?

I DON'T think that if I hadn't known I was leaving for New Zealand in a few days' time, and if—more importantly—the past wasn't psychologically far behind me, I would have dared to traverse even that short space. And when I arrived in front of the dry-cleaner's, and took a first, fugitive glance inside, my courage failed me all the same.

In contrast to the already bright sun that streamed down on Via Meda, the inside of the dry-cleaner's seemed very dark. I just made out, without really seeing them, the rows of suits hanging all around, and on two levels, right up to the ceiling. The counter was at the far end; and there were people, whether customers or assistants I couldn't say.

I went back to the car and returned to the center of the town. I went to the Consulate to take the results of the analysis. In a word, I went on doing all my prearranged duties, methodically, one after another, so as not to think of anything else, though the effort was considerable. It was only in the afternoon, just as I was leaving for Lugano, that I went into a bar and looked up the dry-cleaner's number in the telephone book.

The telephone standing there in front of me was a very simple means of either ascertaining that all this was no more than a homonymous equivocation, a mere similarity, or, if things were otherwise, of confronting the shock.

"Hello, Modern Dry-Cleaner's here." It was a woman's voice, vibrating, decided, strong.

"Excuse me, but is Signora Maria Ferrari there by any chance?"

"Speaking," she said. "Who's that?"

I said my name.

"A ghost from the past!" and she gave a short, frank laugh, without the slightest hesitation. That voice, that laugh, and that relaxed tone suddenly relieved me of a heavy burden. I told her in a few words how I had accidentally come across her address.

She laughed again, lightly.

"Yes, it's true, I told Madame Teresa to tell you anything, but not that I'd come back to Milan! But it's all so long ago! I've two children now, and the girl is just going to be married! If all goes well, by next year I'll be a grandmother!"

I told her I was leaving for New Zealand within a week and that I would be away from Italy for many years. I asked her if I could see her for a moment: there was something I wanted to ask her.

"I'd be delighted. Come whenever you like."

"What time suits you?" I asked.

"Come whenever you like. I'm always here while the shop's open."

I said I'd come along the following morning, if that suited her.

"Whenever you like," she repeated.

Yes, her confident voice had made me realize that all had gone well with her, and hence that there couldn't possibly be the faintest trace of anything between the two of us. We were two strangers who would be talking about two of their friends.

Nevertheless, with the thought that I would see her within a few hours, I couldn't sleep that night.

I ENTERED the dry-cleaner's. At the far end an old man and a customer were examining a suit laid out on the counter between them. As soon as he saw me, he asked the customer to excuse him, came out from behind the counter, and approached me with a polite smile.

He wasn't as old as he'd seemed at first sight: sixty or sixty-five, and still very vigorous. Blue shirt without a tie and opening onto a strong neck, gray flannel trousers: casual working clothes. His face was masculine, rugged, of the people, not vulgar. Little hair, and gray. And the most extraordinary eyes I can remember ever seeing: brilliant, sparkling blue, mischievous and gay; the eyes of a good-tempered medium, who would hypnotize you to sleep. I said my name. He knew it already. He spoke with a marked lilt of Lombardy.

"Just make yourself at home over there," he said, indicating in the corner, and beyond the passage through the counter, a cotton curtain that separated off the rear of the shop. "Forgive us for not being able to receive you anywhere else . . . but, as you realize, in working hours . . . You write music criticism, don't you? You see, I'm one of your readers," and he named the newspaper which used to contain my column. "You're my favorite critic, and I've always followed your advice and never regretted it. I don't understand anything, but I'm mad about the opera. I know that you're going away, going off to distant parts, otherwise I'd really beg you to come and spend an evening with us, a nice little supper, we live above here, I would have enjoyed showing you my collection of records . . . all operas, of course! I think that, at least as regards Verdi, it's almost complete. Please make yourself at home. Ah, here we are."

Meris had appeared at the back of the shop. It was she. But it was also somebody else. Her lovely madonna's face from the Venetian Renaissance was, so to speak, hollowed out: not by lines, but by shadows. Her teeth were still strong, and still her own, but they were too much in evidence, almost protruding. Her hair was in involuntary disarray, and with hints of artificial redness about it. Her dress, a flowered blouse with a black skirt, was a simple working dress. There was something careless and worn about all her person. The coral nail polish was flaked off here and there. I reflected that I had announced my visit in advance, and that thus I had proof that she attributed little or no importance to it. Her eyes: I realized that I had not remembered them well. They were of an even lighter brown than I'd remembered: almost gold; I'd say that they reflected or repeated in a strange way the sparkling laughter of her husband's eyes. But it was the same laugh, the same liveliness, the same ready and natural cheerfulness breathing from her face and her whole bearing, and this confirmed, and even increased, the effect of her voice on the telephone the evening before.

We went through to the back of the shop. She invited me to sit down in a cane armchair. But there wasn't a second one for her.

"It doesn't matter, I'll stand," she said.

Perhaps mistakenly, I interpreted this phrase, despite its cordiality, as an invitation for me to remain standing too, that is to say, to hurry up.

"Now tell me what you want to know."

It wasn't easy for me. But the necessity to be brief helped me in the end. I asked her why she had disappeared in that way, without leaving me a note, without sending a telegram, without anything, and why she had forbidden Madame Teresa to give me her address.

She stared at me in amazement which, I could see, couldn't have been feigned:

"But how do you mean? Don't you know? Didn't your mother tell you anything?"

I answered that my mother died during those very days.

It then seemed to me that Meris collected her strength. She allowed herself a brief sigh: evidently she was remembering something painful. She said in a low voice:

"Two plain-clothes policemen came the morning after you left. They were looking for me. I knew one of them already. He was one of the ones who used to come and inspect . . . They told me I must leave Rome at once and never let myself be seen by you again: in a word, that I must disappear without leaving an address. And all this for your good."

"But they weren't empowered to do it!" I said, dumfounded, indignant, and much more besides.

"Oh yes they were. They could do that and more. They could do anything. They came on behalf of the Ministry. They had orders. If I didn't disappear, you'd be forthwith sent to the front to fight. That's what they said. And they handed me this. I've always kept it, thinking that one day or another, who could tell, we might meet again. When you said you'd be coming this morning, I brought it down. Here," and she lifted the gray felt that covered a nearby table: an orange envelope was disclosed, identical, so it seemed to me, with the one containing my mother's spiritual testament. "Take it," Meris concluded, "I've read it only once; on that day. It was enough."

I took the envelope. At the top was written, in my mother's handwriting, "For Signorina Maria Ferrari. To be handed to her personally."

When she saw my hesitation, Meris went on:

"You can read it later. Now you'll forgive me, won't you, but I've got so much to do. These days customers are getting out their summer clothes, and they want to have their winter clothes cleaned, pressed, and put in mothballs. We have no assistants, as you see. My husband and I do everything. There are machines, but believe me it's heavy work all the same. And life is dear. My daughter is engaged, I've told you already: she's marrying within a month. The boy is studying. If you had an idea of the amount of money we need! Thank you for coming to see me. We can stay good friends, can't we? There's no reason why we shouldn't. Aren't you married?"

"No, Meris," I said. I kissed her hand. "And forgive me."

"You've nothing to be forgiven!"

I plucked up my courage and said what I had thought from the first moment of seeing her again:

"I'll always remember you. You were . . . the loveliest thing in my life."

"Enough of that!" she said with an unbelieving laugh, and led me toward the door.

Her husband was busy with other customers: he waved good-by to me from a distance, from the counter, with a wide and friendly gesture.

This time I didn't wait so long before opening the orange envelope. I got into my car, which was parked a little bit before the dry-cleaning shop, and I read.

MY MOTHER's second letter is still here on my writing desk, like the other one. The date, too, is the same as the other: August 28, 1943. As I pause before copying it out, I see, from the open French window, the meadow that descends in a gentle convex slope toward the sea, between the tall kauri pines, the palm trees, and the giant ferns. In the light of the setting sun, the sea is blue with pink reflections; and pink and white, too, are the villas and houses of Auckland on the hill on the other side of the bay. To-day is December 19 and, like June at home, the beginning of the summer: but at home in Palermo or Catania. The other day I received a cable from Berardo finally confirming all the hopes his recent letters have aroused: legal separation from Sandra is henceforth an accomplished fact, and the maintenance allowance fixed in my favor is the very one we'd asked for. Even after the marriage, it was left to my discretion whether I gave my name to little Ilse or not. Berardo acted well: he held the recognition of the child in suspense until Sandra gave way about the sum of the allowance.

Down there, under the tallest of the kauris, Costantino and Giopa have lit a fire, so as to roast some corn cobs that they found this morning in the Maori market at Pukekohe. In the bright, windless air, the red, yellow, and orange flames look as though they're painted. Jerry, an Alsation wolfhound, is leaping around barking with joy; he, too, probably knows that this is Friday evening and that two days of complete relaxation lie ahead of us. Here is the letter:

Dear Signorina,

Alas, I am aware of everything; and as you will have been able to observe, even before you read these few lines, I have taken the necessary steps.

I am not so naïve as to suppose that you feel for my son Carlo a sentiment even partially sincere. But I hope you have preserved, through the horrors and darkness of your life, some glimmer of Faith. In spite of everything, this glimmer might be enough to show you the beginning of a long journey, the way of repentance and redemption.

But if, to your misfortune, this is not the case, if you have lost all sense of the Good, and try in one way or another, even after some time, to see my son again, I warn you here and now that this attempt will be frustrated.

May God forgive you and save you! This is the prayer I address to Him, and I do not despair that He will hear me in His infinite mercy, and through the intercession of the Blessed Virgin, His Mother.

Now I've finished copying, I have put the letter back in the envelope and placed it beside the other on the writing desk.

I am looking through the French window. Now the flames of Giopa's bonfire have grown higher: they are almost licking the lowest branches of the kauri. It could be dangerous. Perhaps I'd better go and tell him not to throw on any more wood. Jerry is barking louder and louder and jumping higher and higher. I get up from the writing desk and go out into the meadow.

I have taken them with me and, within a few moments, I shall throw them into the flames: the first and the second orange envelope.

Auckland, New Zealand, December 19, 1959